SKETCHER

ROLAND WATSON-GRANT

ALMA BOOKS

ALMA BOOKS LTD
London House
243–253 Lower Mortlake Road
Richmond
Surrey TW9 2LL
United Kingdom
www.almabooks.com

Sketcher first published by Alma Books Limited in 2013

This mass-market edition first published by Alma Books Limited in 2014

Printed in Great Britain by CPI Group (UK) Ltd, Croydon CR0 4YY

ISBN: 978-1-84688-312-5
EBOOK: 978-1-84688-275-3

SKETCHER

To Vera and all the Watson-Grants
I grew up with, including Juhlani

PART ONE

There is a crack in everything.
    – Leonard Cohen

One

Well to begin with, lemme tell you, my pops is the reason we grew up in that swamp. And when I say "swamp" I don't mean that great, big, wonderful Atchafalaya Swamp in south-central Louisiana that everybody talks about. No sir. If you don't know too much about New O'lins, grab a map and go east, almost past Lake Pontchartrain, and you might see the little piece of purgatory I'm talkin' about. I can't tell you any names, cos there are no real names to tell. It's a kind of no man's land, a clammy corridor, part of the muddy mess left behind by the Mississippi slidin' out into the Gulf. So don't blink or you'll pass it.

There were no wilderness tours and jazz music and dancin' and jambalaya tastin' and boat rides coming through where we used to live, cos many people didn't expect *nobody* to be all the way out there. All you'd see out there was wheezin' trees, ankle-deep in the swamp. Most days, nothin' moved except for maybe a dragonfly testin' the water with its toes, or a crow screechin' up in the branches to make even midday look spooky. So the first thing people asked when we told them we lived on that sorry side of the swamp is: "Now, how in da hell did y'all get out *there*?" Sometimes we'd say nothin', but other times we'd tell 'em that our pops had a vision.

Yessir, before we were born, ol' Pops hit the bottle hard one Friday night in the city and passed out. Round about Tuesday, when he came back to his senses, he told Moms he had a vision that he was standin' in a crowd, and all the people saw a desert, a barren land with brown dirt stretchin' from their toes to the top of a mountain on the horizon. In the vision a voice told him he had to journey across the desert to that

7

mountain. So he turned to the crowd and asked for people to go with him, but he couldn't find anybody crazy enough to do that. Then when he spun back around and looked in front of him again, lo and behold, all he saw was butterflies and big blossoms of every kind, with purple and pink, buttercream and strawberry colours swirlin' on top of the greenest grass. He said that he started walkin' and all those flowers felt like silk and velvet under his feet, and everywhere he put his foot a million more blooms exploded in colours that God had not yet invented. And they all made a rainbow road out of the city, from his toes to the mountain top.

Well, my moms said those were all the colours of his lunch that he left in the sink that Friday night. So, yeah. That vision that was supposed to take us into paradise was our first step into growing up in limbo. Now look, I'm not exactly blamin' my pops, I'm just repeatin' the facts like I heard it since I was born, just so you can see where we're comin' from. Now, I heard some of the drama from Pa Campbell – that's our neighbour in the swamp, who'd been around since before that time that everybody loves to jaw about, the *Sixties*. I was born early Seventies, so I guess I can't fully appreciate all that excitement and why everybody in the city and the swamp said *the Sixties this*, *the Sixties that*... especially old man Pa Campbell when he didn't take his chill pills. He always got excited and said: "Skid!... I don't know why they called you that name, boy, but, Skid!..." – *Pause*. "Oooh, the Sixties."

And you better have two hours to sit and listen to him talkin'. It must have been the time o' their lives, the Sixties, what with all that music and bell-bottom tight pants and lots of free love and everything. But I bet they still had headaches and mosquitoes and taxes, so I don't know what all the fuss was about. Anyway, Moms didn't have much to say about all that. Matter of fact, every time you talked about how we came to live at the edge of the swamps of Louisiana, she just got real quiet and stirred them okras a little harder with her lips folded under. And she sighed a lot or she sang a hymn until she calmed down.

See, the way I hear it, when she came to New O'lins, Moms wanted to move into one of those apartment complexes they built back in those days along Hayne Boulevard, "Lakeside Apartments" they called them. Those apartments were fancy and new and for people on the up and up. But my pops, he woke up one mornin' after the "vision" and had a better idea. He said with the oil boom there would be some major construction sweepin' through New O'lins. So he suggested that instead of wastin' money on a small apartment, especially with the first baby on the way, he and Moms should go get a piece of the wetlands much further east. He said he had some contacts, and the land would be dirt-cheap, and if they were lucky they'd prob'ly even find oil on it. But if not, they would just dig in their heels and wait, cos it was only a matter o' time before all that development got into the swamps. I hear my pops would mock-preach about that day, the day they would go to sleep in the swamps and wake up in a better part of town.

"Any day now, Valerie, any day now. Hah! We'll be moving, hah!… without a moving truck. Hah! We won't be movin' out from the swamps, hah! The swamp will be moving out from under us! Take a leap o' faith ba-bay, take a leap o' faith! Amen. Amen."

And Moms would tell him to settle down and stop mocking church, since he didn't go there. At least not to *her* church. Or maybe she just didn't believe in counting your eggs until they're hatched. But then again, maybe it was because Pops is white and he was mock-preachin' like them black Baptist preachers. And that mighta made Moms uncomfortable, I don't know. But look, my pops isn't prejudiced or nothin', so get over it. He married Moms and she's not white. She wasn't even born in America. But I'm the youngest, so my family

didn't discuss those details with me. Anyway, as Pa Campbell
tells it, every evening you could hear Pops coming into the
swamp from the train tracks excited and hollering at the top
of his voice about how far the construction had come.

"Valerie, what did I tell ya! They're all the way up past the
airport now!" – or "Valerie! They're building interchanges on
Interstate 10 now. Hah! It's comin'! Any day now. Just a little
longer ba-baay!"

Well, after a while Pops stopped talkin' so loud about the
whole thing, and then he stopped comin' home with the day's
progress report altogether. Pa Campbell says Pops prob'ly
should not have gotten land so far east, cos by the time I was
born in '73, the whole New O'lins development slowed down
and then stopped dead in its tracks just before it got into the
swamp. And then after that, when Moms would go into town
in the mornings, she said the cranes and bulldozers and all
those other construction machines just sat there by the side of
the road lookin' all tired and refusin' to go any further. And
in the evening, on her way back into the swamp, she would
pass them again, and sometimes she was hopin' to see them
suddenly start up and belch smoke into the air and dig at the
earth and move stuff, but they'd still be sitting there all cold
and lazy. Then, almost as soon as you passed them, civiliza-
tion just kinda surrendered, and you'd find yourself "on a
goddamn safari". The sounds of swamp life would drown out
the city more and more, until you were so deep in the soggi-
ness you wondered if the steel-and-stone city was only something you imagined up. Soon there was a crack on the map, an
area nine-minutes-wide by car. A clear line that showed where
the construction stopped and where the swamps began.

Pa Campbell said the city was "nearly near but fairly far"
– and the almostness of it was heartbreakin'. At least for my
pops. We crossed this distance into New O'lins every day
using a lonesome ribbon of road with bayou on both sides.
There was nothin' but mangroves and open water until you

hit the mainland and rolled under the very first overpass, the concrete feet of the city. This was the stretch between the swamps' desperate fingers and the toes of New O'lins. Toes that stood their ground. So by the arrival of the unexcitin' Eighties, there were four growin' children in the pass: Moms was sayin' we had moved to a "whole 'nother country, just slightly outside of a city", and Pops wasn't comin' home happy. Hell, some days he wasn't comin' home at all.

There was a long period when, every day after sunset, we'd take turns askin' Moms where Pops was. We always did it in order, from the eldest to the youngest, for some reason.

"Well," said Moms when Tony asked her where he was, "if the city didn't come to the man, the man will have to go to the city."

"Well, he's everywhere but here," she told Doug.

"Well, I think he took the scenic route home, son," she told Frico.

Simple answers. I was only eight, but when my turn came to ask, she had to make it complicated. She said: "Skid, I'm so tired a y'all asking me where he is. Why don't you all get on that CB radio and holler out your dad's name and tell him to get himself home."

So we did. Now, we had a CB radio, and in the Eighties that was a big deal. You had to have a CB nickname and all that fancy stuff. And we called our dad "T-Rex" on the radio. And my pops, he was one of the biggest godfathers of Citizen Band radio technology in the South. People knew him, cos he fixed CB radios and boosted their frequencies, and he invented all these sky-scrapin' antennae things that could prob'ly pick up as far as China. So when we all got on the radio and switched to Channel 19 and started pressing the hell out of the key on the microphone and jumpin' up and chantin' "Breaker, Breaker, T-Rex, you copy? Come on home, T-Rex", all the truckers and all the cops and the hunters and the shrimp fishermen and people as far as frickin' California and prob'ly Mexico could hear us. And man, they all started in on the joke, whether they knew T-Rex or not, cos that's one of the things that CB radio people do.

Well, within fifteen minutes we could hear the Ford Transit engine revvin' into the swamp and the tyres grindin' and the door slammin', and the great big ol' T-Rex came crashin' into the house with his claws all out and his teeth sharp. He looked across the room and growled at me, cos he said my voice was the loudest on Channel 19. *Me?* And he made me get back on the CB radio and announce that "T-Rex made it home tonight", and then I had to speak like I was an AM radio announcer, with a big, dumb radio voice and everything. I had to tell 'em what time it was, and do the weather report and tell 'em to "stay tuned for more news". See, in my house they had to get creative with punishment. For example, you can't tell a kid "Go to your room" in a one-room shack. You have to tell a kid "Go to your bed". So when I thought that my radio-announcer bit was good enough, Pops said, "Umm, naw," and made me go back "on the air" and apologize to each state capital and Mexico City individually. And that's hard when you don't have a map and you can't speak Spanish and your brothers are all snickerin' in the background. Moms was sorry for me, even though she had this big ol' smile on her face when she was sleepin' that night on account of rufflin' Pops' feathers. Meanwhile I stayed up listening to two owls matin' on the tin roof while trying to remember which of the capitals I'd left out. "Raleigh, North Carolina!" is what I jumped up and said at about one in the mornin'. The crickets couldn't care less, but out of the darkness Pops said: "It's about time, Skid." I think that phrase had become part of him, cos he heard it so many times comin' out of Moms' mouth. My Moms is real patient, but it seems that as soon as she realized this vision of his wasn't happening, she just got real antsy, and on some days she was plumb fit to be tied, I tell ya. We could hear "It's about time we got out of this swamp" fourteen times a week – seven if we went to bed early. And the poor guy would do his best and say just about anything to make her more comfy. But that's like fluffing someone's pillows when they're sleepin' in a graveyard, or buildin' somebody up like a big ol' dam. Cos one night, right after the sun nodded off, the Valerie Beaumont Dam broke and everything flowed into a big fight.

Two

See, how the cussin' started was we had this five-hundred-gallon water tank outside the house, and it was running low, almost empty, and that was slowing up work in the kitchen. Pops and Pa Campbell had been braggin' that they could use a mud pump and PVC pipe to dig a well until they hit groundwater. But they hadn't done much more than the braggin', cos those two can't stand each other long enough to get anything done. So when Pops made the mistake to ask Moms how far along his dinner was, she answered him the way Doug says women do when they've been stewin' about somethin' for a while.

"They got running water on Hayne Boulevard, Alrick."

At this point Pops could still have escaped by just playin' deaf.

"Huh... what?"

"I *said*, they got running water on Hayne Boulevard."

Once she repeated herself, it was too late. The poor guy dug into a radio he was fixin'. Couldn't even look around to face her.

"Oh... I see. Well... um, we got running water too, baby! And as soon as Pa Campbell helps me dig down to that groundwater, we won't have to be hauling water any more."

"They say you could drink the water straight from the tap on Hayne Boulevard, Alrick."

"OK, but I'm fixin' to dig a thirty-foot well with a distillation unit that's going to be the best damn distillation and desalination unit in the swamps, Valerie."

"You mean this year? This year, Nineteen Eighty-one? You got so many intentions and ambitions, this world is just too

15

small for you and the clock is short on time, Alrick Beaumont."

"Well, what else do you want, Valerie? I know this ain't your Hayne Boulevard, but we doing the best we can – look!"

And that's when he pushed back his chair and got up, and Tony started doing a quiet drum-roll sound effect with his mouth, cos he knew it was time once again for the *Grand Tour of our One-Room Swamp Shack*. My old man stood in the middle of the room and turned around three-sixty degrees, pointing with his left hand at things you really couldn't see, cos they were prob'ly outside in the mud or hidin' behind the mountains of stuff he was repairin'.

"Val. Look. We got a 45-kW generator with a Caterpillar D90 engine – brand-new – plus four eighteen-wheeler batteries for back-up. We got two four-by-two-foot KeroGas stoves for cookin' and bakin', a forty-channel Cobra CB radio – that's the latest, with more output than they allow in these parts. It's peaked and tuned and it's got a thirty-foot antenna outside, so you can talk to whoever you want. We got two HF-1200 walkie-talkies jus' in case someone needs to go into the woods. For godssake, we got the city right next door, Val!"

She just kept choppin' carrots without lookin' up. Instead she answered real soft, like the Wisdom Book of Proverbs say you should:

"You're right Alrick: we got everything we need *right* here. Everything... *except* running water and rice. That's right. Between makin' sure we all got home when you're out doin' your 'evening activities' and me trying to keep my two jobs cookin' and waitin' tables for other people, your wife forgot that we're out of rice. So, Alrick – look: we got five ounces o' lean ground beef, one large onion diced, ten ounces of sun-ripe tomatoes, green chilli chopped and one pound o' red beans, but we need about six or seven ounces of Zatarain's right about now. And where we going get it, Alrick?

And don't say 'Lam Lee Hahn'. Those Chinese people know exactly how to shut down shop and head home at night. They know that nobody 'cept the Beaumonts would be coming to make groceries this time o' night. Those Asian people, they opened a shop out here in this hellhole... but they're smart. They live in the city. In the *city*. So, you goin' get it, Alrick? Just pop into the city and get us some rice somewhere... since it's 'right next door'."

I wanted to point out to Moms that the Lam Lee Hahn family – who were genius to set up that small grocery shop out near the train tracks to serve swamp folks and make money – were actually Vietnamese. But this cussin' was goin' good, and I wanted to hear the endin'. Well, to be honest the endin' was disappointing at first. It was just Pops sayin' the usual "*bordel*" under his breath and me saying to myself, "You know, Skid, cuss words might be the only French your Cajunish father knows" – even though he liked tellin' us all about The Great Expulsion from French Canada back in Seventeen Fifty-something, as if he had been there.

Now from where I was, I could see Frico in the old dresser mirror, in his usual place on the floor beside the bed. That's where he liked to sit and do his sketches – where we couldn't see him. Moms told us to always look out for Frico. She said to make sure he had his glasses on when he was sketchin', and then pay close attention to him, cos sometimes that boy would be concentratin' so hard on what he was paintin' or drawin' – he'd forget to breathe. He'd just kind of fall asleep sittin' straight up with his eyes wide open. Yep, he'd blank out and wouldn't budge for hours. So we'd shake him – and if that didn't work, we'd prob'ly have to slap him. They wouldn't make me slap him, cos sometimes I didn't know my own strength.

Anyway, there he was: I'm watchin' him in the mirror and – would you believe it? – all of a sudden he just jumped up with the sketch pad and walked out of the house into the pitch black of night. Now that may sound simple, but you don't just walk out of Valerie Beaumont's house in the pitch black of night without someone accompanying you or making sure there are no black bears or water moccasins or demons lurkin' about the swamp. Furthermore, Frico was only nine years old. How dare you walk your nine-year-old self out of the house and let the screen door slam behind you like you can't stand all that fightin' in your ear? And especially *without* your glasses? But see, that's the kind of crap that Frico Beaumont got away with.

Now, I'm not sayin' I'm innocent. I'm jus' sayin' I couldn't catch a break, like with that CB incident – but Frico, everybody treated him like he was some kind of special, even though Skid Beaumont is the last Beaumont – the *baby* Beaumont. While me and Doug and Tony wash dishes and haul water and go borrow somethin' from that crabby ol' lady Ma Campbell across the fence, Frico gets to take Calvin, our yaller dog, on a lovely stroll to the shop or to go paint by the train tracks or deeper in the swamp. But even then, that's during the day. So when he stormed out of the house that night, I was waitin' to see if he was finally gonna get it. But Pops, he just stopped his Cajun-cussin' and said: "Y'all go on and get your little brother."

Of course, even if Doug and Tony weren't doin' no homework, they weren't gonna get up first, cos they were just tired of goin' after Frico. So I jumped up like a good boy, made sure the screen door didn't slam when I ran out, and waited to see if anybody was goin' to come after li'le ol' Skid and protect him from black bears, water moccasins and demons. But no, sir: 'twas just me, myself and a million crickets.

Now, even though I don't personally believe it, older folks say that strange things from hell walk under the old cypress trees after dark. So, if you ever go walkin' in the swamps, here's a few rules for ya, just like I heard 'em.

If you see a shadow walkin' out on the water, look away.

If you hear someone whistlin' or singin', don't join in.

If a voice calls your name in the woods, walk in the opposite direction. Quickly.

Watch out for a hairy man with his head in the trees: that's the Loogaroo werewolf man.

Look out for the little bald-headed girl walkin' fast – and don't follow her.

And most of all, you need to look out for James "Couyon" Jackson and his gang, who'd dope up on crack before coming in a black van to cut out your kidneys and leave you in a tub full of party ice and rock salt. The way I heard it, you'd rather bump into the Loogaroo man after dark than run into those crack-pipe-hittin' types in the broad daylight, I tell ya.

So yeah, Pops told me all these stories and then he let me go out alone. Anyway, all that waitin' in vain on the doorstep made me lose precious seconds, so by the time I chased after Frico he had disappeared, almost like the darkness was a stretch of water and he'd done gone under in it. Well, after walkin' blind for a while, I realized I didn't know where I was. See, in the pass, we lived on a little piece of land, shaped more or less like an "L" – a cul-de-sac, really. The top part of the L was connected to the mainland and led in from the train tracks that ran through the swamp. You went down a grassy slope from the tracks when you entered the L. Then, a little way in, there was a footbridge with a decent enough creek runnin' under it. You crossed that bridge and went on for about two hundred metres on a dumped-up marl road before going round a bend into the bottom part of the L, which is where we lived along with Ma and Pa Campbell. Their house was right across the chicken-wire fence from us.

Now, all around that L-island, as I call it, there was some murky swamp water filled with alligators and lots of drowning opportunities. So at night, without a light or a full moon, you could easily end up going off the corner of the L – and that would be the end of it. Furthermore, after the dry season, when rain broke a drought, big ol' sinkholes could be anywhere. So I stayed put until I saw Tony and Doug way behind me with a flashlight and I got a sense of where I was.

Doug was callin' out, "Skid, wait!" – so I walked in the opposite direction. Tony, who was the eldest at thirteen, began yellin' something scary about some vampire guy that he used to watch when my family had a TV. I wasn't goin' to look like no baby, so I took my bearings from the light and just kept walkin' until I saw the flashlight bobbin' up and down, on the ground and up in the cypress trees, so I knew they'd started runnin' after me. I took off at top speed and just kept lookin' behind me from time to time.

Now, I don't know how soon it was, but I just felt the ground getting soggier and soggier, and then I heard a voice from heaven say: "Skid, stop." Actually it was Frico's voice – but that was good enough. He sounded like he was up above me in a tree somewhere – and that was weird, but that's ol' Fricozoid for ya. Then, when I stopped and peeled my eyes and looked dead ahead into the night, there – right in front of me – was a steep slope straight into the dark swamp water.

"Don't move."

Hell, like I needed him to tell me that. I started reversing slowly, and he said again from up in the tree: "I said don't move – till I tell ya."

That's when I saw the eyes. Just above the water surface, right in front of me. One massive bull alligator, about a twelve-footer, right behind the grass, just waitin' for me to keep walkin' forward. Even though I'd just finished runnin', I felt colder than a dead eel and I started wondering where the hell was Doug and Tony when you need 'em? When they finally caught up, Tony was pantin', cos he was kinda pudgy. In the dark I could still see that Doug had a "what the hell is wrong witchoo" look on his face. He had dragged on his soccer uniform back to front and he had only half-pulled out his cornrows when all the chasin' started. He shone the light on the bank in front of me and said: "Look, fool."

I saw that I was standing in an alligator slide – that's the long slide marks that an alligator's belly makes in the mud when he's gettin' off the river banks to prob'ly get dinner. And that gator just sat there down in the water like a flesh-and-blood submarine and gave everybody the evil eye. Then Calvin came up and started yapperin' just to impress us, and the alligator raised his head and hissed just to let us know he wasn't off-duty. So I walked backwards slowly and Doug started givin' me a lecture, while Tony took the light and swept the area. He shone it into that monster's mouth and saw those teeth and started with the vampire stuff again until Doug, who was a year younger than him, told him to grow up or shut up, whichever one came first. So just to annoy him, Tony put on his nerd voice and looked at the sky, pointin' out that US satellites look different from stars and they can move them around from secret locations on earth – and Daddy knew, cos he helped build a rocket at the NASA Assembly Facility over in Michoud and blah blah blah.

In the middle of all that science fiction and Doug lecturin' and Calvin overdoin' the barkin' thing, here comes Frico's voice again from up in the tree, real slow and soft in the darkness: "See, this is exactly why I got out here in the first place. Can't catch a break from y'all. Jeez."

And Tony swung the flashlight into the trees and Frico shielded his eyes and nearly fell off a branch. The guy had climbed into a tree with some branches that hung out over the water. Moms said it was a tamarind tree. It was tall, but still smaller than those big old cypresses and beech and willow trees. It had low branches, so it was much easier to climb. We always went up into that tree durin' the day, cos it was like our lookout point. From up there, we could see clear across the train tracks over to that scrap-metal junkyard where those mean Benet boys live, north of us. Beyond their dungeon was an old clogged-up canal that could give them access to the far-east end of Lake Pontchartrain. Lookin' east, all you could see was train tracks. You couldn't see the end of the tracks, but we knew that one train went to Slidell – which when you're in the swamp is another city a whole world away. Turnin' around to the south-east, we could see the stretch of bayou in front of our house that, like I said, was built on the bottom part of the L shape I told you about. Along the underside of the L, you'd see Pa's sugar-cane strip, the mud levees we built, then some lonely crawfish traps bobbin' up and down in between the mangroves of the open pass. Beyond that there was nothin' but a lake and the eternal Gulf of Mexico way out south. Moms always said we came to live in the drainpipes of America. To the west was the best part, cos on a clear day you could see New O'lins with all those glass buildings lookin' liquid behind the shimmer.

Frico went "Shhh!" when Tony started climbing the tamarind tree and shakin' it. He made us stop halfway and promise we'd shut the hell up while he was drawing. It took effort, especially at night, but I climbed all the way up to the top where Frico was and told Tony to pass the flashlight, even though Frico had a cigarette lighter up there and everything. Frico had his back against the main part of the tree, and his legs were wrapped around a branch beneath him. Clutchin' a No. 6 pencil in his right hand, he stuck it into his shaggy hair. His left hand gripped a small sketch pad that was also restin' on his knee. I shone the light off to the side of the sketch pad, so that only the outer circle of the beam caught the drawin'. Frico was lookin' across the stretch of water towards our house. He was tryin' to sketch the swamp night scene, though he could barely make it out, cos he left his glasses plus the half-moon was just draggin' herself in over the Gulf. Then, when I turned around and looked west, my breath got stuck in my neck, cos for the first time, from up in that tree, I saw the city from the swamp at night. Downtown New O'lins was blazing and throbbin' – and when you moved your head, you could see all kinds of colours twinklin' through the trees. The high-rises, with all those fluorescent lights inside their windows, reached up like a crown covered in diamonds. Then again, around the base of the buildings, the gold glow of the street lights over in tourist town made the whole city look as if it was hoverin' on jet boosters – like something that just came down from above. But man, if there was someone out there in the city lookin' back at us from a window in one of those fancy buildings, all they'd see is pitch black.

Frico had finished the outline of our swamp shack peeking out from the cypresses, so he started filling in the night sky. The soft scratch-scratch of pencil on paper and a sudden light breeze from the east lifted the heat from the swamp floor and made me sleepy in no time. I sat in the fork of two branches, rested my head back, closed my eyes and thought of Pops' vision. I saw the buildings of New O'lins comin' closer and closer. I could hear them: a soft rush at first, like faraway rain. Then the rush became a rustle that broke into a rattle of glass against steel and steel against stone. Faster and faster, buildings popped up from the swamp floor until they all came crashin' through the trees in front of us. Fragile blue cranes and woodpeckers flew away, and suddenly we were so close that we could lean across and touch the cool walls that swooped into the sky. We could peep inside offices and leave oily forehead prints on the windows.

Then the light breeze stopped, and a mosquito started blowin' a jazz horn in my ears. It was off key, so I opened my eyes and killed it and wiped my palms on the tree. And my dream-city dried up and went away as well.

"Shhh!"

Frico didn't appreciate the noise, but something had distracted him before I did.

Lower down on the branches, Tony and Doug were pointin' to a light out on the bayou. Someone was prob'ly night-fishin' for bluegill near to our house. Pa Campbell wouldn't like that, cos whoever it was, they weren't from our little L of land. The boat with the light came across the water until it was right next to the bank and up under our tree. Then, all of a sudden, a big ol' rock came flyin' through the leaves of the tamarind tree. We hollered out and hung on for our lives. There was laughter from the darkness below and then a metallic sound came clangin' up through the branches. I swung the flashlight to see a grapplin' hook barely miss Frico's face. I ducked down, and the hook wrapped clockwise around a thick branch right behind my head. Someone started pulling on the rope and whoopin' and yellin', tryin' to shake us out the damn tree.

"Let catch ourselves some Beaumonts, Squash!"

It was the Benet boys, who called themselves "Broadway" and "Squash", our regular bayou teenage terrorists. They weren't much older than Tony, but they were tall and stout like footballers. Each one looked like half a house, and I heard they even had beards before they were eleven. *Freeze frame.*

Now see, these Benet boys were vicious. They'd do just about anything to make life in the swamp a little more miserable for everybody. They'd been expelled from too many schools to count. They hunted in and out of season, killin' things just because they could. Their father owned a junkyard, and they just set down all day and welded together new devices to do the worst damage possible. One torture tool was called the "eye-catcher". That was a catapult made from tin and tyre tubes. It shot nuts and bolts and could take an eye out. And don't bother tellin' their old man, cos he was worse than them.

Now it seemed the Benets were testing out a new weapon and they wanted us to be the guinea pigs, but we knew the drill when these demons came around. Holler and run. Doug was racing down the branches and Calvin was raisin' hell, when my pops came out of nowhere and stood under the tree.

"Stay where y'all are!" he shouted.

Then he took out his knife and, while the hook was still attached to the tamarind tree, he reached up, leant over the water and grabbed the rope stretchin' out towards the boat. He cut the rope and let it fall back into the bayou. Two voices cursed out of the dark, then everything was still again. Pops called up:

"Come on down boys, and let's go – seems like those Benet boys need a good whoopin'. I'll go across the tracks and talk to their ol' man in the mornin'. Right now I need to go get the rest of *my* whoopin' from your mother."

Say what you want about my pops, but nobody was goin' to mess with us and get away with it, even though that time he let those Benet boys off easy.

So we're walking back to our house and the Benet boys are behind us on the bank, wet like swamp rats and swearin' about what they were going to do us next – but they kept their distance. Then Pops – I watched him, that man – he took Frico and put him in front of himself as if to shield him from any other Benet missile. Then it got worse. Pops took off his jacket and wrapped Frico up and took all his pencils and stuff and carried them for him.

Now, when I looked at Doug and Tony, they didn't see nothing strange about all that mollycoddlin' and that special treatment. I mean, I know Frico's kinda feeble and he was born premature and all, but he's the one who jumped out into the night air. Now, in Pops' fancy suede jacket, Frico was a warm, fuzzy bear and I was feelin' like the slimy serpent.

When we got back to the house, Pops told us to go on inside, and he'd be right in. I thought he was goin' to visit old man Pa Campbell (even though they weren't on good speakin' terms ever), to tell him about the Benet boys hurling hooks and stones from their boat at us. But when I peeped outside through a crack between the boards that made up our swamp cabin, I saw him take something from his pocket. He looked this way and that way and stooped in the dark and dug at the dirt with his bare hands. Not like I didn't see him do this before, but he always told me, "Skid you ain't see nuthin' now, y'hear?" So I asked Moms what he was doin' there in the dirt this time of night.

"Planting his dreams, son. Just remind him to leave his work shoes on the porch."

And she used the sarcastic voice only cos she just had a fight with him. I mean, you could see she loved the guy. She just hated the swamp life, and that fight with Pops was like the beginnin' of sorrows. And that's when it hit me – like a hickory nut in a hurricane: the one stone I could use to kill two birds. I got to thinkin' that the way to get things back in shape in my family and make them have some respect for people other than Frico Beaumont was for me to get the city that had been sleeping for years to start movin' into the swamps again.

So how was I plannin' to get that done? I wasn't sure yet, but right round that time when things were looking pretty bad, I just kept thinking how everybody in my family was proud of Frico's skills on paper. Moms thought his paintings and drawings were somethin' special, and Pops said Frico's gifts were going to "put the Beaumonts on the map once and for all". Frico had won school competitions since kindergarten, and they even put a painting of his on greetin' cards for sick kids over at Charity Hospital in the city one Christmas. Doug and Tony liked takin' him places to impress girls. So if anything was really goin' to help us out, it may very well be this boy's talent.

But lemme tell ya – for me, it was much more than just talent. I knew things that the rest of my family had no idea about. See, when I was really young I used to follow Frico everywhere, cos that's what little toddler brothers do. And when I thought about it hard enough, I could remember that when I was about three years old, out by the train tracks, I saw Frico sketch on paper with his left hand... and he made some strange things happen. It had been a while, but deep down I *knew* what I saw. That boy was more than artistic. He had somethin' in his left hand… a strange power to *fix* things with a pencil. But just like the lazy machines on the New O'lins development, he had quit that kind of sketchin' and he wasn't budgin'. So my job was to figure out how to get him to do this thing again, in time.

Three

Rewind a li'le bit. So like I was sayin', when Frico was four, he sketched a picture of a cat that had a broken leg. And the cat got better and walked away. Man, that cat was so excited about havin' a brand-new back leg he just got up and hit the train tracks and walked and walked for miles and never came back – I swear. In kindergarten Frico drew himself pissing under a plum tree in the schoolyard, and the tree withered and *died*. Look, I'm not making this stuff up. I can't even stand the guy sometimes, but I was there. And that's what happened.

Now, I know I'm not talkin' hogwash, cos the rest of my family also told me about some li'le things that happened before I was born. Take for example, there's this story in my family about Frico Beaumont wakin' up as a baby and seein' a big ball of blue light over his crib and him reachin' out and touchin' it with his left hand. Doug was awake and saw the whole thing and told Moms and Pops. But they couldn't get around to agreeing on what it meant. Moms was saying the blue light was an angel, but Pops said, "Yes, angel from *hell*!" He said that any ball of blue light in the swamps wasn't nothin' but a damn *fifolet*. That's a spirit that was left to guard French treasure, centuries ago, he said. Meanwhile Frico thought all that blue-light stuff prob'ly never even happened. Doug just wanted an excuse to call him "*folet*", cos that's the closest you can get to callin' your brother "fool" without gettin' a lecture from Valerie Beaumont. Well, after that, that name is the only thing that stuck for a while. The real details of the story all went foggy, like "L-Island" before the rain moves in.

If you think that story doesn't mean anything, lemme tell you a little bit about the VW panel van Pops used to drive. Now, I heard that Pops was proud of that van and he always waxed it and parked it right on a slope where the sun came through the trees, so that the windshield could catch a ray of light and shoot it across the yard and straight into Pa Campbell's house. That would make the old man wonder "what the hell" and come to his window and see the van glistenin' and get jealous or just plain pissed off. Doug said Moms said she didn't know why Pops was showin' off, cos that panel van was NASA property and he shouldn't even be drivin' it home from the "facility" in the first place. Pops was a genius, but he wasn't no bigwig at work. He was one supervisor out of a hundred on an assembly line that helped put together rockets and other space vessels. Pretty cool.

Anyway, the VW van was there, all waxed and parked on a slope, glistenin'. Doug said he was sittin' in the back with Frico when Tony, who was about six at the time, went into the driver's seat and released the handbrake. I wasn't walkin' yet, thank God, so I wasn't caught up outside in the whole mess. Well, that VW panel van came rumblin' down the slope and Tony, he couldn't reach the brakes or anything, so the vehicle damn near missed a tree, but it scraped along Pa's chicken-wire and wood fence, until Pa Campbell ran out of his house, barefooted with cigarette in mouth, and jumped into the shotgun seat and pulled up the handbrake.

Well, everybody got shook up, and the van had a long scratch on the side. Now you can imagine, our pops is comin' out of the house yellin' at Pa for God knows why, Moms is taking her kids out of the van and shoutin', I'm inside screamin' for my grits and Pops and Pa Campbell start ballin' fists and knockin' the snot out of each other for no reason. Moms puts Frico down to stop the fight, and by the time they're finished tusslin' – *poof* – that scratch on the van was no more. Then everybody saw little Frico sittin' on the ground, drawin' a detailed version of the van in the dirt with his left hand. And they all stopped arguin' and said "aww" and gathered around Frico and told him he was amazin' – and I'm still inside screamin' for my damn grits.

Anyway, ask Tony Beaumont right now for his version of that story and he'll prob'ly tell you that it wasn't the first time he was "driving" Pops' van, so he had everything "under control" until Pa Campbell jumped into the shotgun seat and "threw him off so bad he had to scrape the fence". He'll also tell you that Pops' VW van had doors that slid all the way back, so when Moms retrieved her kids from inside it, she slid the door open and kept it there to hide the scratch on the side until the ol' T-Rex cooled down. Well, look here, you'll learn not to listen to Tony Beaumont's stories too much. Cos, first of all, if there was still damage on that panel van when Pops went to work, it would have gotten him fired. And the way I hear it, when Pops *did* eventually lose his job, it was cos he went to the NASA facility and tested out some biofuel that he invented from swamp duckweed and sugar-cane juice, and they caught him and said he was selling moonshine on government property. That scratch disappeared long before all that.

Well, *fast forward* again to Nineteen Eighty-one: after that night in the tamarind tree, we were still broke as hell and livin' in swamp and all, and I started off my plan by suggesting to Frico one day that we try to make some money with those powers of his. When I told him what I had in mind, he cleared his throat and scratched his red head and took off his tiny glasses and rubbed his freckled nose, and said that it was such a long time ago and we had prob'ly made up the whole story just to fool people, so it was all a lie about the cat walkin' and the tree dyin' anyway. Well, Frico's a real hard-headed bastard who would beat you up if you bothered him too much, so I took it easy. See, all he did at home all day was draw and paint. And like I said, the boy was good. So, nobody didn't

31

want to disturb him when he was doin' a masterpiece. He got away from me annoyin' him the same way he got out of going to make groceries at Lam Lee Hahn. He simply took out his brushes one at a time, chose watercolours and headed out to the train tracks. So many times I wished I could be that boy. He was talented – and he had it all figured out. Me? My talent was to make money, even though I had nothin' to show for it.

So, anyway, Frico was just play-actin' about the sketchin' bein' fake, cos before long *he did it again*. Now, this wasn't part of the plan, it just happened.

See, I borrowed this newspaper-boy tweed cap from my big brother Doug, though it was bigger than my head and fell down over my eyes most times. Doug said it made me look like the sax player in a New York jazz club. Tony said it made me look like an idiot, but he's the eldest: he didn't know much about what was cool any more. Well, it just so happened that Frico had a pair of tweed shorts with the same patterns as my newspaper-boy cap. Now, it's a tradition in my family to wear the other guy's clothes when he's not lookin'. We call it "bandwagonin'". See, you could ask to borrow somethin' from a guy, but that's no fun. So, with bandwagonin', the idea is not to get caught. If you happen to wagon a guy's shirt or shorts and you're lucky to see him comin', then you got to hide up in a tree and pray that the guy doesn't need his clothes right away. Oh, and if your feet are big and flat like Tony Beaumont's, you can't possibly be serious about wagonin' somebody's shoes, cos seriously – that's the end of them. Tony would wear Doug's church shoes, then come back in, clean the mud off and park them under the bed like nothing happened. That's what caused that big ol' Sunday-mornin' Mother's Day fight.

Everybody was all gussied up and ready to go to church. Doug was dapper in a coat and tie. But when he pulled out his brand-new church shoes from under the bed, they looked like a duck had been wearin' 'em for days and days. Man, you shoulda seen him and Tony rollin' and splashin' in the mud in front of our house and Ma Campbell callin' out to them from across the fence in the name of Jesus and Holy Mother Mary – and them standin' there tired and muddy as hell in their church suits and Moms just shakin' her head in disbelief. Poor Moms... but it was funny though.

Anyway, like I was sayin', one day I wagoned Frico's shorts to go with my cap. I couldn't bother to ask if I could borrow it, cos I was only goin' to go make groceries for Moms at Lam Lee Hahn. It was a good day, until that young Vietnamese girl at Lam Lee Hahn, the tomboy, she saw me come into the shop.

"You come heah yestuhday an' you come again today, good good."

"No."

"You no come yestuhday?"

"No."

"Hmm. Then, you have twin brodda, yes?"

"We're not twins."

"Hmm. Well, your brodda look like you. You have same clothes too!"

Sometimes the best answer you can give is "OK", so that's what I said. I was a little annoyed, cos I used to get that a lot. But I don't look like Frico. We got the same frizzy reddish hair, but he's skinnier than me. He has Pops' brown eyes and he wears specs. I got my moms' dark eyes. But I guess wearing Fricozoid's shorts didn't help matters neither. Then, as I was walkin' around in the store picking up groceries, the girl was followin' me around and tellin' me it was the Year of the Monkey and about all the things they do for the Vietnamese New Year. So I said, "That's nice, do you give discounts?" – cos I really wanted to keep some of Moms' change to drop into my savin' can or get some candy. Well, the girl, who was prob'ly ten or eleven at the time, she just smiled and kept smiling until her eyes disappeared, and she was so cute when she gave me a proper cussin' in bad English about how it's bad luck when the first customer for the day comes into the shop and starts bargainin' for discounts so early.

She said: "Leetle boy, you want to spoil da whole day?"

And I felt bad, 'specially since I was only buyin' bitter melons for Moms to put into her diabetic stew. So I said sorry and she made me promise to come back and spend more money and help her learn more English. I knew she outsmarted me, so I liked her style, and we stood there talkin' the whole time, while Moms' pot was waitin' on the bitter melons. Mai, her name was. Her family had moved to America seven years before. They were farmers, so they were fixin' to set up a farm out in the swamps behind the grocery shop to grow greens and raise chickens and catch fish out in the Gulf. She said you can't do all that in the city. Plus the swamps reminded the older folks of the country village where they used to live in Vietnam before the war – a pretty place at the end of the "Great Mekong River that runs from the top of the world to feed the Delta," she said like a teacher, but in broken English. Then, when she was describin' it some more, an old Vietnamese man, her grandfather I thought it was, he came out and spoke to her real hard and loud in Vietnamese, so I assumed I was distracting her from her shopkeepin' duties and I got out of there real quick.

But when I was goin' back home, the Lam Lee Hahn family dog, he got all excited by the old man's shoutin', and he barked and growled and dug under the fence and chased me and bit me on my right ass cheek. And that dog stood up on his back legs and held on with his teeth and rocked his head side to side and tore out the whole damn seat of Frico's goddamn borrowed pants. Man, that bastard Frico was so pissed at me he only sketched a picture of his tweed shorts all properly sewn up and left my backside with those tooth marks in it. Well, I wasn't gonna let him sketch my ass anyways, so whatever.

I told Moms it was the Benets' dog that did it, cos I didn't want to get my new friend Mai into any trouble. When Frico said he was goin' to tell Moms the truth, I had to give him the Snickers bar I bought plus two dollars' hush money. Anyway, I didn't mind. I was glad that at least I got that bastard to sketch something back to perfection, so those were the best bites of my life and money well spent.

Well, after that demonstration of his powers, I felt it was about time I called a meetin' about Frico's sketchin'. I needed to reveal Frico's powers to more people and create a plan to manage it going forward. Of course, before that I didn't brag to nobody else about Frico's powers, cos people always want too damn much. You know, they would want to tell him what to do and bring all their bullshit to get fixed without my permission or without payin'. Hey look, I was Frico's manager: I invested a Snickers bar and two dollars into that whole business. Shiit.

So that tamarind tree I told you about was our official conference room. Hell, we had to book it and everything. Not with an actual book, but you can't be having a serious conference and then ol' freckle-face Frico decides he wants to climb up and paint some bluebirds and tell us to shush. That boy loves critters. Got it from his mother. So anyway, you had to just tell the rest of the Beaumont boys, "Look, I'm in the conference room," and then pray they didn't come spyin'.

So I called up the crew. At the time it was Marlon the wannabe child star and our cousin Belly, who was really like a brother, but lived out at Honey Drop Drive close to Marlon's house. Honey Drop Drive was in an area they call De La Roulette, a little roundabout community north-west of us that's not built-up city, but it's definitely not swamp. It was supposed to have been a little gamblin' town, but that never happened.

Anyway, like I told you, us Beaumonts, we didn't have no phone, so roundin' up the crew for a meetin' could be one elaborate affair. I had to get on the CB and turn to that same Channel 19 that got me in trouble – cos it was the truckers' channel – and holler: "Breaker, breaker Tall Horse, Tall Horse you on the frequency, break?" "Tall Horse" was Belly's dad's CB nickname – or "handle", if you want to use a technical term. That name "Tall Horse" was also an automatic cuss word that my moms couldn't stand to hear me say in the house, so the longer Tall Horse took to answer the breaker-breaker, the more likely it was that Valerie Beaumont was gonna shut down the whole call. So, I'd shout out to Belly's daddy (who drove a sweet eighteen-wheeler over in Atlanta) and hope he was in his big rig. When he got to a rest stop, he'd shout up ol' Belly's house on Honey Drop Drive from a payphone and suffer through a lecture from my Aunt Bevlene about how Belly had too much free time on his hands and no fatherly guidance and needed a good talkin' to, plus some more maintenance money, cos he was only ten and eatin' everything in sight. And if some hitch-hiker girl giggled in the background, he would get another earful. So he just hurried up and told her, "It's long distance, Bevlene. Times a-wastin', time, time!" And Belly would come on and take the message that there was a meetin' in the swamp. Belly's daddy was cool like that. Then Belly would take another half an hour to lace his tennis shoes and primp himself and ride a quarter-mile to Marlon's house on his BMX bike and wait fifteen more minutes while Marlon practised bein' a child star in his garage.

So I was lookin' out from up in the conference-room tree, wonderin' what I could fine one of them for, and I saw Belly pedallin' towards L-Island along the train tracks. His plaid shirt was wet under the arms. I could fine him for that. Marlon was on the handlebars of the bicycle in one of those cool promotional T-shirts he got whenever he auditioned for a commercial. Belly was bobbin' his head and looked like he was talking to himself, while Marls had on those portable cassette-player headphones. As usual he was rewindin' cassettes with a pencil and singin' Air Supply at the top of his voice. Truth is, that boy couldn't carry a tune in a bucket. So as soon as they rode up, I climbed down and told Marls to pay a fine. He grabbed the headphones off.

"Fine? For what?! The conference ain't even started yet."

"For singin' in the swamps."

"Since when?"

"Since Pa Campbell told me that in Peru you shouldn't sing in the jungle, cos spirits will sing along with ya."

"Peru? Yo, look man, we live in America!"

"Peru *is* in America, moron. *South* America."

Belly jumped in, clappin' his hands: "And we live in the South... of America, South *A-mer-ica* – you got that? So... pay the money, man, c'mon, time, time! Matter of fact Marls, why don't you just make it easy on yourself and go get us some *bánh mì* and some cheese at Ham Lee Lamb?"

"Lam Lee Hahn. And some cold drinks," I said.

Marlon looked at us like he was being robbed. Which he was. He leant his head to one side.

"Wait just one minute, I wasn't the only one singin', man... Didn't you see Belly—"

"Naw man, I was *rappin'*. And that's different. Don't confuse the issue."

Marlon was nine at the time. We prob'ly treated him like a little boy, cos he was so short. And he chose to hang out with Belly, who was only ten and over five feet tall – and that wasn't goin' to help. Anyway, he said we'd all soon stop laughin' at him when he became a child star like his uncle up in New York said he would. Of course we all gave him a hard time about that, 'cept Frico, who believed in the guy ever since he got a small part in a McCozie's Furniture commercial when he was seven. It was a TV commercial, but you only got to see ol' Marls for a smidgen of the thirty seconds. He sat in a sofa with his "TV family", singin' one line in the jingle: "*Oooh... up to forty per cent off!*" That was funny as hell – cos seriously: who sings about a damn discount anyway? Anyway, when some kids along Honey Drop Drive started singin' that Marlon was "forty-per-cent tall" or "forty-per-cent small", Belly had to step in and rough these guys up, sayin' he was actually Marlon's half-brother and therefore the only one authorized to say nasty things to Marlon's face. Those kids bought it, even though Belly was touchin' the sky and Marlon was scrapin' the earth. Marls took all those blows like a champion, especially on his birthday. Every year, when his birthday rolled around, we'd say: "A child star needs to be a *child*, Marls, wha's happenin'?" And he'd say his uncle wanted to start right away, but his grandmother didn't understand the industry, cos she said he could only become a star when his grades improved.

Well, when he came back with the *bánh mì* and cheese, we climbed up in the conference room and I started breakin' open the middle of the bread and stuffin' the cheese in it. By the way, *bánh mì* is really French bread that thinks it's from Vietnam. Before long, Marls started back up with that child-star-dreamin'.

"I bet I can be a black child star like Gary Coleman."

"African-American, that's the new term."

"Yo Belly, look man. I'm not gettin' into all that South American, North American, African-American thing with you no mo', man. Whatever that new term is... I'm sure it's gonna be expensive. So I'm-a just be black, straight up!"

Well, it seems like things always came home to me in that tree, cos that was prob'ly the first time I was thinkin' about what Marlon was sayin'. Not the child-star part: it's what I would call the "who we are" part. You don't care too much about things like that when you're younger, but I was nearly nine.

But the way I saw it, we Beaumonts weren't "straight up" anythin'. My family couldn't call themselves Cajun just because Pops' greatest-granddaddies came from Canada and settled in the Atchafalaya Basin. He abandoned that lifestyle a long time before, and he was so far away from the culture he couldn't tell us much about what Cajun meant except for some of the superstitions, some cookin' and some cuss words. And we kids, we weren't quite country, but we weren't city boys neither. We grew up in a place that was like the soggy meat between two slabs of city. Of course, livin' out in limbo didn't help us look "normal". We'd turned up to school in clothes that showed we didn't live in the city, especially hip boots when it was rainin'. Meanwhile our friends would wonder what was up with our hair. Reddish-brown at the ends and black at the roots and off in every direction like nut grass. Plus, Moms made us all wear our hair in topknots – until we said we hated it. Frico never minded it, though, and soon the guy grew dreadlocks that he tied into three topknots that stuck out on top of his head. Made the guy look like a matchstick on fire – but he's an artist. Artists get away with anything. Anyway, I told our school friends that our moms is black and our pops is white, but I wasn't sure if it was all that simple to be called "Creole", even though a dictionary might tell you that. By the way, I'm not sayin' we weren't good-lookin'. Hell, we all got our daddy's height and frame and our mother's face and her smile, which means we were tall and handsome, we Beaumonts. You could see my moms and pops in my face, but there was someone else there in the high cheekbones, like a kind of riddle.

Some kids liked callin' us "weird" or "red-boned" or even "*mestizo*", even though we had no Spanish blood. But my creative-writin' teacher, Mrs Halloway, she would intervene and tell them that all those words didn't "adequately describe anybody's complexity". I liked Mrs Halloway: she used words that sounded crispy, or crackled like a snack wrapper.

So after a few seconds of thinkin' about all that, I said to hell with it and just followed what my mother said when she was experimenting in the kitchen: "Mix it all up and see what happens." Well, thanks to Marlon aka Child Star, I felt like I had the mixed-up part down pat.

Now, between all that deep thinkin', the bread and cheese and my plans to cash in on Frico's talents, I forgot that I should have been watchin' out for those hyenas, the Benet boys. So – by the time I saw Squash Benet – he was at the foot of the tree with a damn chainsaw. He pulled the recoil. The saw buzzed. Then he looked up and tried to shout somethin' above the noise.

"I can't hear you. Turn it off!"

He turned it off, and then, every time I tried to say somethin' else to him, that bastard pulled the recoil and started the buzzin' back up again.

"Whauut? I cain't hear ya from all the way down here! Speak up Beaumont!"

Broadway, the bigger Benet, appeared at this side. I glared down at both of them, but I reckon that from their perspective they could see all the way up our noses, and that's not a very menacing look at all. Broadway motioned for Squash to turn the saw off. He squinted his eyes and scratched the fuzz on his face and spoke like there were three dots between his words.

"Um… Yew boys… fixin' ta… eat all that… baguette by yusselves?"

Belly acted real quick. He slid down two branches and leant over to talk to Broadway and Squash.

"Yow, look, Herbert, Orville, I know it's been hard—"

Pause. Now, Belly knew these boys from Lanville Elementary over in Jefferson Parish. They prob'ly came in on the first day of school and started classes and then beat somebody up by second period and got expelled by recess. So I thought it made sense that he took a shot at talkin' to them. See, my cousin told us the whole story behind these Benet boys as he heard it from school – and it wasn't pretty. They weren't just mean: they had reasons to be miserable. For starters, they both had asthma and had to walk around with animal skins on their chest and inhalers in their pockets all day. Their mother had gotten up in the middle of the night and ran off and left their old man and had taken up with some rich guy from Shreveport, and it damn near killed old man Benet. So they left the house exactly as she last cleaned it, waitin' for her to come back. Belly rode past a few times on the train tracks and inspected the livin' room through the window. He said dust was so high in that house you'd have to shovel your way across the floor, with a tractor. There were dirty dishes in the sink and two dead sunflowers in a vase of green water on the mantel, prob'ly from the last time Mrs Benet put up a fresh batch, and the whole place was still decorated with dusty sunflower drapes.

Belly told us that their drinkin' water well had been contaminated real bad, cos their old man brought in illegal machinery and handymen and decided to dig for natural gas and oil by hisself. Now, the Benet part of the bayou looked like sludge: the fish couldn't swim in it, and that rotten egg smell wasn't just Broadway's armpits. It was stagnant water and animals decayin'. The whole natural-gas project failed, but that old man Benet was convinced that the gas was just deeper down in the limestone. He was determined to keep diggin'. They needed money bad, and Benet was desperate. Now, Belly knew all that. But the one thing my cousin didn't know about the Benets was that you should never, *ever* call the Benets by their real first names. Yup, that family was messed up. Their birth names sounded like insults in their ears. Even their old man called himself "Backhoe". The guy's real name is Tracey, for godsakes... with an "e".

So anyway, as soon as Belly said "Herbert" and "Orville", Squash's face turned red and Broadway just got the look of a murderer. The chainsaw rattled back up again and started gnawin' at the trunk of our tree. What's funny is that they made sure to drop their dainty little protective goggles over their eyes before they started splittin' wood. Anyway, when Marlon and Belly saw wood chips flyin' and felt the vibrations of the chainsaw, they started hollerin' for help – and I did what any sensible Beaumont would do: I dropped the baguette and cheese. Yep. I can't believe we gave up our refreshments like that, but look: these guys were choppin' down our conference room.

Now, it didn't matter to the Benets that the bread fell into two inches of mud on the bank. They turned off the saw, we breathed out, and Squash went and picked up the bread and brought it to his big brother. He looked up again and sneered at us.

"Tell yer pops... that we want... our groin-grabber back. Tell him to come around... to our house any time and bring it, cos... my poppa's been fixin' to have some words with him."

I looked up at where the hook had landed that night, and it was still there, snug around the branch. But now that I knew what the purpose of the hook was, a grabber for groins, I wasn't goin' to just toss it down and let them try and jingle our bells with it. So I said, "Sure, OK, I'll tell him" – and they walked away chewing on our bread. I was hopin' they'd bite both ends, so they'd have bad luck. Squash called out with his mouth full. "Oh, and yah might want to encour'ge that mongrel o' yours to stay out of our oil fields. It's dangerous out there."

It's real funny how your mind works, cos every time I remember watching those boys walk away over the tracks, eatin' our food, I can still hear the song that Marlon was makin' up about the whole thing. Imagine... we were mad and this guy was singin'. And that bastard knew we couldn't fine him again, cos he said he had no money left. What's worse, that song was catchy as hell.

As for the conference – well, after that bread-and-cheese robbery, I warn't in no mood to tell them about Frico's powers. But I still went ahead and told them anyway. And that was a bad move, cos I don't think I sold it very well. Belly and Marlon, they just looked at me and burst out laughing until they nearly fell out of the tree. Then they started in on me about how the Benets' underground gas was gettin' into my head and lots of other mean stuff that went on for half an hour and got so bad I'll only tell you the endin'. They said they'd only believe in the sketchin' if it could do the absolutely impossible.

"Hey, Marls, let's see those powers turn you into a child star."

"Fuh-geddit man! Let's make your daddy come back home without a hitch-hiker girl."

"Wait, wait, or... or make Skid get a girlfriend."

And they had to hang on to the tree while they were haw-hawin' and chokin' and enjoyin' themselves – until they were drunk on laughing at ol' Skid. I was happy I could make them laugh after the Benets robbed us. Furthermore, if I was the only believer in the Frico Church or the only investor in the Frico Enterprise, then I'd be the only one to get the blessin' or the benefit. So whatever. Those two clowns climbed down and rode away and left me up in that tree with only those good-for-nothin' tamarinds to keep me company. Those things are so tangy they set your teeth on edge and make your stomach bubble.

Four

Well, after that things just got worse between us and the Benets. Pops never went over there when he said he would. One Sunday, some decent church folk from Long Lake Free Gospel took the time to come baptize Tony in the creek, cos they said he was of age. Even though I was usually suspicious of city people who came into the swamp, it was a real nice occasion, cos they sang with harmonies and nothin' 'cept tambourines. *Freeze frame.* Church folks dressed in white, standin' waist-deep in the water. They all put their hands in the air and they're singin' and swayin' like trees. At their fingertips, cotton-ball clouds are polishin' the sky crystal-blue.

As soon as the service was over and the people went home, we were just relaxin' in the water, cos gators don't usually get into the creek, even in the deeper parts. Well, there came the Benet boys, who were watching the service from out on the bayou. Squash ran up and cannon-balled into the water and tried to pick a fight with born-again Tony. We ignored them at first, but we couldn't ignore the fact that all of a sudden the water got real warm and our legs started itchin'. That guy Squash came near to us and took a leak in the creek, and it was right in the spot where they had just had a *baptism*, for godssake.

Now, that was wrong on so many levels. So we jumped out of the water to throw this guy in with his own pee, but his big brother pulled a shotgun from a wheelbarrow and said: "Stand down boys. No use... goin' to meet yer maker... so soon." And even though we reckoned he didn't have no bullets in it, we weren't takin' no chances, cos I wasn't sure if Frico's powers could work on gunshot wounds. Then Broadway used the shotgun barrel to pick up all of our clothes that were on the bank and throw them into the water, and we had to watch him do it.

The next day, I took the groin-grabber out to the train tracks and called out and threw it over to their side, thinkin' that's what they wanted. I told them to leave us Beaumonts alone after that, but they just laughed and came and grabbed me and held my head down on the tracks until the eastbound freight train was about ten seconds from my goddamn nose. I had nightmares and smelt diesel for weeks.

During those weeks, ol' Tony Beaumont invented a rocket from an empty chlorine-bleach bottle. I told him that thing would never reach the moon.

"It's doesn't have to, punk. It just needs to reach the Benet house."

"Ohh, a *missile*."

Then, when I saw him stuffing the bottle with some fireworks that Mai gave me, I didn't like that, and we had a tussle. Mid-fight he stood up like a war general and put one hand on his chest and used the other one to hold me off by my forehead. He made a speech while I was swingin' fists. He said givin' up those fireworks was part of my "destiny" and my role in the "Beaumont retaliation for family pride and glory". That sounded so cool.

So we launched that missile at dusk. It glinted purple-blue up against the ground, then rattled and jumped off into the air, smoke and sparks trailin' behind it. We cheered, but it didn't reach the target. It fell plop onto the train tracks and made a colourful fireworks show. Then I remembered about Belly's natural-gas story, so I told Tony the bleach-bottle bomb was a stupid idea that could have gotten us all killed. But really I was just mad that all my sentimentally attached fireworks went up in smoke for nothin'.

Well, Broadway and Squash found out we tried to bomb them, and one day after school they blocked the footbridge when Tony and Belly were tryin' to cross over the creek.

Those Benet boys prob'ly learnt new words that day, so they told Tony that *gens de coleur* have to swim across the creek. Tony didn't mind, cos the bridge was getting rickety anyway, and Pops and Pa Campbell hadn't gotten around to fixin' it. So him and Belly took off their shoes on the bank, and while crossin' under the bridge Tony told them, "Y'all can't even spell *gens de coleur*." That floored them, cos it was true.

So they leant over the bridge and dropped spitballs on Tony and Belly while tellin' them that all Beaumonts were tryin' to "*passe blanc*", which was their way of sayin' we were tryin' to look white. Well, they didn't take too kindly to Belly sayin' that they were tryin' to "*passe* smart" and "*passe* handsome", so they chased him and Tony with a big ol' huntin' knife.

At that point Moms did what Pops shoulda done. She marched all of us over to talk to Backhoe Benet. She never called his name or nothin'. She just stepped up on his porch and said good evenin'. But he wouldn't come out to us and talked to her through a window behind the dirty sunflower curtains as if he didn't care. So she stood there and made a statement:

"My kids came runnin' into the house today, chased by your boys. And it got me thinking that whether we all came here last year, thirteen years ago or hundreds of years ago, we're all running from something. We're all refugees here. And… this refuge is the worst of 'em. It's… it's not even a ghetto. It's a swamp. And it's not even a decent swamp. Nothin's even s'posed to live out in these parts 'cept for the critters. And they're not making much of a fuss other than they s'posed to. So if my chil'ren can't catch a break here, then where the hell are we supposed to go?"

When the figure behind the curtain just laughed softly, she realized it was no use.

"Well, we can all go to hell if that's what y'all want. So let me know."

Somehow, Pops never got involved in all that. He was always walkin' on a slant, so to speak, until one night he came home sober and the Ford Transit lights showed him somethin' that popped his head gasket. See, Pops had this aluminum sign that he was real proud of. He painted it himself and put it right at the entrance of our little L of land. It was about two by three foot and it said:

REPAIR 'EM LIKE BRAND NEW!
KeroGas Stoves, Televisions
CB Radios and Appliances
CALL INSIDE NOW

Well, the Benets took the sign for target practice. They shot holes through all the letters that had a space to shoot through. Pops stayed up all night paintin' a new sign and cussin'. He put it up the next day on a piece of ballistic steel that he borrowed when he used to work at that Michoud facility.

When they couldn't shoot through that, the Benet boys just went ahead and tore the whole sign down and lay it flat on the ground and threw paint all over it. So Pops said "Hell no" and went across the tracks to talk to them. He told us to wait by the tracks while he walked across with the sign in his hand and the pole draggin' behind him. The sunflower drapes moved. It was Backhoe Benet. We saw the rifle nozzle pointin' at Pops. We saw the flash, heard the shot, and saw our Pops jerk backwards when the bullet hit the sign in his hand. Pops was still standing. Backhoe laughed out loud and said, "Jus' checkin', Beaumont!" He motioned with the barrel for Pops to leave the bulletproof material out in the yard. "What's in my yard is mine, includin' you!"

The door opened. We saw the dead sunflowers on the mantel, then Pops disappeared and the door shut. Well, we weren't movin' until we saw our pops again – and in about three quarters of an hour he came out with the glummest look on his face. He was carrying a cardboard box with six puppies in it. They were cute little critters. All brown mutts with black mouths. One had a white mark on his right front foot like a sock. We walked alongside Pops. He was walking fast and talkin' real quiet. We had to jog to keep up.

"Mr Benet says these six kids belong to Calvin. Said he doesn't want mongrels in his yard, and we should keep our dog off his property, or else. You boys'll have to chain him for a while, y'hear?"

So it seems Calvin went and got himself entangled with the worst people in the swamp. Calvin, why? Why not at Gladys', that sweet ol' widow from further down the tracks? She had girl dogs and she'd keep the pups too. Why not Evin Levine, that hunter guy in the busted-up boathouse who could prob'ly use a couple more mutts in his huntin'? But no, Calvin had to go cavortin' with Ol' Medusa Benet, the worst dog possible, even though dogs can behave much better than people sometimes. All in all, that didn't matter too much. What was real puzzlin' for me was that I knew my daddy didn't go face to face with the Benets just to talk to them for forty-five minutes about a shot-up sign or about Calvin knockin' up their dog. So when everybody was oohing and aahing over the pups, and Frico was sketchin' them bitin' his toes, and Calvin was nappin' on the porch like he had nothin' to do with all this, I sat down on the floor beside the bed and I wondered: "Everybody sees the puppies Pops brought over... but can't nobody see the monkey on his back?"

Five

Well, I don't think I have to tell you how deflated I was feelin' after those two laughed at me up in that tree. However, just when I was really low, things got better. Round about that time we went to this Easter Break Baptist youth camp somewhere along the Gulf Coast. It was Harry T's idea, cos he had joined the Cub Scouts by then and said he knew everythin' about campin' and knots and signal fires and morse code and all that stuff. Valerie Beaumont let us go, even though it was such short notice. We sat on a couple of broke TV sets in the back of Pops' Ford Transit and he dropped us off with our makeshift campin' gear. Nothin' fancy. It was me, Frico, Marlon, Belly and Harry T, and we got there early to help set up for the rest of the camp kids.

Now, when the bus came at sunset, this little city boy Peter Grant, who never got out of his house much, he was runnin' beside that bus for about half a mile, and all the kids on the bus were cheering him on until he tripped over a rock in the dirt road and fell and busted his face wide open. Pow. And everybody said, "Oh my gosh" – and he was bleeding bad and the camp nurse wasn't there yet. So they washed him off, and we went into our cabin and – guess what – Frico actually took out his sketchpad and fixed ol' Peter Grant up real perfect. I held the flashlight so Frico could draw his face proper, and we didn't even charge the guy a dime. You should've seen that midget Marlon and Belly eatin' their words like cold soup. But to this day Harry T keeps sayin' the nurse came and I slept through the whole thing. Yeah, right. All I knew was that even though Frico was still reluctant to sketch, him fixin' those shorts and patchin' up ol' city boy Peter Grant's face meant that soon we'd be in business.

Of course I knew that when camp was over, Marlon and Belly would go back to pretendin' that they didn't see what happened at camp. So as soon as we got back to school, I hatched a plan. See, that statement about the impossibility of Skid getting a girlfriend really hit a nerve. So I said to myself: "I'm goin' to do better than gettin' a girl. I'm goin' to go for the best one there is."

Now, I should tell you: I love older women. Loved them since I was, like, six or thereabouts. And why not? Older women are so fine. Anyone who knows me will tell ya, there's somethin' about a woman many years my senior that makes Skid Beaumont act up like he's on catnip.

That's why when little Suzy Wilson first came to Long Lake Elementary in '82, I wasn't interested. Suzy Wilson was the most popular girl in school, even though she was skinny and too talkative and her chin was all pointy and whatever. She came from a sleepy corner of Canada, the French part, like my pops' great-great-grandpopses, where it prob'ly snows all year and everybody stays inside. And I suppose there's not a whole bunch of people to talk to on account of that. So when Suzy landed in Louisiana she had a hell of a lot of catching up to do. Man, that little girl would yap and my ears would just fall asleep.

So, to be honest, the only thing I liked about Suzy Wilson was her aunt, Miss Fiola Lambert. *Slow motion.* Miss Lambert was this sweet-lookin' teacher at Long Lake with a French accent and curls in her hair like a little girl. But man – there was no mistakin' she was a woman. She was like warm toast soaked in syrup, or a cup of that camomile tea they serve in fancy restaurants – hot and dreamy. They said she had "European charm". I wasn't quite sure what that meant, but it sounded real delicate, like those heels that made her legs look so long. Even Pops, when he came to the school and couldn't remember Miss Lambert's name, he kept referring to her as "Miss Jacob's Ladder", cos he said her legs "went all the way up to heaven". Of course Moms gave him hell for that. Anyway, when all the guys were salivatin' over little Suzy and her lemonade stare, I closed one eye and took a look at her aunt, thirty-year-old Miss Lambert, just so I could imagine Suzy in the future. And I gotta tell ya, future Suzy Wilson was hot as hell.

Meanwhile, Marlon, Frico, Harry T and this other dude Kevin, they all liked Suzy. Man, it was like a circus. Everybody came with somethin' to try to impress that girl. But Marlon, he took the whole thing to another level. He got all cheesy and started writing songs for her. Well, actually he was just making up new words for Michael Jackson songs and singing them back to her, like she wouldn't notice. Psssh. That hypocrite Suzy would just sit there on the steps during recess sipping the cold drink Marlon bought her day after day, pretendin' to love those tunes. After a while Frico couldn't bear to see him sufferin'. So he told Marlon: "Look. Lay off the lunchtime concerts, man. She's laughin' at you." My boy prob'ly thought Frico just wanted to thin out the competition, so he kept up the karaoke. But my brother knew what he was talking about. That Suzy Wilson is damn lucky Frico didn't use his sketching powers to make her ugly, cos I reckon he wouldn't have had to sketch too much. Now, in spite of everything, Suzy didn't really bother me apart from the yappin' and takin' my friends for a ride, but then somethin' happened one day during recess.

I was listenin' to some music on Marlon's cassette player. While I was tappin' my fingers to the beats, Suzy Wilson comes and pulls off the headphones and asks how come I didn't hang around her like Marlon and the others. I wanted to say, "Cos you're a yapper." But I thought that would be nasty, so I tried to be clever. I told her, "Naw kid, you're too young for me. I'm really into your aunt though." Soon as I said it, Suzy's jaws dropped, her eyes bugged out and I knew I was dead.

So there I was in Principal Phillips' office watchin' this half-willin' ceilin' fan havin' a borin' conversation with a type-writer that was clickety-clackin' in the back room, when Moms walks in, demanding to know why her son was sent to the principal for saying he liked one of his teachers. Now Phillips, he's the principalest-looking principal you'll ever see: he pushed back his glasses with his finger, stroked his double chin as if he had a brand-new point of view, and as usual started with a quote from some long-ago guy:

"Mrs Beaumont, have you ever heard the saying, 'A child unbridled is a public report of domestic misdeed'?"

"So my kid is a horse?"

That was prob'ly the first time I saw Phillips stop dead in his tracks. He just sat there silent, and the smell of fresh exam papers came out of that room with the noise of the faraway typewriter, and it just made me feel sick all of a sudden.

"You see, Mrs Beaumont," says the principal in the end, "it's not so much what your son said that got him into trouble: it's what he was doing when he said those words... Terence, do you mind showing your mother?"

Aw, dammit. Now, I honestly didn't remember what I was doin' at the time. And I meant no disrespect for Miss Lambert. I was just tryin' to look cool in front of her niece. But now ol' Screwdriver Phillips wanted me to demonstrate some dumb thrust-and-grind move for Moms in front of pointy-chin Suzy. Look, I can't even dance, man. And lemme tell you, Moms hates anythin' that looks like disrespect for other people. So yeah, that day I got punished twice because of damn Suzy Wilson. But I didn't care about all that: that goddess Fiola Lambert and I were meant to be together, even if Suzy would be my niece-in-law or whatever you wanna call it.

Now, even though I always put my hand up in her class (and that made the others call me *mon petit chou*, which is supposed to mean "teacher's pet" or somethin' like that), technically speakin' Miss Lambert didn't know how I felt. So

I figured I had to get her attention. And it couldn't be that whole corniness of a present or an apple on her desk. Hell, who does that? Plus I ain't got no money for no presents. Of course, even though I had just turned nine, I had a brother who could sketch a picture of me and magically make me look all grown up and handsomer in real life, but he was being a jerk and not using his powers much at all. So – guess what – I decided to try some magic sketchin' for myself. Yeah, you heard me. You can laugh, but see, I figured me and Frico, we shared the same womb and all, so maybe I had the same powers but I just didn't know it yet.

So I tried sketchin' myself a few times, but then I got scared, cos only the kinky, red-hair part of that left-handed drawing looked like me, and I didn't want to get stuck as a stick man for the rest of my life. Well, I stepped it up. A few days after that, I got this eyebrow pencil and locked myself in the bathroom and reckoned I could just sketch a moustache and beard on my reflection in the mirror to see if I could grow them real fast. I figured my powers would be weaker than Frico's, so I doubled up. I did the moustache-and-beard sketchin' every single day until Moms, she started asking who the hell kept smudging up the bathroom mirror. So one morning I was using some vaseline to clean that smudge off the glass when Moms, late for work, barged into the bathroom and caught me with one hand holding an eyebrow pencil and the other hand in her jar of vaseline. She took the Lord's name in vain, and Doug and Tony came running.

Of course, after that the mirror-sketchin' had to stop. I figured I was prob'ly going about it all wrong anyhow. Maybe Frico sketched with only magic pencils or somethin', or maybe he said some secret words before he did the drawing. But man, I was as confused as the very first bug to hit the very first light bulb they ever invented. I didn't know where I was going with this sketchin' thing, and the longer my powers took to kick in, the more my bigger plans were gettin' delayed.

Well, after Prize-Giving that year, the guidance counsellor at school wrote to Moms and asked her to take me over to see this lady doctor in New O'lins proper, right by the Lake. Apparently, this lady would see me for free. I wasn't quite sure why we had to go to this doctor lady, cos I felt OK. But I figured on the way there that it might have something to do with that eyebrow pencil I'd borrowed from Miss Lambert's handbag. Or the whole vaseline incident, or me taking all of Frico's pencils and then lyin' about it. Well, whatever the crime, I didn't mind doing the time, cos man, this lady doctor looked like she was in her thirties and she was *fine*.

"Hi there, I'm Dr Barton. You can call me Lisa." She had a dusty, baby-powder voice and the cutest, slightest gap between her two front teeth. *Wow.*

"Hi Lisa. I'm Skid. I'm nine... almost ten."

Moms told Dr Barton I wasn't gettin' along with the girls at school. Hell, it was just *one* girl. The doctor asked me to talk about that. She sat forward and smiled and looked at me with her eyes all soft and bright, like two full moons over Lake Ponchartrain. *Aww man.*

Now, I decided I wasn't going to start off with some immature story about Suzy with this fine lady, so I said: "Well, my mother's right. I don't like girls. I like women."

Lady doctor nearly died laughing. After that, things got less funny. She kept asking me how I felt about my mother and Pops and a bunch of other serious stuff I can't recall or can't see why they were important.

Then she asked me what made me afraid. To be honest, even with all that junk about the Loogaroo and Couyon and whatever else, the only thing I was really afraid of was not havin' any cash at all in my pocket. But before I could tell her that, she gave me this big ol' sheet of black paper and some neon-coloured chalk and asked me to use my left hand to draw "whatever it was that protected me from what I was afraid of", or some such thing. Of course, I could only think of drawing my big brother Doug, cos look, the poor guy would give me all of his lunch money every single day if I told him I lost mine. So that was easy. Then the doctor asked me to draw a picture of myself. *Aw, hell no.* My sketching powers could kick in any time now, and like you prob'ly figured out, I couldn't draw to save my life, so I didn't want to start doing that again and risk screwing up my looks. Especially since the left-hand drawing I did of Doug just looked like crap. Plus, that Dr Barton would get to keep my sketches, and I wouldn't be able to destroy the damn things if everything went to hell in a hurry. So nope. There was no way I was gonna draw an image of myself ever again.

Now, I like volcanoes for some reason. So instead, I drew a massive volcano, rising up through the clouds, with jagged edges at the top. It was roarin' to life with a red, boilin' crater at the top and smoke and ashes above the cone, and there was a long, lonely road leadin' up to it. My drawin' was cool – even though if artsy-fartsy Frico saw it, he wouldn't be too impressed with it.

Well, the doc, she looked at my drawing and said: "OK, so where exactly are you in this drawing?"

I told her me and my older brother Frico, we were right up there on the road closer to the volcano, too far along for anybody to see us. We were goin' to go fix the cracks in the crater. Then she smiled and looked so sad in her full-moon eyes that I wanted to ask her if I could draw somethin' else. But then she asked Moms to let her speak to me alone.

When Moms went outside, the doctor asked me if there was anything else I had to tell her, and I told myself I wasn't going to say anything about Frico to this lovely lady. But she prob'ly hypnotized it out of me. You know how sweet these ladies can be. So I just found myself babblin' on and on and tellin' the doctor about the sketchin' and how I was working on my own powers and stuff.

I was talkin' like I was tumblin' down some stairs. You know, like when you want to stop yourself but you just can't?

And the whole time, that sweet lady, she's looking at me and smilin' sad, but she was so beautiful that I just went on and on about Frico and the cat and the plum tree and the shorts and Peter Grant's face and how my brother wasn't sketchin' enough and I wish he would... cos everything in life was broken and needed fixin', especially New O'lins and all. You gotta say stuff like that to a woman. Women like it when you're sincere and poetic. At least that's what Doug told me.

Then it was Moms' turn. The doctor took me to a room with some other kids so she could talk to Moms alone, but I snuck back and lay flat on my belly and listened under the door. I couldn't hear what the doc was sayin', but whatever it was, it was making Moms fall to pieces. I could hear her talkin' between tears.

"Yes, Dr Barton" – *sniffle* – "it's not goin' so well between their father and me. He used to be a wonderful man" – *sniffle* – "sweet 'n' kind when we just got married and I came over with him. But he's not himself any more, and it's ruining everything... my poor chil'ren."

Well, hell, I didn't know what that was all about. After all, I was the reason we went into all that trouble to get dressed up and bother old man Pa Campbell to drive us into town to see the doctor – so why was Moms cryin' about Pops and tellin' all her stuff to this sweet lady?

I listened some more, but then this security guard that looked like Colonel Sanders, he came and lifted me up by the belt and set me on my feet and said: "Go on now" – and that made me miss the best parts.

Anyway, Moms' eyes were all red and she kept rubbing my shaggy head the whole way home. I took the opportunity and got her to buy a Po' Boy for dinner. That's a big ol' Louisiana sandwich and a once-in-a-blue-moon meal in my family.

Well, we never went back to that sweet baby-powder lady doctor Lisa. And for a while I wondered if I went too far with the Frico story.

Anyway, that day I couldn't wait to get home to see if Doug was still in one piece, cos like I said, I drew him all screwed up. So I ran into the house and there he was, sittin' in that big ol' tangerine armchair behind the door. I stopped and stared at him.

"What you lookin' at, Skid?" he hollered at me after about ten seconds of me starin'.

"You doin' OK? You feeling all right Doug?" I went closer to inspect him.

"Yeah, I'm fine, fool, what's the matter with this one, Momma?"

"Don't call your brother those names, Doug."

She stepped towards us, her eyes all angry.

"I don't care what nobody says, y'all are just fine. And y'all gonna be fine!"

And she just broke down again and started bawling in the middle of the room. And Doug, he said he was sorry and came over and hugged her – and I was hugging her too, but meanwhile I was looking Doug over from head to foot, and it looked to me like he was in one piece. So when I was sure that he was feeling all guilty about making Moms cry, I just told him: "I lost my lunch money today again, Doug."

Six

"Alrick Beaumont is a brilliant man.
He can fix anything, and he can
shock dead radios back to life,
resurrect old stoves gone cold…
He makes sleeping TV sets open their eyes
and assembles rockets that go
high up on the blue shelf of heaven,
blazing bright above our level."

September 9, 1983

OK, I know it sounds all artsy-fartsy and real pretentious, but that year my pops was payin' me ten dollars to write that crap about him. And since ol' Skid didn't get much for his birthday, I needed the money. See, on your birthday you got a good breakfast, lunch money and dinner just like other days. If it was on a weekend, Moms would bake cornbread. But generally, she gave you a kiss and prayed for you, Pops slapped you on the back and told your brothers to grab you by the arms and legs and bounce your butt on a rock ten times for good luck and then toss your ass in the bayou – and that was it. "Happy Birthday till next year, y'hear!"

So when this poem thing came about three days after I hit the big One Zero, I sat down on an old car seat beside the house facing the bayou and tried to write something. Now, that car seat is real comfy, cos over it there's an old bedspring leant up against the house that's covered with some herb vine that Moms calls *cerasee*. She says it's good to drink for purgin' the blood. Well, all I know is, that car seat and the bed spring covered with cerasee vine both make a nice, shady spot for fallin' asleep. So every time I tried writin' I just drifted off into Pops' vision.

So after that, I got Doug and Tony to help me write it, but I didn't tell them about the ten-dollar prize. Doug came up with that "blue shelf" part. Now, I didn't know exactly why Pops needed me to do this, but I think it had somethin' to do with him and Moms. But hell, adults are always weird that way, so I kept my mind on the prize money and wrote proper English like I learnt in school and like Moms taught me. I really wanted to start writin' all my poetic stuff in a journal, but you ain't got no privacy with three brothers and one room. Anyway, the first line of the poem gave ol' Pops goose pimples. I swear the man teared up and I got my ten dollars and went straight to Lam Lee Hahn with it.

I bought a stash of cold drinks and dried plums and a sketch pad for Frico just in case we needed it. I stashed everything up in the tamarind tree by securin' it with copper wires from inside an old standin' fan. Then I banked the other six dollars in that empty propane canister behind the dresser. Apart from the money, I was proud of myself cos I had beaten ol' Fricozoid at somethin'.

See, Pops asked Frico first to write a composition about his father. Told him he'd get the ten dollars and everything. But ol' Frico he just couldn't help himself. He had to tell the truth. He wrote somethin' about Pops not knowin' how to love and care for a woman, and how women need to be cared for, especially the mother of his children – and all that. Well, look: I agreed with Frico one hundred per cent, but that ain't goin' get you no money.

So I sat down, gathered my big brothers around me, took out my dictionary and wrote Mr Alrick Beaumont a poem. Not a composition... a poem. Oooh – you shoulda seen that money comin' out of his wallet. He wanted to give me one big, borin' old Ten Spot just like that, but I told him I needed ten one-dollar bills, so I could throw them up in the air and count them over and over. *Freeze frame*. And for his honesty, Frico got squat.

Of course, Valerie Beaumont found out about the whole poetry-sweepstakes thing and she silently raised hell.

It was one of those whisperin' arguments done inside when we kids were out in the yard playin' soccer penalty shootouts. Pa Campbell had just come over to help Pops raise the porch again. We had to do this every year or so because of the subsidence in the swamp – and the porch, which was on the softer side closer to the water, always sank faster. Pops used to say if I shut up long enough I could hear the house sinkin'. Anyway, they dumped a load of marl and gravel and took apart the porch, and while Pa was busy hammerin', Moms and Pops used the noise for cover.

"I don't know what the big deal is, Valerie."

"Oh, you mean apart from teaching your child to gamble and using money we don't have?"

"Gamble!"

"Yes, gamble. And bribery. Tryin' to buy their loyalties. To prove you're special."

"What's botherin' you, Valerie?"

"Do you know why we're here? Cos I've always believed in you. I look into the sky at night and I know that the man I married helped put rockets all the way up there."

Her voice went softer, so I had to press my ear up against the frosted-glass louvre. It was cold.

"Alrick – he can do anything. But one thing he can't do is take us out of this swamp."

"Is that what's botherin' you?"

"What's botherin' me is that your chil'ren are losin' the father they know... that we're poor... that we been here too long."

"Here we go again. You've never—"

"See that old PVC pipe out in the yard? The one that leads from the tank? That plastic pipe is a symbol for me."

"Jeez…"

"It's above ground, Alrick, *above* ground. And do you remember why? Cos when we just got here, you said: 'Let's not
even bury that pipe, cos it's only temporary… all temporary.'
Soon the city'll be sweepin' through here and we'll be in a
better place. Now congratulations on finishin' the well, but
that pipe is still there."

"Look, Val—"

"No, *you* look around you, Alrick! I'm still here – we're all
still here – taking it lying down just like that plastic pipe. The
city is afraid of these backwaters. And meanwhile, you think
it's OK to give your chil'ren money to feed your vanity?"

And then Pa Campbell hammered up a storm – and I was
happy, cos I didn't want to hear any more. I went up into the
tree for a cold drink and looked into the city.

Well, by early the followin' year, we started goin' to church
more and "spendin' more time as a family", as Moms put
it. On weekdays, as soon she got home from cookin' and
waitin' tables, she would help us with our homework by
herself. And then before dinner we'd light a small fire outside behind the house and put some wild bushes on it to
help chase the mosquitoes and the gnats away, cos especially when it rained and you heard those sad ol' cypress
trees weepin' into the water, you knew the bugs were comin'
out to feed. You heard them coming. Then after dark the
crickets took over and worked the night shift – thousands
of them chirpin' all night to the beat of one raindrop at a
time, sliding off a leaf into the swamp water or drumming
into one of Moms' cookin' pots through the tin roof. That's
how you'd pass time when it rained: counting drops and
cursin' crickets. Then all you needed was Pa Campbell wai-
lin' the blues on his harmonica for you to feel like you could
lay down in the bayou and blow bubbles like a bullfrog just
so you couldn't hear all that sadness. But when it was dry,
we'd all sit on this makeshift bench at the back of the house

and watch the sunset. Calvin would be close by, scratchin' himself or runnin' from his kids, and I'd look at the edges of the sky change from blue to blush and listen to the critters and wonder why God spent so much time decoratin' a day that was dyin'.

One time Moms said that the clouds were lemon custard with the edges toasted golden and the westbound birds were like sprinkles, and those frogs going glug-glug-glug were prob'ly singin' their li'le ones to sleep. So I thought, "Wow, that's really nice." Then right after that, Pops came home smack in the middle of the crème-brulée clouds and the lullaby singin'. He'd been away for two nights and smelt different and sounded tipsy. There was a big peace sign painted on his face, and he had these fancy new clothes on. And I just went right back to thinking that God was wastin' his time decoratin' a day that was just about dead.

Now, usually we all went to Long Lake Free Gospel Church on the weekend, but one sleepy Sunday mornin' Moms got up and after breakfast she told me she wanted me to go with Pa Campbell into Gentilly on a mission for her. I wasn't too keen on the idea till she said I was goin' to do it "like a ninja". We didn't have no television at our house, so at the time I had no idea what a real ninja looked like, but I heard Harry T talkin' about ninja shows all the time. That boy watched a hell of a lot of TV, and I think it must have messed with his brain a little bit. He believed some impossible things just because they came over the tube, I tell ya.

Harry lived over in the city, but that boy loved diggin' for adventure, especially in the swamp, so I wouldn't even call him a real city boy. He'd hitch a ride on his bicycle in someone's truck all the way to where the asphalt disappeared and the dirt road began. Then he'd ride the rest of the way into the swamp and drop by just in time for some food and then haul his ass back home to sit in front of his damn TV set till he fell asleep.

Now, me and Harry, during the summer, we used to plan missions just to mess with angler fishermen or daring tourists who believed in brochures and prob'ly thought they had found some place "untouched by human beings". So we'd see them all peaceful, in their little fishin' boat out on the bayou, and we'd just ride up suddenly and look all queasy and tell them to get out of our toilet.

So when Moms said "ninja mission" and my brothers didn't sound interested in going with me, I decided the best person to tell was Harry T, cos sure as the sun he'd be comin' into the swamp early that Sunday.

Well, would you believe it, when Harry turned up at our place, I couldn't recognize the guy. He had bought some kind of Jheri-curl kit and put it in his hair, and it was dripping all over his bicycle like he'd fallen into the bayou a coupla times. Plus, he had on these sunglasses two sizes bigger than his face, and he was wearing a leatherette jacket and some extra belts with big buckles. He also kept grabbing at his pants. I asked him if that's what a ninja looks like, cos there was no way in hell I could tell at the time that he was tryin' to look like Michael Jackson or whatever. My father only fixed TVs: we didn't have one for ourselves. Well, that just started the ninja mission off on the wrong foot, cos he was mighty pissed at me – and when Pa Campbell dropped us off in Gentilly, he just kept pedalling the bike the rest of the way real fast with me ridin' on the handlebars, till I got scared and told him he did look a li'le bit like Michael Jackson and he slowed down. The truth is, Harry Tobias couldn't look like Michael Jackson even if he prayed for it. He kept tellin' people he was half Cherokee, half black and half something else, so he couldn't even get his fractions right... idiot.

So, there we were in Gentilly, and after a while I hopped off the handlebars and walked up to a clean, white wrought-iron gate with *"Deux Cent Quarante-Deux"* written in gold cursive on a black iron plate. Behind the little gate was one of those gardens I saw in the magazines that Moms used to buy. She knew all the flowers in French gardens by name. She wanted a garden based on that Marie Antoinette lady we studied in school. So she'd stay up nights readin' and wishin' she could grow boxwood bushes, pink petunias, white roses and peonies – but all that salty soil in the swamp don't allow for that kind of daydreamin': we had to settle for some aloe vera, peppermint or periwinkle in a couple of Sherwin-Williams paint cans out on the porch.

I pushed the gate and went up the narrow walkway with the flowers nodding at me on both sides, while Harry T waited by the kerb, looking in a little mirror and fussing with his Jheri-that-didn't-really-curl. The house was baby-blue with French windows and white mouldin' that made it look like a birthday cake. Tiny peach-and-brown birds bounced around a fancy concrete bath in the courtyard, and through the trees little sequins of light came down and sprinkled a few wrought-iron chairs and a table in the garden shade. *Ahhh yes.* You could sit there all day in the shade and have tea and soup, if you wanted to – though with so many birds above your head I don't think it would be a good idea.

I stopped at the door and fished around in my jeans pockets for the note Moms gave me to deliver. She said Pops would be at 242 Plume Noire. He would be there calling on a customer to fix a stereo, and I was to go give it to him, this note. As usual she was very specific. She said: "Now, when you knock and the person comes to the door, say good morning, ask for your father and hand the note to him." I said OK, cos that sounded real simple for a ninja mission, but somehow as I stood there looking at the note in my hand, something began to stink about this whole thing.

The damn door knocker seemed to know it too. It was one of those knockers that you see all the time with a mean-lookin' lion bitin' into a big ol' cast-iron ring. But this pa'ticular lion was grinning like he was saying to me: "Go ahead and knock, if you have the balls, kid." So I did. Well, after the fifteenth knock-knock-knock, Harry was getting antsy, cos his hair was melting in the sun and I was all ready to quit this mission. But someone peeped through the fancy fleur-de-lis latticework over the top of the door. Then the latch goes kruck-kruck, I hear the bolt sliding out slow, the door groans open, I look up and... I'm standing face to belly button with Miss Fiola Lambert.

I'm thinkin' Moms set this up cos I'm always talkin' about Miss Lambert. This is obviously my belated birthday party – and I was expectin' to walk inside and everybody would be there to shout "Surprise!" And here comes the Sunday-morning breeze suddenly sweepin' down the slope and rufflin' Miss Lambert's curls and pressin' her green silk nightgown closer to her skin. She brushed some of her little girl curls from her face, and the white roses and peonies threw butterfly confetti all over the place. *Super slow motion. And freeze frame.*

"E-Skid-eh?"

I heard music. I loved it when her French accent made a little sandwich of my name and left dainty sounds at both ends. Ahhh.

She bends down and smiles at me. And even in the breeze there is sweat on her upper lip, and there's another drop of it runnin' down her neck, and her curls are messy now. Her eyes are jumpin' left and right, and I'm suddenly nervous and confused, cos I'm in love with her and I hate that I'm in my worst clothes, that I didn't have my moustache yet and that I came here with Harry T and his ridiculous hairstyle. And when I was busy hatin' Frico for bein' so damn selfish – who appears in the doorway behind Miss Fiola but my pops in his sad ol' boxer shorts? My eyes bugged out. His eyes bugged out.

"Why – what are you doing out here?!"

He dashed behind the door, so I said to hell with handing him the note. I just pulled my eyes off Miss Fiola and started to read Moms' note:

Behold, Alrick Beaumont. I know thy works!

This wasn't the first time Moms was usin' her King James Bible verses to express herself – but hell, it was the *worst* time. And Heaven knows I wished I hadn't come. I reckoned those bastards – Frico, Tony and Doug – knew about these ninja missions and must've thought it was my turn to bear the bad news. But something tells me I was the only one who ever completed one of them.

Well, Miss Fiola, she ducked inside, but my father rushed at me through the door in a pink bathrobe that he had obviously just dragged on. So I start runnin' like a lucky Thanksgivin' turkey, cos I've never seen my old man so mad. He's gallopin' behind me cursin' my mother and me. And Harry T, he's laughin' and ridin' right alongside me just ahead of my old man, hollerin' that I should get on the bicycle handlebars. But a whoopin' with that bedside slipper in Pops' hand is more likely at this point, so I just keep goin' until my old man decides it's not very decent to run about the neighbourhood in his drawers and a pink bathrobe.

So I get home, and Harry T is wonderin' if the mission is over so he can go watch TV. I'm quietly sobbin', not quite sure if I'm sorry for Moms or angry because my father was fixing Miss Fiola's stereo on Saturday night.

Then, right after the ninja mission, Pops moved out of the swamp, and I felt like it was my fault, even though it was Moms who told him she didn't want him and his ways no more and he was never to come back. His Ford Transit van took him away, together with all the stuff he was repairin'. And Ma and Pa Campbell, who were on the porch when he was packin' up, they just went back inside and turned off all their lights. Soon I could hear Pa Campbell on his harmonica brewin' up some bittersweet breeze, and I wanted to just hurl a rock at his house.

When Pops drove out, I ran to the corner of the L and watched as the van splashed through the creek and rode up the slopes and got to the train tracks. And the back lights, those back lights, they just burned red-hot and then went dead-dead cold. And the van turned right and disappeared behind the mangroves out at Lam Lee Hahn, and there was no sound except for the whole swamp sinkin'.

I saw Pops set foot back there a few weeks later, after dark, as I was dousin' a mosquito fire in the yard. I knew someone was out there, but Calvin, he wasn't makin' a fuss, so I wasn't too scared, until I saw this tiny red glow bobbin' through the trees and I was thinking it was one hell of a firefly or an angry baby *fifolet*.

Then Pops stepped out of the darkness behind a cigarette and stooped down beside me. I hadn't seen him smoke in a long time, so he smelt weird, but I wanted to hug him. That would have been even weirder than the cigarette smell, though, so instead I just said, "Hey Pops." Then he whispered to me that he was sorry, but he needed one of Moms' pictures so that he could keep her close to his heart. That sounded good, so I brought it, gold frame and all, and gave it to him without askin' her, and he went away without even saying thanks. All he left me was that smoke curling up.

By that Thanksgivin', we were broke as hell and, like they say, it was hard in the Big Easy and outside the city limits where we lived. So hard that one day, me and Doug, we even saw Moms leaning against the house and crying in the rain after coming back in from Lam Lee Hahn. Man. You never ever get that out of your head. See, in that high-water wilderness, you could prob'ly catch panfish or crawfish or some small game, but not quickly or easily enough to feed four growin' boys. At least not without bein' adapted to it. We were like fugitives who ran away from the city but were sittin' waitin' for it to come catch up with us. Even after so many years we still weren't ready for country livin'. We had no serious practice huntin' or fishin'. We couldn't predict the tides that came in from the Gulf, not to mention those storm surges that either chase you out or lock you in for days. We could try it, but my moms, she wasn't ready to adjust. She had hardcore beliefs and practices, includin' the culinary ones. Thanksgivin' mornin' we heard her mumbling to herself that "on Turkey Day or any other day, me and my kids won't be eating no rattlesnake or squirrel or possum pie, or any kind of chit'lin's. Where I come from we don't eat that stuff." Me and Doug decided it wasn't the best time to tell her that we'd been samplin' swamp rats over at Pa Campbell's. And those suckers weren't half bad.

Anyway, with all the tough times, at least we had entertainment. I was fully ten years old before we got this beat-up colour television set from Pa Campbell. Tony hooked it up to the CB antennae, and I got to see what a real ninja looked like.

Meanwhile, I was still trying to get Frico to sketch Harry T and make him look like Michael, the King of All Music Everywhere. Now, even though Harry T didn't really believe in all this sketchin' business neither, at least he was ready to give it a shot, cos he was always up for adventure and all that. And – would you believe it – Frico *agreed* to do it, but he told us to go search for the best picture of Michael that we could find so he could use it as some kind of reference.

Well, Harry T and me, we saved for weeks and rode around to record stores to compare prices. We checked phone boxes in the city for spare change and of course I asked Doug for money. But he said he was saving to buy some fancy white tennis shoes and some soccer boots, even though Moms asked him where inside these swamps he was goin' to wear white shoes. So anyway, we only got enough to buy two cassettes after all that. Harry took out the cassette jackets and borrowed some ol' magazines from a barber shop, but every time I thought we had found the perfect MJ photo, he said he could find a better one. It was always "he don't look like that no more" or "that one isn't new enough" or "his hair is more curlier now" or some other story. So every couple of days I would glance into the dresser mirror and see Frico beside the bed, lookin' at me and smilin' weird, cos I guess he knew that the King would keep changin' and that me and Harry T wouldn't be able to agree on one damn photo.

Seven

"That's blood, not ink." Moms was smellin' the writin' on those strange letters that were delivered to our house one full-moon Saturday night. Well, not delivered, more like flung into the yard: nobody actually delivered mail in those parts. So it was creepy when me and Frico came into the kitchen Sunday morning with sixteen bright-yellow envelopes in our hands, all addressed to "VALERIE BEAUMONT & HER OFFSPRING".

"Where did you get these?"

Moms wiped her hands. The envelopes had strange diagrams.

"Outside. The whole yard is littered with 'em. There's more. It's the same letter again and again."

"Well – did y'all hear me say it's *blood*?"

Sixteen envelopes fell to the floor.

"Go wash your hands. And next time, don't *nobody* take this kind of thing in here, y'hear me?" We nodded. Her face was a rock. She bolted the doors and blocked out the kitchen windows with cloth from under the sink. Then she picked up every letter except for one and dumped them all in a rice box. When she opened the last one, the place smelt really bad. She turned to Tony.

"Florida Water... candle... cupboard... top shelf."

She wrapped her head with the reddest piece of cloth I ever seen, stuck a blue pencil up in it and poured the Florida Water onto her hand. She folded the letter seven times and put it in the middle of the kitchen table. Then she sent for her King James, dropped the book on top of the crumpled letter and pressed it down.

"Hold hands round the table."

Goddamn it – now, this was serious. In my house Moms would do this stuff from time to time, so I didn't think anything of it. But we didn't hold hands to pray until some real trouble was brewin'.

For a few days that box of stinking letters sat there on the kitchen-area table with the King James Bible turned east on top of it. A brass padlock was in the middle of the book, holding down the pages to the Book of Psalms. Next to the Bible was the big Catholic candle, even though I thought we were Free Gospel or somethin'. It had a picture of a lady saint and it kept burnin' all night. It smelt like roses. On the last day, Moms tied her head with the red cloth again and lit some incense. I'm not quite sure what the incense was, cos she said we weren't supposed to even repeat the name of it in the house. Man, that stuff smelt worse than the dried-up blood. Then she took the blue pencil out of the head wrap and wrote a name on a piece of paper and burned it along with the letters in the mosquito fire while she was readin' the Psalm out loud – but backwards. Her eyes were closed and her face was all golden in the blaze. She said somebody was trying to conjure up some magic – trying to put a goat-blood spell on us – but they couldn't touch us now, so we shouldn't worry. And for the first time I wished my pops was there to protect us – until we figured out he was the one doin' the damn conjuring. Then I wished Frico would do something about that. But you know that bastard.

Well, I was in middle school and eleven by then, and by that time I had given up thinking that I had any sketching powers. I had done lost interest in Miss Lambert anyway, and furthermore she had turned on her heels and high-tailed it out of New O'lins after that stereo-fixing occurrence – and bless God she had taken ol' Suzy Wilson with her. It was a good thing I gave up tryin' to find out if I had powers too, cos that experiment had gotten me into no ends o' trouble. Hell, I still got into trouble, but at least it was some brand-new nonsense – like that Sunday when I borrowed Belly's new bicycle.

See, Belly, he always got some cool stuff from his daddy over in Georgia. Now, at that time Belly was six foot one, though he was only thirteen years old. If it wasn't for his knocked knees that boy would prob'ly be six foot three. But still he was taller than my older brothers, and because of that, everything his daddy sent for him had to be super-sized. So this new bike was as big as a horse. We called it the "Beast". I remember it was a classic, restored 1950s Bendix bike with the brake in the hub. Now, if you don't know what that last part means, that's OK, cos I didn't either. See, Belly and Doug and Tony were all helping me ride this bike. It had a real steel frame, fat black-and-white tyres, a dynamo and a bell… yes, a bell. So they all helped me get on the Beast and shoved me off, and I'm zigzagging down the dirt slope in the swamp and ringing the bell and comin' around the corner singin' and Pa Campbell's lettuce-patch fence is coming towards me, so I need to stop. But I notice there are no brake levers on the handlebars. But Belly is jumpin' up and down and shouting that "the brake is in the hub". Well, that's a relief. Now all I have to do is find the "hub". So I take my eyes off the marl road and I'm lookin' around the handlebars prob'ly expecting to see some labelling in big block letters that says "HUB". But there's no such thing, and this doesn't make sense, and I'm ringin' the bell for Calvin and his kids to move outta the way.

"Well, Skid," I tell myself, "whether it's in the bayou or on a bed of lettuce, you're goin' down."

Next thing I knew I was lyin' on my back, countin' clouds. The Beast was OK, but Pa Campbell's lettuce-patch fence and a coupla heads of salty lettuce were written off completely. Moms got really mad. You'd think it was *her* forehead that was gonna have chicken wire printed on it for weeks. She insisted that as punishment I should help Pa put his fence back together, especially since when the bicycle crashed, Pa's goats got excited and went on a rampage and got into their house and ate twenty-two dollars from Pa's trouser pockets.

And that's how, while workin' off my mistake, I got to talkin' to Pa Campbell every evening for a week about some serious stuff. Round about Sunday evenin', when I thought I could trust him enough, I told him about the goat-blood letters, and that Moms thought Pops was conjurin' spirits, but I personally didn't really believe in such things. And when he turned slowly and looked at me with his filmy cataract eyes and shook his head up and down, all he needed was a flashlight under his chin and a campfire to make me piss the place up.

"Now hold on deah, Skid. Now look heah. Whatchoo mean you don't believe? Look heah. The worse things in this heah swamp don't walk on fo' or two legs, y'heah me? They ain't bears or big cats or even Bigfoot. They cain't be hunted. They ain't dead and they was nevah alive. Theah is things in this god-forsaken backdoor of Noo Orlins that can*not* be described, y'heah me? This place is a *crossroads*, y'heah? It means people come here to cast spells, and they leave stuff in the soil heah. And long ago theah was a town heah for fishermen and miners an' all dat, and folks say they got wiped out by a witch who sent bad weather back in Nineteen-Fifteen, y'heah me? And befo' dat theah was early Chawasa and Apalachee tribes and all, plus American forces fought the British in these parts, so many godforsaken soldiers went to hell right here where we standin'. So spirits be heah! So don't be disbelievin' in invisible forces! Cos if you sit real still and lissen close, you can hear theah voices... whispering... Shh. Lissen!" So I leant forward and he farted. And we laughed hard until Ma Campbell, she heard it from the house and shouted at him to come get some tea, cos he hadn't eaten a thing since lunch.

Pa got gassy and was always jokin', and that made it hard for anyone to take him seriously. But it would do you good if you did. He'd been around for a while. He knew stuff. He had

one of those white beards coloured by smoke and sweat. He
was baldin' at the front, so he usually wrapped his head with
a black bandana like a bike-gang leader and then pulled his
long, white plait over one shoulder and let it hang down to his
chest. You couldn't see any lips on this guy when his mouth
was closed, on account of the forest on his face. His mug was
all wrinkled, as if time was a liquid and he had his face soakin' in it for too long. The rest of his skin was cracked till you
couldn't tell what those tattoos were supposed to have been.
The back of his neck was always red and criss-crossed, like one
of those fancy Christmas hams. He had on this silver ring with
the bluest turquoise stone in it – like a little pinch of summer
sky. He said it reminded him that there were "new horizons
somewhere". All I know is that ring bit so deep into his finger
it couldn't pos'bly make its way back over his rusty knuckles.

"Don't take Pa too seriously son: he talks lots of bull when
he misses his pills. And he believes in *everything*." Ma Campbell threw the old man a nasty pair of eyes as if to say: "Shut
the hell up". But by nightfall Pa Campbell had told me so
much I felt brand new, and I didn't even feel like he was Suzy-
Wilsoning me, cos what he was saying was useful.

Right about the time Moms would be lighting the mosquito fires, me and Pa, we called it a day and went into his house.
The old man rummaged through a wooden chest and fished
out this American Indian-looking cloth. Wrapped in it was a
big ol' photo album that used to be white.

"Now," he said, "what was you sayin' to me earlier, Skid?"
He flipped the album page after page, licking his finger each
time, more out of habit than anything else. I knew he was
talking about the goat-blood letters, but I wasn't gettin' back
into it, especially at night. He stopped at a page and turned
the photo album around so I could see.

"Recognize that fella?" His grubby fingernail was tapping
at a Polaroid that had gone almost fully yellow. It was a photo
of three white men standin' up among some darker-skinned

people dressed in white with drums and pineapples in their hands. They had really white teeth and were excited about the camera. You could tell. The same way I could tell that most of them had been pulled into the photo late and everybody had to make space to accommodate them. From the looks of it, they were all down inside this huge hole. Someone had taken the picture lyin' down on the ground and lookin' up at the people and the sky. It was a really nice shot. You could see the edges of the hole above them. I recognized one of the white guys as my pops, lookin' younger. He was standin' beside another man, handsome guy, in a beige bush jacket with a crispy starched collar, a fake ship captain's cap and one of those see-through sunshades that doesn't block any sun at all but only makes the whole world look all yellow.

I had seen another picture at my house with him and that same guy in that beige suit and glasses goofin' off. But Moms always said she hated that picture, cos it made Pops' friend look like that preacher guy Jones, who they say was a wonderful man till he killed all those church people in some place called Guyana not long after I was born. That was a crazy story if I ever heard one.

Anyway, the third guy in the photo was obviously Pa Campbell, who looked pretty much the same, but his hair was out like a hippie, his teeth were whiter and his beard wasn't. Then I remember thinkin' that this was the first time I had ever seen Pa Campbell and my pops standin' close together. It was almost like he read my mind.

"Me an' Alrick, your pops, we go way back."

"Really? And where's that place y'all at?"

He breathed in and let it all out slowly.

"That place... is out in the sun, kid. That place is San Tainos," he said, like it was a declaration of some sort. "It's a little island aways from here. Paradise really. If the whole world was on one island, that island would be San Tainos. Ooowee. Your pops and me, we used to get off the grid and go hang out in San Tainos for a bit in the late Sixties. It was girls, beaches, rum. Then—" He paused.

"Then what?

He laughed. "Your father forgot how to be free. He fell in love. Look heah." Pa flipped the page and tapped another photo. It was on a beach with the prettiest ocean water you ever seen.

On the horizon the sunshine looked so warm it must have popped those fresh popcorn clouds hangin' out over the sea. Now, I was fixin' to fall in love with that sweet, dark-skinned lady in the picture he was pointing at when he said, "That's your momma right theah about fourteen-fifteen year ago." And I just hated myself for a little bit. But Moms was as pretty as ever, though. Her skin looked like she polished it, and her red-lipstick smile was bright and comic-book perfect. She had on a smooth orange stone danglin' from a chain round her neck and one of those colourful cloth bands holdin' back her hair from her forehead. You could see her hair was long, even though it was styled in a topknot on her head. A red Coca-Cola tank top and a tie-dye skirt to match the headband made her look like a doll from Pops' VW dashboard. There was light in her eyes to match her smile and the glint off her hula-hoop earrings. She looked like Pam Grier. Not the bad-ass Pam Grier: the sweet, smiling Pam Grier.

In another picture, they were in the water. She was laughin' because Pops had her in his arms and that yellow-glasses fella (he didn't take them off) looked like he was about to splash both of them. It was weird, like those two in the picture were not my parents but some other happy couple who were still down on that island lovin' each other.

"Now, I'm not sure I should be tellin' you this, but your mother's from San Tainos, son. She was born there."

"I think I heard that."

"Whatchoo mean 'you think you heard'? That mean they never told you. If you ever heard about San Tainos, you'd *know* you heard about San Tainos. Your momma was born in one of the prettiest places on earth. The gods made that place special. She came heah with your pops when things turned ugly in the late Sixties."

"Ugly?"

"The Sixties was part of a nervous time with e'rybody threatening to drop a big bomb on e'rybody else, till the whole world got so goddamn scared nobody dropped a bomb on nobody at all. But then even if nobody dropped jack, you still needed to know which one-a da bomb-droppin' sides you was on. So the long and short is, San Tainos started makin' friends with the wrong side, so the ol' US of A wasn't their friends no more. And when things got tougher in paradise, your Moms, she married Alrick and came to Florida first and then eventually headed heah to Noo Orlins."

Ma Campbell was off in the kitchen area, fixing some Unidentifiable Fried Object on the stove for their supper. Pa Campbell, he kept looking to see how far away she was. Meanwhile, I saw she was listening to how much he was tellin' me.

"Now Pa, I told you to keep your trap shut and stop scarin' that boy with them swamp horror stories."

She limped over with his pills. At the same time she dropped a big ol' plate full of some poor critter's fried skins between us, and I told Pa that I'd be headin' home, cos Moms would be waitin'. He said Moms been waiting a long time, so she wouldn't mind. He said there was lots that I should know, so I should go ahead and crunch on some o' them skins real loud so Ma Campbell couldn't hear what we were talkin' about.

"She's half-deaf as it is anyways."

"I heard that," she hollered from the kitchen area. "I may well be half-deaf, Lobo Campbell, but I'm all you got! And you still can't handle all this."

Pa laughed and farted and continued. It turned out that my pops became a hoodoo conjurer after he went to San Tainos, met Moms and fell under her spell, so to speak.

"Your pops, his hoodoo was third-rate. He had to keep comin' to me to fix his conjurin'. But your momma's folk magic was special, cos she mixed it up a bit. She became known as a mojo queen, a root doctor, prob'ly one of the most powerful conjurer in these swamps before she stopped doin' them spells."

Well, my head and neck were on fire like I had seen a ghost. Now I wasn't jumpin' to no conclusions, but that might start explaining Frico's sketchin' powers and all – but I wasn't about to say anything more 'bout that to nobody. Plus, this old man was on a roll, and I wish I had one of those new tape-recorder things that Pops promised to buy me.

"So, by the taam she was pregnant with that second boy theah, your other brother, she started goin' to that Long Lake Free Gossip church. And even though they say theah ain't nothing wrong with gettin' a little help on earth when God's got his hands full up in heav'n, your momma decided it was taam to stop all that mojo-conjuring." He paused, then he looked up and leant forward, glaring at me all cataracky and filmy. "What I'm really try'na say, son, is that people say – don't quote me, but I hear tell that just by whistlin' – your momma could raise up things from under these muddy swamp waadas that could make Godzilla look like a god-damn gecko."

I looked at him all blank.

"Aw, dammit son, you got a TV now! Watch some more, kid! Or ask your wannabe-Cherokee friend who Godzilla is. Jesus! Or look it up in da library fo' godsakes, I ain't got the taam wit' you kids these days! Anyway…"

And he went on about Moms and her skills in some Caribbean conjuring they call *obeah*, that is one powerful mixin' of African and Christian rituals and English magic – and she also knew the power of somethin' he called "Amerindian art". I didn't catch what he said about that, cos as Pa Campbell went on and on, I could only see the pictures in my head of

Moms lockin' the doors and lightin' the candle and crushin' the goat-blood letter and burning somebody's name in the fire. And then it hit me and I said to myself: "Shit, Skid. Your old lady is a witch and your brother is a damn wizard."

Well, you can bet I didn't sleep all week, and every time I looked up from my bed in the darkness, there was ol' Frico's outline, sittin' up, lookin' back at me, like he knew I found out somethin'. Hell if he was gonna get me to talk, though. I wanted solid proof of the originations of these powers before I went back to bribe him with somethin'. So I just rolled over and went back to sleep with one eye open.

PART TWO

An old broom knows where the dirt is.
— Everyday proverb

Eight

"Load up!"

It was Saturday, so Pa Campbell would be taking the gators in his old Ford truck over to Al Dubois Fish and Seafood in New O'lins East, and Moms said I could tag along. Harry T couldn't make it, cos he said he was "keepin' the Sabbath" that weekend, which prob'ly meant he would be recordin' movies on the second-hand VCR he bought off Belly, as soon as he figured out how to put the thing back together. I reckon he borrowed the VCR and pulled it apart and didn't know what screws went where, so he ended up buyin' the scraps. But it was no problem if Harry T didn't make it. I was diggin' Pa Campbell's stories, and on the way, he told me some more.

"Your pops and I don't get along no more, on account of yo' mother wantin' to stop all them conjurations. I told your pops, 'Alrick, let her be.' He said if Valerie knows 'bout the spirits in the swamps and if she wanted to stop conjuring, that would be her entitlement, but she shouldn't be preventin' him from protectin' his chil'ren. So each taam one a y'all was about to be born, your pops made sure the baby would be under guard."

"Under guard?"

I thought he was gonna blast me again about not watching enough TV, but he said, "Yeah. Now, this ain't necessarily hoodoo, but nine days or so before the baby is s'posed to be born, theah is a tradition to supplicate and ask an archangel to come protect the newborn." I shivered. "Yeah, dat's right. These are things you need to know, son. Right now, I'm appointin' maself your Godfauder, and since I'm half-Catholic, that means ol' Pa Campbell is responsible fo' your spirichual upbringin'. Now, lissen. They got spirits that like to harm li'le children, so that thirty-foot archangel is s'posed to hover over da house whirlin' all six brass wings and beatin' them forward like blades on his bronze armour. Terrible sight, if you saw it. He's a warrior angel, so he's ready with a fire sword in one hand and a burnished-metal mirror – yes – a mirror in the other hand. See, the only thing 'cept Almighty God dat can scare the ol' Devil or a spirit away from a poor soul is the Devil's or the spirit's own reflection. So the archangel goin' hafta hold that mirror up high so dat they can see themselves and git back, you understan'? And if they don't fly away, then the ol' sword of the Almighty's goin'-a hafta come down hard and discourage 'em some more, you understan'?" I shifted in my seat. Maan, that angel sounded scarier than the Devil.

We turned into the Fish & Seafood place. "Well, your momma, she found religion while she was pregnant, and told your pops that the archangel Michael, he knows his job already. Your pops asked me to intervene and git her to agree to ask for protection, cos if there is disagreement between the parents the archangel ain't gonna visit. But I said no: that was between she and him and God and the archangel. So, up to this day, your pops thinks I betrayed our years-long friendship and, worse, he's dead sure that the archangel never showed up and a female spirit called Old Hige, she flew up from the Gulf and rocked a cradle or two many nights."

Well, I reckon that when he said that, I should've been all freaked out or riled up or I should've just thought Pa was plumb nuts. But no. Matter of fact, that was the best damn news I'd gotten all year. This was confirmin' that *fifolet* story and the fact that Frico had some kind of energy in him. But then again maybe Pa Campbell was missin' his pills or was kinda walkin' on a slant on account of that whiskey flask he kept throwin' back when he thought I wasn't lookin'.

The details didn't matter – but if that bastard Frico had powers, then I was sure I was born to help him use them. I wish

I was him to be honest. But with my luck, if I wasn't "under guard" and some entities came crowdin' around my crib, I'm dead sure all those bastards brought me was the gripes.

Anyway, Pa went in to the Fish & Seafood guy, Al, and while they were hawkin' over prices, up drove a noisy Mitsubishi Montero beside Pa's truck – and who was in the passenger seat but little Miss Vietnam, Mai. Her mother was takin' a nap in the back seat.

"Oh Mai, Mai, Mai," I called out as soon as I saw her, but she didn't get it. When I was about to explain the joke, her grandpa, he leant across from the driver seat and looked at me. He had bags under his eyes, ready to pack every bad thing you ever did, and the permanent knitting of his grey brows was sayin': "Back off my granddaughter" or something worse. So I kinda slinked down in my seat and waited till he had taken two buckets of jumbo shrimp inside. Then I jumped back up in my seat and tried to flirt with Mai again. But she was all business that day. They had to drop off pounds and pounds of shrimp that they were growing themselves right in the swamp across from us, and then they were going to pick up somebody who just got in from Vietnam.

"You should come meet Kuan, you'll like her."

I said, "Sure," even though I wasn't no great fan of her grandpoppa and his talking eyebrows. Well, out comes the old guy again with Al Dubois behind him, and I see somethin' he does: he lets Al give Mai the money for the load of shrimp, like he didn't want to touch the dough. Strange man. And that Mai, she was so cute, she just unrolled that big coil of money and told Al to wait while she counted it, like she was some kind of responsible adult. Then, when the Montero rattled up again, Mai's mother woke up and counted the money one more time.

Well, they left as Pa Campbell was walkin' out, and he climbed back into the truck with money and one of those corny pine-cone air fresheners. He knew his van smelt like stale fish. Now it would smell just gorgeous. He passed me two dollars. "You deserve it, cos I ain't talked to nobody like this in fourteen years, you heah?" I was goin' to say thanks when he said: "Now I jus' paid you to shuddup. So lissen, let me wrap up the story." So we took off and he told me how my parents had both put bottle spells on each other.

"That's when you get a good sturdy bottle and you put cinnamon and spices and some hair or a picture of the one you love in it and seal it up real good. And the idea is that they should stay with you for ever, cos you locked them in."

As much as it was hard to imagine my parents with that sorta groovy, magical relationship, I started feeling sad when Pa Campbell said it ended even before Pops moved out. After Moms started going to church and was born again, she decided to break her bottle, saying that love shouldn't be locked up. Pops got drunk and broke his soon after.

"He shoulda sealed up those bottle spells and thrown them in the Gulf o' Mexico, I tell ya. Dat's what I did with Ma Campbell – and now she's with me every single goddamn day that the Lawd sends! Hell, I cain't even go to the grave by maself!" He laughed and farted. "Anyway, after the bottle spells got broke, your folks just found it harder and harder to stay together. And you shouldn't blame yaself son. It has nothin' directly to do with you. Grown folks are strange and stay in the worst of places for all the wrong reasons. Matter o' fact your pops came back to me to conjure up a new love bottle spell after he moved out, and I said no. Seemed he was try'na win her back, but I tell ya, theah ain't no earthly power stronger than a woman who's made up her mind, y'heah me? Hell, he even drew three Xs on that priestess, Marie Laveau's grave, and made a wish to git your momma back. Now... your pops, he seemed OK 'bout me sayin' no to doin' another love bottle spell at the time, but then three week ago he came into the swamp and bought a goat kid off me sayin' he wanted to try 'something different' for Thanksgivin'. Now, I sold him the goat, but goats don't go 'gobble-gobble', so I knowed somethin' was up. And now you're telling me your momma got a goat-blood letter, right?"

"Letters."

"Goddammit, Skid. He made multiples to give the spell at least one chance ta work. Or prob'ly just to scare her into takin' him back, I reckon." He paused. "Well, son, we need ta pray hard, cos if you're saying dat your momma blocked out the windows and crushed dat letter and burned all of them along wi' somethin' else... then in a coupla days, your pops has a serious conjuration comin' right back to him like a boomerang."

We headed across the Lake. On the causeway, Pa Campbell stationed the radio. Shoehorn Johnny, a great street-performance old guy from downtown, was finally gettin' to playing his jazz trumpet live on the air.

"Well, at least somethin' is new for somebody roun' heah."

That's when Pa gave me a grand tour and some history. "You know, your pops was a visionary. Do you know why I came to live in the swamps, kid? I came to live in the swamps to escape, to get off the grid again, perm'nently. To renunciate society."

"Renounce society."

"Yes, renunciate it. It means 'to give it all up'. Look up the word son, I told you I ain't got the taam. Anyways, there were some other reasons, but deep inside I reckoned since e'rybody was waitin' for a bomb to be dropped, I might as well go somewhere I could be self-sufficient if there was a big kaboom. Close to a river with all the critters we could eat. Just kinda lay low until all this Cold War thawed out, if nothin' really happened. And you know you cain't lay any lower than Noo Orlins! This place is below sea-waada level, son. Somethin' else for you to look up. Anyway, Ma Campbell, she stuck around, and while her folks and my folks all got together and headed off to dig some bomb-shelter complex in the desert, she came to Noo Orlins wi' me. Now... your pops, he came to the swamps for the opposite reason. Progress. And he was on to somethin'... well... sorta."

Later, when we got back from across the Lake and drove along Michoud Boulevard close to the crack on the map, Pa stuck his hand out the window and pointed. "See that whole area, kid? That was supposed to be a sprawlin' community called 'Pontchartrain' or 'Orlandia', dependin' on who you ask. They even built the levees for dat development."

I looked where Pa was pointin', and all I saw was water and marsh. At one point, we passed a road that zoomed in over our heads off the highway and then just crash-landed in an open field. It was a ghost exit, a road that went nowhere. I reckoned that it was supposed to be one of those interchanges that Pops was excited about back in the day before I was born. The road headed into the bushes, and you couldn't see the end of it, like it just sliced into the earth and went all the way down to hell. I felt a chill. It was a strange sight. Pa went on:

"After a while your pops was figurin' he could get more business in his repair shop as soon as the community grew up around him. But now that the oil's gone bust, all that development is dead. These days, you can still see that big ol' concrete sign somewhere near one of these exits that says: 'NOO ORLINS EAST'. They made that sign when they tried to get things goin' one final time. Well... some people say that's a gravestone, son, cos the project died. And your daddy's plans, they broke apart like that swamp soil does in the summer."

My chest felt heavy. Pa was killin' me now. But he couldn't tell, so he kept on.

"But to be honest, I always wanted the swamp to stay the way it was. Even though in truth: it was never the same ag'in. I reckon all those critters that lost theah homes and survived, just had to keep coming east, cos they were wonderin' where the hell theah home went. Soon we had tons of 'em when the development came to a halt. But gen'rally it was OK. Like they say, if there ain't nothing broke, then nothin' needs to get fixed... or something like that. I don't recall exactly. I ain't taken that damn pill t'day, and Ma Campbell is goin' to shoot me."

Nine

When we got back home it was after dark, and the mosquito fire had gone out early, on account of a sudden evening shower. Moms was standin' on the dark porch in the doorway of the house. The light behind her made her look so witchy I felt better when the truck lights hit her and showed her face. She shielded her eyes and walked towards us before the truck even stopped.

"G'night, Lobo. Can I talk to you for one minute?"

Damn. Pa was in for a Valerie Beaumont lecture – and I was out of luck too.

"I don't know what you been telling my son," Moms told Pa. "I don't care exactly. I just want to tell you that from here on, I'd like to keep some things private. You know how Alrick feels about tellin' them too much about…"

Pa scratched his beard and nodded.

"And one more thing, Pa. I don't appreciate you feedin' my children them swamp rats, y'hear?"

Dammit, she knew. That gossip Ma Campbell must've told her. Guess that explained why me and Doug were gettin' doused with cerasee tea for two days straight.

Moms continued. "Pa, you know. You've been there. Where I come from—"

"Yes, yes Val, I know, where you come from you don't eat that typa crap. I know. Y'all prefer a big plate of curried goat meat or some salted codfish for that blood pressure of yours," he said, tryin' to laugh things off. But Moms wasn't amused. So Pa said he was sorry and offered to do anything to make it all up to her. She said she'd let him know as soon as she came up with some good punishment.

"And you'd better make sure you keep your word, cos I've got a witness."

"Really? Who?"

"This same last boy of mine that you just hauled in here all odd hours of the night." And she looks me dead in the eyes as if she wants to cast a dark spell on me.

I didn't get punished, though. So I took it that I should count my blessings and just get to sleep, even though I wanted to ask her a few things. But Moms, she kept rakin' Pa over the coals a li'le longer – and she was riled up with ol' Ma Campbell too. You'd think with all the trouble her fugitive son had been causin' up and down the Mississippi, Ma Campbell would want to mind her own business... but no.

Pause. Remember that guy James "Couyon" Jackson I told you about? Well, before he was a notorious gang leader he was just poor ol' Ma Campbell's slow-learnin' son. When people in the swamp and the city talked about James Jackson, they kept their voice down like they were talkin' about Beelzebub hisself. That's because James Jackson was known all along the length and breadth of the Mississippi for a heartless way of huntin' animals – and it was even rumoured that he hunted humans. One night, he supposedly shot a fishin' partner for a tin of chewing tobacco and dumped him in the Rigolets waters under the train bridge. They say he called it an accident and got off scot-free cos of no evidence. And I heard that all that time he's talkin' to the judge, he's chewing the dead man's tobacco in the courtroom.

Now, I'll be the first to tell you that last part don't sound possible, but everybody said it's true, and you know that's how gossip turns to gospel. Furthermore, Pa said that good-for-nothin' boy was actually chewin' Court Case Root. That's some powerful herbal chew, similar to John the Conqueror root, if you know about that kinda natural magic stuff. I heard people sayin' that James spit a cheekful of Court Case

Root on the courtroom floor, repeated a Psalm and walked free. Judge didn't know what hit him.

Now Ma Campbell, she was so scared of what her son had become. Every time there was a nasty murder or robbery you could expect ol' Couyon Jackson to show up in the swamp and lay low for a few days. Poor Ma Campbell she'd be happy he was OK, but anxious for him to leave before Pa called the police or traded blows with him. Pa had grown James up like his own boy. He sent him to school and all that, but when James had trouble keepin' up with the other kids in school, Pa would say: "Ma, I told you that boy James is *couyon*."

Now, you wouldn't want to be called "couyon", even though it sounds like nice Cajun French. Well, neither did James, cos it simply means you're an idiot. As you would expect, James hated bein' called that name so much, he'd still go wild if you said it to his face. People say six dead men did.

Anyway, when we went inside, I followed Moms with my eyes. We were in the house all by ourselves. I was goin' to say somethin' sweet to her and make friends and just call it a night – but the night wasn't over by a long shot. She switched off the porch light and spoke without lookin' at me.

"Your brothers are out searchin' for Calvin. He didn't come for any food today. I just hope he's not gone back over into that man's yard."

I didn't like the sound of that one bit, and I started itchin' to get out there and help. Well, before long she switched back on that porch light and said: "We're going out, and I need you to go on up ahead to the tracks and tell them to wrap it up until tomorrow. Calvin can bring himself home."

I sure hoped she was right. We had to be feedin' the poor pups with medicine droppers, cos Backhoe Benet separated them from their mom, so I wouldn't want to imagine what else he would do. When we got closer to the tracks, I saw the flashlights first. Doug and Tony were out there. I guessed that as usual Frico had prob'ly been allowed to go do some weird night-time sketchin' and could come home any time he wanted, but I was bein' given the cold shoulder for ridin' with Pa.

Anyway, I caught up with them at the slope: Tony was lying down on that little gradient that goes up to the actual rails of the train tracks, in a jeans jacket and hip boots with one of our walkie-talkies in his hand. Doug was on his belly in the wet dirt, in a zipped-up black sweater and hip boots as well. They had taken a small boat from Pa Campbell and rowed across from our house and come up the side of the bayou. They were scopin' out the Benets' place, and I said to myself: "Damn, Skid, you just ran into a full-scale military mission with the big boys." This was the big leagues, so there was no way I was going to tell them that Moms said to come on home. You don't tell soldiers their mom says to come on home.

Well, exactly one minute after that decision I was mad as hell, cos Doug told me *they* were the ones who sent Calvin over to the Benets "on a mission". Tony said he had heard Pops' van comin' into the swamp, and from up in the tamarind tree they verified that the Ford Transit was parked around the back of the Benets' house and Pops was inside talkin' to Backhoe. Somethin' strange was goin' on between them since that day with the puppies. So Tony came up with the idea to strap one of the HF-1200 walkie-talkies to poor ol' Calvin, duct-tape down the microphone key and then take him to the train tracks, turn him loose and let nature take its course. That dog was so hooked on the Benets' Border collie that he'd dash across the tracks once a chain wasn't holding him back. So there we were listenin' to the other doggie-walkie-talkie to see if we could hear what Backhoe and Pops were talking about.

"Shhh! Skid, keep quiet on the gravel. Doug, where's Calvin now?"

"Should be under the Benets' house. Expecting to hear audio any time soon."

It didn't take long for all of us to agree that that walkie-talkie-Calvin thing was a bad idea. I couldn't believe these dudes sent my dog into danger like that, but overall this was some cool stuff. And I wish I could call for back-up – but it was too late for Harry T to get down into the swamps and, like I said, gettin' through to Belly and Marlon took some serious long-distance communication.

So we were it. The team and the back-up. All we could do now is listen. But all we could hear was dog hair. Yep. See, if those geniuses had asked me, I woulda told 'em that Calvin would be draggin' hisself on his belly in the mud under the Benets' house and whimperin' and pantin'. That's not a good idea when you're tryin' to listen to something. Well, the dog-draggin' sound continued for about another minute – and then suddenly, as clear as day, we could hear Pops' voice from inside the house.

"I told you, Tracey... Backhoe... whatever you call yourself these days... there's nothin' over there!"

"Yew sho' you checked ag'in?"

"Yessir."

"With all the nec'sary methods?"

"And then some more."

"Now, Alrick, yew owe it to me to keep on lookin'."

"I don't *owe* you jack... (*static*) We all 'greed on this a long time ago. Shared ownership of any gas we (*static*) or take the losses if we didn't find any – simple."

"And I'm sayin', it's too early to call it."

"We've been searching for twenty years, Benet!"

The radio frequency was actin' up. To make matters worse, the sky suddenly flashed on and off, and we felt the first drops of the rain returnin'.

We pressed our heads closer around the walkie-talkie. Backhoe was gettin' antsy.

"Look, Al. There's got to be somethin' over on your side. Look around and (*static*) already checked over this side. That side of the swamp is pure Mississippi limestone, there's got to be some gas pockets under there. Check again or (*static*) your people off my land and let me get the pile drivers and the drills in here myself. I owe people and we're runnin' out of time. Remember, what's on my land... is mine. And I'm sure you don't want that to include sweet Mrs Beaumont, do you?"

We heard a scuffle comin' from inside the house or under it. Right at that minute, the noise overpowered everything.

"Tony, there's too much static!"

"That's not static, man: that's Calvin's backside."

The static turned into a thump-thump that could only mean one thing: Calvin was under the house with Medusa tryin' to become a daddy again.

Tony spoke in his nerd voice. "It appears Agent Calvin has gone rogue and is cavorting with the enemy." We started laughin' until we realized there was silence from inside the house.

Then all hell exploded. More raindrops were drummin' on the Benets' tin roof. Backhoe heard Calvin thumpin' through his floorboards and shouted to his sons, who ran around the back. They flung the groin-grabber under the house. Calvin yelped. They hauled him out. He was snarlin' and growlin', but we could hear when they ripped off the walkie-talkie and hit him in the head with it. He howled and bit somebody, or maybe the both of them, and they hit him in the head again and again. Then we heard Pops' van start up and saw him hightailing out of the swamp in the rain with the back doors still open and Backhoe runnin' behind the Ford Transit with a plank. Backhoe stopped when he saw that Pops was long gone. He put his hand to his forehead, looked at his fingers, then stomped off to go join his boys. I jumped up mad and excited at the same time.

"I'm goin' in!"

"No, you're goin' home." Doug grabbed my collar and turned me in the direction of the house. Right then I heard a *zing* by my ear. Either it had started rainin' horizontal, and the drops were balls of fire or... Then there was another sound. Somethin' you feel through your pores before your ears recognize it. One. Two. Six. Eight gunshots. I made for the tamarind tree and monkeyed up onto it. Calvin came out from under the Benets' house and bolted across the tracks – ears back, tail under. Then came the whole Benet family, stridin' after him. They were gun-confident, steppin' fast across the border, blazin' shots at our dog in the dark. Hot nozzles coughed out deadly red. Each time the poppin' lights showed the Benets' faces for a few seconds before they turned into shadows again. The explosions bounced among the cypress trees like pinball. I couldn't believe this was happenin'. Doug and Tony dropped flat again and crawled in the mud towards the footbridge a little ways off.

"Skid!"

Doug was shoutin', but I was long gone up in that tamarind tree, and I wasn't comin' down. I was watchin' the whole thing from above, soakin'-wet and scared as hell, but I held on and kept my head down.

In the flickerin' from the sky, I saw everything frame after frame. Backhoe swung down the barrel of his rifle and started workin' the lever, pumping shots as Calvin zigzagged through the trees. That dog was a champion runner. Backhoe was cursin' mongrels, but somethin' told me this madness had more to do with Pops than with our dog. Then Moms, who was waitin' for me the whole time, she heard the shots and came runnin' and screamin' at the Benets from the other end of the footbridge – but either they weren't hearin' or they were too pissed off to care.

Backhoe had crossed the train tracks and came chargin' down the slope, rifle-ready, Broadway and Squash flankin' him like outriders. They had a six-shooter each, hammerin' out bullets that cut down leaves and slammed into tree trunks. They blew three rounds each and then fell back to reload without even lookin' down at the handguns. I saw clearly what they were plannin' to do next. While their daddy looked around for Calvin, they focused on the footbridge. As soon as Tony and Doug raised up to run across that bridge, those Benet boys took aim at my brothers and started squeezin' off shots. Their father thought it was the dog and joined in with the rifle. Bullets tore up one end of the bridge. I called out loud, and Moms put her hands up high in the dark at the other end, either callin' on the Lord or castin' a spell. Maybe she was just tryin' to make them see her and her boys, I don't know. But the smoke in their eyes from all that shootin' and the water and noise from the sky wasn't helpin'. There was gunpowder in my throat, and my hollerin' went silent for a second, like in those terrible dreams you get when you have a fever.

As Tony and Doug hurried over the bridge, Broadway and Squash ran after them like it was a feedin' frenzy. My brothers leapt off the bridge and stood in front of Moms. They faced the Benets. Squash walked up slowly. He laughed a little, then got serious, pulled back the hammer of the pistol and took aim. His eyes grew wide.

"Squash... Broadway. That's enough, boys," Backhoe called out from the dark.

Squash shouted back: "It's self-defence, I heard!"

"No, that's enough, c'mon, let's go!"

Two feet behind him, Broadway was ready to blaze. His voice was lower, but just as menacin'.

"That's funny, Squash... huntin' accident's what I heard."

Moms still had her hands in the air, with her palms holdin' up the sky. Tony put his five fingers out, as if they could block bullets. His other hand was clutchin' the walkie-talkie. He was swearin' and beggin' at the same time. Doug turned his flashlight towards the hunters. In the shaky beam, the rain was slantin' into Broadway's face and drippin' off his peach fuzz. My bones started rattlin'. His grin turned into a grimace one second before he and his brother squeezed those triggers… hard. I was screamin' when the nozzles flashed. Stupid words with no meanin' come out when you're terrified. Moms brought her hands down at the sounds, maybe to shield her face, but those bullets, they went high. Just before the bullets, there had been a loud crack with a squeak in it, like a heavy door breakin', and even in the darkness we could see that somethin' crazy was takin' place. All of a sudden, the ol' footbridge broke under their feet. You could hear the wood split and hit liquid. Then came the sound of their bodies droppin' hard against it. They rolled off the broken bridge and lay there, sputterin' and lookin' 'round, frightened as hell, in the creek that was now swollen because of the rain. They picked themselves up quickly and stood waist-deep. They blamed each other, then found their guns and waded in towards the bank, more determined to do damage. But the creek, it bubbled up and the banks where the bridge used to sit just crumbled in and shoved them down into the water again. Things got real muddy, so they put up their guns and tried to hold on to each other in the muck and the downpour.

"Orville, Herbert, stop yer strugglin'. That's a sinkhole!"

Backhoe was on his belly with a big branch stretchin' out towards his sons and shoutin' above the thunder. He looked up at Moms but he wouldn't call for help. Tony and Doug were halfway to helpin' them and halfway holdin' back. Then, while they were tryin' to grab hold of the branch, we all heard it. At first I thought it was thunder, but it was a groan comin' up from the ground itself. The earth moved and the creek was a big ol' cauldron comin' to a boil. That spot where the bridge had fallen in opened up some more, like paper does when a candle burns under it. The shakin' got worse. I held on tight, and everybody on the ground rocked this way and that. Broadway and Squash started cryin' out for help, but the sudden sinkhole got angry and boiled up some more. It swallowed up the footbridge. It swirled round and round and when Squash's hand was just an inch from the branch, the boys both disappeared under the bubbles and the darkness and the noise, sucked down into the earth along with everything else. My eyes and mouth were wide open when the shakin' stopped. The surface of the creek settled down. Crickets complained and water gently sprinkled the earth, as if the atmosphere had been innocent the whole time. The slender creek now had a big lagoon where the bridge used to be. From up in the tree, it was a great python that had swallowed somethin' it could never digest. Moms, Doug and Tony stood huggin' on one side of the sinkhole; Backhoe Benet knelt in the mud on the other side. He was halfway into the creek grabbin' at water and mud and whimperin'. Then, in the silence, a light flashed right above my head. It wasn't lightning. It was Frico Beaumont, perched on a branch above me, quiet as a shadow, a cigarette lighter below his chin, the fire flickerin' in the rain on his glasses, a soaked sketch pad resting on one knee. "Shhh," he said. And a blue pencil was in his left hand when those boys fell into hell.

Ten

Two human beings died that night.

That's what my mother said I should never forget. As if I could. We were all there when the squad car came, washing the trees in an antiseptic kind of blue. After the fire truck arrived and the place burned red, the coroner's vehicle, a sleepy stainless-steel panel van, rolled in. There was no ambulance.

The coroner's driver refused to come down the slope for fear of more sinkholes. So they squabbled a bit with the firemen about bringin' the bodies up to the surface of the sinkhole that was now full, and when they did, the squad car's fluorescent lamp cut through the dream light of the moon. It streamed across the wet ground and came to rest on that water gateway into the earth. I felt sick.

Moms took a quick breath and stepped back and called us away from the sight. She just hugged all of us and rocked back and forth and kept whisperin', "Jerusalem, Jerusalem," for some reason. Even with all the water, Broadway and Squash were covered in heavy grey mud, and you couldn't tell them apart. They tried revivin' them – and when they couldn't, Tracey Benet just knelt right there in the mud, goin' hopelessly back and forth, holdin' this one's face and then that one's head. He slapped their cheeks softly and said words that I couldn't hear from where I was, like he was tryin' to say, "OK boys, joke's over, you can wake up now."

Now, when they finally covered them up and carried them to the van, a second squad car came and a lady who looked familiar, she came hurryin' down the slope and passed the coroner's van and came up to Tracey, who was talkin' to the police. Tracey turned around and just stared at that lady for an eternity of seconds – and that was when I heard Moms say: "Pauline". It was Mrs Benet.

After a couple of screams and otherwise silent, sad gestures, Tracey hugged her and she punched him, and he hugged her again and then he took her up the slope to the van. I heard the back doors creak open, and the coroner guy who stuck his head inside must've been tired or annoyed that he had to undo the sheets that he had wrapped around them, cos he took a while doing it – and Pauline, prob'ly watching him unwind the cloth while those cop lights went blue-blue-blue, she just fell to the forest floor in her decent clothes and screamed and held her belly for a long, long time. And when it was done, the policemen, they questioned Moms, but she told them we weren't being chased. I don't think the policemen believed her, cos they took Tracey away to question him some more about what he was callin' a huntin' accident. They prob'ly wanted answers about a gun they found in Broadway's hand and how so many shells were found on the train tracks.

The second squad car waited until Moms had taken Pauline and given her some herbal tea from her best china in the glass display case. Pauline refused to come inside. She sat on the front porch of our house, and when she spoke between sips of camomile and playful growls from Calvin's kids, she sounded like Moms just a little bit. She had jet-black hair cropped close at the sides, and the top was frizzy and went up in the air like a pop star's. She put down the teacup ever so often and took out a mirror to fix her make-up, even though the place was only half lit. She pulled down her cheeks to straighten out the bags under her eyes, then pulled back her cheeks towards her ears as if she was tryin' to iron out wrinkles that I couldn't see.

Pa Campbell, who was out there with his rifle from the first shots that were fired, he went back into his house and took off his bandana and put on a hat, just so he could walk up to Pauline and take it off and say he was sorry for her loss.

Pauline looked at him with his hat in his hand and gave him the kind of smile that showed she appreciated every word he said. And when they ran out of words after discussin' the earthquake again and searchin' for answers, they all suddenly looked like three little kids who had played too long and now needed to go find their parents. Then one of the policemen, a baldin' guy, saw that the porch had become uncomfortable, so he said it was time to go, and when we all trailed behind Pauline and Pa Campbell and Ma Campbell and Moms, we saw that they had put black-and-yellow tape across the creek right around the sinkhole with "POLICE LINE DO NOT CROSS" repeated on it, as if we needed to be told more than once.

Then one Fire Department first-aid guy, he said that with all that happened we should prob'ly all get checked out at the hospital. Well, I wanted to ride on the fire engine, but Moms said this was no time for fun and games, so instead they tossed me into the back of the squad car with Pauline and Frico. I didn't know what to say to her, so I kept my mouth shut. Tony and Doug went with Moms and Pa Campbell, and that whole ride into the city after 10.30 in the night was bizarre.

First of all I'd never been in a police car before. We rode along in pitch black with only the dull beams of the squad car hurryin' a few feet in front of us. Then, when the first overpass went slidin' by and we burst out into the light, I could feel the heat comin' on, like we were rollin' into an oven. The broken lines in the middle of the road slid under the car and made me think of those black-and-white keys on a piano playin' the same notes – the same sorrowful notes, over and over again, like the saddest thing in the world was happenin'. And it prob'ly was.

Look, I never reckoned Frico would go over the edge like that. I wanted him to stop dilly-dallyin' and do stuff, but I wasn't plannin' on *that*. I watched him in the cop car rear-view mirror, and apart from his eyes lookin' like he was really tired, it didn't seem like the whole thing bothered him one bit. Every time we passed a street light, those diamond-shaped shadows from the cage that separates police from prisoner in the squad car just kept sliding across his face. Even in the back of a police car, with his face in a shadow mask every few feet, that boy still looked innocent. But so did those Benet boys when they pulled them out of the earth. I closed my eyes to block out the image, but instead I trapped the whole thing in my head. Frico. Squash. Broadway.

I remember the crickets chirpin' slowly after we got back that night, like they were listenin' how many quarters Doug was countin' out into a can. He did it so slowly, prob'ly tryin' to make sense of what happened or feelin' guilty that he and Tony started the whole thing. Or maybe he just wanted to see how much money he had to help Moms pay back Ma Campbell for helpin' out with the hospital. He was like that. He said money was the only magic he believed in. Cool. But you wish he'd just make noise and get the countin' over and done with and stop the damn torture.

Speakin' of torture, I hope Calvin died in a hurry. Yes, Calvin died. Backhoe and his boys blasted our dog two times in the rampage. The second bullet, a full-metal-jacket, was to his head at close range against the foot of a tree where Calvin had curled up after taking one in the hindquarters. So, like Moms said, I made sure to recognize the tragedy of the human beings first.

Now, let me just say that Calvin was like a regular guy as well. He didn't give no trouble except for goin' under people's houses and likin' the Benets' girl dog. You could hang laundry on the line and that dog would walk away just out of respect, especially if it was white sheets. If he stayed near the sheets, it was just to guard them from those houseflies that make a hobby out of leaving nasty little specks on your best things. Calvin would watch a fly out of one sleepy eye and then – clop! – he'd take that speck-maker down and chew on him a bit before droppin' him on the ground in a mangled mess. In the evenings, Calvin would jump and hug you with muddy feet just because you came home to the godforsaken swamp – and he still thought the world of you even when you failed a test or whatever. It's horrible how the Benets died. And Calvin, he didn't deserve to get shot and killed like that either. I'm just glad he made little replicas of himself before he left.

But back to Broadway and Squash. I thought about them for days and days. I told myself that in another life away from this swamp with its muggy nights and jungle laws, we could have all been friends. Our parents would all be super-rich and we'd share our bologna lunches and those little Hostess cakes with the cream fillin' in the middle that get advertised on the back of Archie comics. We'd go to one of those private schools where kids wore a blazer with a nice crest on it and everythin'. And they would've bathed regularly and combed their hair and known their grammar, and they wouldn't have minded being called by their right names.

Anyway, we didn't go to the funeral, but Moms, she got a programme from the church service, and on the front of it, they called them Herbert and Orville. Maan, after that I wanted to talk to somebody about everythin', but I had slim pickin's this time. Moms had warned off Pa Campbell about the gossipin'. Tony was goin' on and on with his nerd voice and explainin' how "sinkholes are natural occurrences in the wetlands – or maybe all that experimental frackin' that Backhoe started in the swamp a while back had caused the limestone to get weak". Doug would just keep on countin' his money, and Moms, well, I was beginnin' to wonder what her hands in the air meant when she stood in front of those boys and their guns. Seems like she brought her hands and the bridge down at the same time, if I remember correctly. Or was it all Fricozoid's doin'? Or maybe she hit down the bridge and he conjured up the hole under it. Damn. Now, if those two were really workin' together, I was goin' to have a hard time gettin' anything done. Maybe Frico was takin' instructions from her or the other way around. In any case, I was up a creek, so to speak, but I'd work it all out and keep goin', even with all the confusion.

Pa Campbell stood on his porch for four nights after the funeral, staring out towards the Gulf as if waiting for somethin'. It was September again, and the breezes were already shakin' paprika onto the trees. So he complained that he was cold all the time and he put on that woven Native cloth I told you about and started walkin' back and forth on the porch, shakin' and hummin'. He'd lean against the railin' for a long time, till I started thinkin' he was sleeping upright. Ma Campbell always came to take him back inside. Truth is, that old bastard was waitin' to talk to me, but under the circumstances that wouldn't happen for a while.

Now, usually on Turkey Day every year Moms would say we had a lot to be thankful for. But that year – Nineteen Eighty-five, man – she was right. That year she also said we couldn't have dinner and leave other members of our family unfed, even if they didn't deserve to eat. She had gotten a big ol' Butterball turkey from the owner of the restaurant where she worked and she carved off a piece and put some "real purdy gravy" with potatoes and some squash stuffed with shrimp in that gravy dish with the pink flowers on the side. She was experimenting with that tamarind sauce, but we didn't like it. Then when she was wrappin' the whole thing in foil to keep it warm, I heard Pa Campbell's truck startin' up, and he was honkin' the horn and makin' a hoopla. Momma told Tony and Frico and Doug and me to load up and go with Pa Campbell to visit Pops and bring him some Thanksgiving Dinner. That was a bit of a surprise – but the bigger shock was when Pa drove up to St Mary's Hospital in Slidell. Seems that Pops had taken a bad beatin' from God knows who, but I suspect Benet had somethin' to do with it. Pa Campbell always said that man Benet had questionable connections in the city, and they'd do him a favour every now and then. One of Pops' hands was fractured, and his whole body was all swollen up like a tree trunk. They had to be keeping him hooked up to a hospital bed for observation on Thanksgivin' night.

"Took a tumble over some appliances, boys."

"Yeah, some ninja stoves and radios, we copy dat." Tony was hilarious, but that was not good timin' for sarcasm or makin' any kind of remark. Guess he was upset and wanted Pops to know that we knew he was in some kind of deal with Benet, but as usual Doug told him to shut it. Pops obviously didn't even know that his wife and kids had been almost gunned down after he bolted out of the swamp that night. He only heard that the Benet boys died in an accident and he mentioned it to Pa Campbell. Pa had nothin' to say about it, even though they did talk for a while and made up good after all those years. Twice Frico started sketchin' Pops's fractured arm – and twice he erased it. It's like he knew better than to mess with a boomerang spell, especially if it was Valerie Beaumont's work.

We were way outside visiting hours, so a sweet nurse in a tight uniform, I remember, she came by, smiled and threw us all out so nicely. Pa and Pops, they shook with left hands as we got up to go. On the way out, I let everybody walk ahead of me. Then I turned back when they weren't lookin' and went back to Pops' bed. He was surprised when I took a whiskey flask bottle from my back pocket with cinnamon, nutmeg, some paper with Moms' name and some of her hair in it. He didn't know I knew about this stuff.

"I want my moms' picture back," I told him.

And I was surprised when he pulled it out from a knapsack beside the bed and handed it to me. I rolled the photo and tucked it into the bottle and gave the whole thing back to him.

"Now put your name in there and go toss it into the Gulf of Mexico for godssake… I want my pops back too."

You could see that he wanted to hug me and everything, but he had only one hand workin'. Plus, like I said before, that would just have been too weird.

When we got back into the swamp it was late, cos Pa Campbell took a hell of a long time in the restroom at the hospital. I studied Moms' face to see if she was in the mood to answer any questions, but you can't read a woman that easily. I figured it might not be the best time to ask her about the archangel, so I decided on something intelligent-sounding like it could be for school or something. I asked her who Marie Laveau was, even though I knew already. She told me that Marie Laveau was a mixed-race voodoo priestess who was born free in Louisiana, and she'd been dead for over two hundred years.

"And by the way that is voodoo, not hoodoo, so don't be ignorant about that ever."

And then she went back to clearing the table. I asked her if she knew that Pops went to the grave in St Louis Cemetery and made a wish to get her back. She smiled and said: "He can do whatever he wants, cos in my opinion, a woman who was born free ain't doing nothing to keep another woman in bondage."

Her cheeks were all shiny again, and I was hoping that she was a little flattered that Pops could go to that extreme to get her back. But then all of a sudden the smilin' got weird and she was staring at me with no teeth showin', and she looked real creepy, like she could read my mind. But Tony always said: "Never watch a woman's smile: watch her eyes." So Moms' eyes started lookin' disappointed.

"What?" I said.

And, would you believe it, the woman pulls out the same goddamn whiskey flask bottle I gave to Pops in the hospital and slams it on the kitchen table and calls out my full name in such a slow, quiet voice I felt cold.

"Now look, little boy – don't you go gettin' involved in things you don't know nothin' about, y'hear me?"

I swallowed hard. "Yes, ma'am."

I shook my head and felt stupid. Dammit. I'm dead again. See, you really don't want to be on the receivin' end when Valerie Beaumont gets all bowed up and ready to strike. She leant into my face.

"You want to cast a spell, boy? Then go to school and grow up and get your ass out of these goddamn backwaters, y'hear? Cos at this rate, with all the idlin' you been doin', it will be a damn surprise, I'll tell you that! And that goes for all o' you!"

She swept the room with her index finger and her eyes, and everybody stopped breathing.

"Now y'all might miss your father, but you can't take magic and fix everything, y'hear? You got to work with what you got... you understand? Y'all need to remember that. Work things out in other ways, every single day. Even the good Lord walked this earth, but he wasn't into showing off with no miracles. God is good, but we got work to do too. So make somethin' of the little you already got. That's the *real* miracle."

She took a hammer and broke the bottle in the sink and washed the hair and the spices down the drain. Then she said real soft: "Now go put my picture back where you found it. Matter of fact, I can't even trust you no more. I'll go do it my damn self."

My brothers, they were gigglin', and I was frozen solid – couldn't move. I couldn't finish a sentence.

"How?..."

"How what? How did I get this?" She held up the neck of the broken bottle and then chucked it in the garbage before swingin' right back around to glare at me again. "Well, mister, maybe it's true that your momma can whistle and raise anything up from under the waters here and over in the Gulf. Or maybe Pa Campbell just took it right back here from the hospital and gave it to me. And let that be the end of it, y'hear?"

Eleven

Now, before the end of the year, I wanted to tackle Pa Campbell for takin' that whiskey bottle back to Moms and rattin' me out. I also made up my mind to tell him about Frico. If he believed me, I'd let him in on the whole Benet boys' killin'. So I made an occasion for it. I went to the fence and called him – and he hobbled out. I told him I wanted to learn all about the crawfishin' part of his business, cos I saw he might need some help. Well, he just half-grinned and winked and told me to go back inside and be ready at a moment's notice.

Soon there was a knock on the window and ol' gossip-monger Ma Campbell came callin' on Moms with a cup of hot water ready to mooch some herbal tea. By and by, after gripin' about the goats and the government, she got around to talkin' about her son. I was gettin' impatient, but I wanted to hear the latest on the legendary James "Couyon" Jackson. Turns outs he had gone and gotten a price on his head. A hundred thousand dollars. He was layin' low and workin' as a cowherd in Texas, but the farmer saw a news report that there was a reward for him. So the farmer nabbed ol' Couyon by lockin' him inside the cattle chute beside a dairy cow one night. Now, a cattle chute is a slender little steel cage for controllin' a big ol' fat cow. Throw one good-for-nothin' gangster in there and that's a tight fit. Anyway, the legend goes that Couyon Jackson milked the cow, shook that milk into butter, greased himself, slid through that steel cage and had gotten clear across the Sabine River border into Louisiana by the time that poor farmer came back from callin' the police. All the Texas cops got was some damn good butter, fresh from the farm. Well, whatever the story was, Couyon was wanted and runnin' loose. Finally Ma Campbell got around to sayin' Pa wasn't doin' so well and needed a hand gatherin' all those crawfish traps and sortin' through them mudbugs, and she was wonderin' if Moms could send one of us young ones over for a few hours.

When Moms' hollered out and asked me if I done my week-end assignments, I shouted back "Hell, yes!" before I realized I damn near gave the whole plan away by being too enthusiastic.

So I'm in the pirogue – one of those small aluminum boats – with Pa Campbell and I deliberately called him "Lobo" to get his attention – but that wrinkled old man, he was lookin' at the next crawfish trap comin' up. See, to catch crawfish in a serious kind of way, you gotta set traps in a line all along the mangroves. You gotta put some dead fish or somethin' delicious in that wire trap and let those mudbugs crawl through the openin' to get it. Then when they realize they got a meal, they'll also discover they can't get out the way they came in, cos their claws and all their pointy parts and the thing they're holdin' on to gets in the way. So you get out there in your boat and as you pass along the line of traps, you haul them out the water one at a time and you dump those suckers into a plastic bucket or the front of your boat if it's a small pirogue-type boat or whatever, and you move on to the next trap and so on.

So Pa Campbell, he's rowin' and stoppin' at every trap and dumpin' crawfish in the front of the boat, and the crawfish is crawlin' and clatterin' against the aluminum boat – and I'm so fascinated with those bugs I forgot that I wanted to have the upper hand in the conversation. So Pa, he threw a giant crawfish in my lap, and while I'm struggling with the thing he just comes out with:

"Pay attention kid. The wind is changin' in this heah swamp. You came heah to talk, but you betta go on and lissen, cos I don't have much taam... and I don't mean today-taam – I mean taam, period."

The old man was scarin' me again, but he was always too dramatic. He dumped the last trap in the boat and, as he was throwin' out the rotten bait, one of the mudbugs hung on to it and dangled over the water. He picked him off the dead fish tail and dropped him in the boat.

"All the questions you came into this boat wit' will be answered if you just tune into what I'm sayin'."

"See kid? Life's hard, but it don't hafta be miserable, y'heah me? I travel the Industrial Canal and around the city and all the way across to Metairie, and I heah people talkin' about businesses closing and it's never been like this since the Great Depression and how God turned his or her back on us. Of course life is hard! But happy's in your heart. The people who don't know that happy's in your heart and not in what you have, they the ones who say God left this planet heah like a goddamn crawfish pot and went off and did somethin' else. Dunno, maybe she went to grab an ice-cream cone. And heah we are steppin' all over each other tryin' to survive. And in all this survivin', there's still a whole lot of plain old grabbin' and greed."

I imagined a picture of God gettin' up off his throne cos he heard the ice-cream-vendor van comin'. I thought it was ridiculous to think of the Almighty just sittin' around on a great big armchair all day anyway, so I started laughin'.

"Don't be laughin'. And look at me – lemme get to the point. Forget all that talk about ice cream an' whadeva."

Pa Campbell steadied the boat – which had started rockin', cos he was throwin' up his arms at me. Somethin' told me he wasn't so steady himself. He jumped right into another topic like we'd been talkin' about it long before.

"What those Benet boys got was comin' to 'em. Now, I'm not happy they died, but they were headin' theah before they was born. I mean, it was a curse."

"Before…"

"Yes *before* they was born. It was a curse he put on his own flesh and blood by bein' too greedy."

"He who?"

"Remember that man in the yellow glasses and beige bush jacket in those photographs from San Tainos?"

"Oh, the Jim Jones guy."

He looked at me weird. "What? Anyway, that's Tracey Benet. Him, your mother, your pops, me and Pauline... that's Mrs Benet... we were friends for a long time. All of us were the toast of San Tainos. Those days we were damn near famous and all very good friends."

Man, I couldn't connect the idea of that handsome fella being ol' hard-face Backhoe Benet. Worse, I couldn't imagine that the man who killed my dog used to be Pa Campbell's good friend. So I stared off over the lake and then back at him, and he looked away.

"I know, I know. Heah's what happened. Backhoe had money from natural gas that his fauder found in Pennsylvania dem days. That boy grew up rich and ambitious. They had property from here to the Yucatan, so we used to drive down to Mexico in a Studebaker – it's still ova dere in his junkyard – and we'd go to the Benet beachfront property in Merida and then sail to San Tainos right off the coast. We used to call him 'Captain Benet' at the time, cos he even found time to serve in the Coast Guard right out of high school. So he's the one who used to drive the boat out to San Tainos. We called out there the 'Tiny Antilles', or the 'Mini Caribbean'. Ooowee. We were livin' the life, man. Up in the mountains learnin' from the tribes one minute, the next minute on the beach and thinkin' of never goin' back home. But then, greed got in da way. One day, when the girls were playin' beachball, Tracey said he knew a place jus' outside Noo Orlins that might have some oil. Now, maybe it was the damn mojitos or whatnot, but we spit in our hands and made a deal that we would all go camp out on the land for a few months and see if we thought it might have some deposits. He was convincin'. He said: 'Look, this land is good for gas, and my daddy bought me some acres. And if we get reason to believe that theah's really oil or gas under it, then we're in theah with pile drivers and drills, or whatever, and we'll split the earnin's. We'll be rich. Hell, yew bet your life… I'll drive the backhoe maself!' That's how he got the name. So we came here, to this swampy place you see around you, and we camped out. Well, by the taam I was way into my thirties we hadn't found nothin', even with several companies comin' in and tryin'. Many times unregulated by any authorities, to be honest. But Benet wasn't backin' down. He just kept on plungin' into the earth until it got illegal. Well, your pops went back into the city and got more interested in natural magic from San Tainos and even more interested in your mother. He couldn't wait to get down to San Tainos to see her, and that was a problem. See, we always went together. And more importantly, at that time Backhoe was your mother's boyfriend."

I flung away the crawfish and grabbed the sides of the boat. "What? No way!"

"Easy now son. That was…"

My head felt heavy.

"Backhoe?! What? You mean…"

"I said easy, Skid. That was a *long* time ago."

"You… you mean I came that close to lookin' like *Broadway and Squash*? Oh God!"

He stopped rowin', and the boat – that was goin' in a straight line – started wobblin'. He just looked at me and frowned and leant his head like a dog who just heard a tea kettle.

"Is dat what you're gettin' from all dat I'm sayin' to you, son? Dat's your concern? Jeesus Saviour! Cos I ain't got the taam witchoo taday."

The boat was really wobblin' now. I was wishin' he would stop lookin' at me like that. He sighed and narrowed his eyes and started rowin' again.

"So anyway, I told Alrick not to go to San Tainos by himself, but he did again and again, and by and by things changed.

Backhoe found out and wanted to hang him by the toenails. But your pops, he was in love. So when things got rough and he married Valerie and came to America, Backhoe went down to the island for Pauline. Now, that was just to make Valerie feel bad, cos that Pauline was like a young Miss San Tainos at the time – yeah – beauty-pageant winner and all. And by the way, I know you mighta heard stuff from his own mouth, but don't be thinkin' that man Tracey is prejudicialist. He's not. *Bitter* is what he is. And he's been so for a long time. He taught his sons to harass y'all, so y'all would just pack up and head on outta the swamp and make it easier for him, cos he still got feelin's for your... for Valerie. But... look what happened. It's all karma."

All that time in my head, I'm still back in the Sixties with Moms and Backhoe. Imagine... Skid *Benet*. Daaamn.

Pa kept goin'. "Anyway, where was I? Yeah, late Sixties. After a while, Backhoe called up Alrick and reopened his offer, sayin' that the gas and oil was deeper down – and he wanted to get it like we all agreed. Of course, at the time, Alrick was just tryin' to settle in with his new wife, plus he knew under all that calmness Backhoe hated the fact that he took away the love of his life. But Backhoe said: 'Look, business is business, no sweat, I'm happy. And I hear that you're the man for the job.' What he meant was that somebody over in Alabama told him they found oil underground by usin' divinations."

He didn't wait for me to ask.

"Divinations is when people use magic to find out somethin' that science cain't. It's all over the Old Testament, kid. Ask your Harry T friend. Anyway, in this case, Backhoe knew about Valerie's conjurin' powers and wanted Alrick to get her to find out where the oil was under the land. See now, he had to be cautious, cos the place was in a mess and people were talkin' about it. So that's when Alrick came and told your momma that they should invest in a piece of swampland and the city would catch up later on."

"So, he didn't have a vision?"

"Course he had a vision, cos when Valerie found out the trick and refused to help with the divinations, he prob'ly *wanted* to believe something good would happen evenchually. Like the city would actually come into the swamps. That was his Plan B if there was really no oil or gas. 'Twas on his mind day an' night. Plus, he had to get your mother here for a long enough time, in order for her to feel the energy of the place and conjure up where exactly the minerals were located. So he told her the vision. And she is a spirichual person, so she gave it a shot. And ol' Alrick, he was a sneaky one: he went ahead and got your momma pregnant, so that apartment idea she had wouldn't look so good any more. But when your mother came into the swamps, like I said, she found religion and refused to do any more spells 'cept for protection. And Alrick, he flipped a wig when she wouldn't do it, and he went and did some reckless magic himself, I tell ya. Started planting seals and conjurin' spells all over the place. Been doin' it for years. Now, with the subsidence year after year and all the gravel and marl we dump on this land from time to time, he can't find those seals anywhere. That land we live on is a magic minefield, you heah me? Don't you play with magic if you ain't ready for the constiquences! And that's why I say the wind's a-changin', son. Earth balances herself. At first I thought that as soon as Backhoe and Alrick realized there was nothin' in this swamp, then they'd just relax and I'd kick back with my old lady and enjoy the view right here. But greed is a ghost! I love this place, but this swamp is haunted by greed. And it's heavy with spells. Hundreds of powerful seals are buried in the earth right heah, and all that power is about to balance this place out. Those poor, misguided boys dyin' is just the beginnin' o' sorrows. Now, I never told you this when you came to me and said y'all think your pops was conjurin' against y'all, but he was prob'ly desperate and just tryin' his best to scare your mother off the land, cos he cain't imagine what all those seals he planted are about to do. But of course, that goat-blood letter, it backfired and he hurt his own self."

Now, after that bottle-spell incident I knew I shouldn't ask this, but I couldn't help myself, especially since I remembered Pops in the darkness diggin' at the dirt with his bare hands that night.

"Plantin' seals, Pa?"

"Have you been lissenin'? Now, don't you go trying nothin'. There are enough spells goin' on as it is. That's why I gave that whiskey bottle back to your mother. That's it."

Pause. And I just sat there and looked at him and looked down and played with the clambering crawfish and looked up again and sighed and looked away. That old guy looked at me out the wrinkly corner of his eye till he couldn't help himself. I gave him ten seconds more, and by the time I'd gotten to six on the countdown in my head, he rolled his eyes and went on.

"Dammit – awright! But just for your edjufication: the seals are from *grimoires*, son. Ancient spell books. There are seals... symbols that people bury in da earth – and if theah are minerals or riches or oil or gas or wha'eva, then it's s'pose to bring it right up. Seen it maself with ma own two peepers! But most people use good magic for greed. Then they say the Great Spirit turned her back on them. But it's them who give up on their good selves."

It was sunset almost, and the high tide had snuck up on us and was lop-loppin' against the boat and makin' it unsteady. The autumn breezes tunnelled into my ears, so I missed most of what Pa said after that. Then when we were rowin' back to the house through the trees, a big lazy cloud bank came stretchin' sideways from over the Gulf all the way across to the swamp – and it looked like a giant heap, hundreds of feet high. The sun was right behind it, so it gave it this gold lining at the top that looked like a big ol' mirage of a mountain.

Now, Pa Campbell, he thought I didn't notice, but as he rowed back through the cypresses with the water now higher

up on the trunks, I could hear him whisperin': "Hey Bigfoot
– hi Old Sarah." And I looked around and realized he was
talkin' to the damn trees. Well, I wasn't so emotional about
trees 'cept for my conference room, so I was snickerin' and
playin' with the crawfish, until I looked up and saw that as
we came through the trees, the duckweed, that green carpet-
looking thing on top of the water in the swamp, it just kinda
closed back up and made the surface look so solid you felt
you could prob'ly hop out of the boat and run on top of it
and jump over those water hyacinths with the purple-and-
gold Mardi-Gras-coloured flowers – and walk on water all
the way up to that big cloud mountain that wasn't really
there. And that's when I told myself that I *really* believed
in Pops' dream. And now that I knew the whole back story,
it was eye-opening, like wakin' up with conjunctivitis until
Moms rescues you with some saline.

To tell the truth, I didn't even care if my pops still believed
his vision or if it was somethin' to get Valerie Beaumont into
the swamps. I just had the same premonition – and Frico had
the power, even though the boy had taken a really bad turn.

Pa Campbell brought the pirogue around to the landin' at
the front of our house, and we used a plastic shovel to scoop
the crawfish into an ice cooler. It wasn't even crawfish season,
so the shells were hard and noisy. I did most of the shovel-
lin', cos suddenly Pa started shiverin' like he was cold. He sat
down at the edge of our landin' and then, when I could no
longer see his face except for the flickerin' white in his eyes,
he said to me like it was a benediction:

"You are also from San Tainos – at least a part of you.
Know what that word 'Taino' means, son? It means 'good
people'. But it also means you got ancestors that was on this
side of the world for thousands of years before ol' Columbus
came pokin' his sword all over the place. Soon as he came, I
believe deep down they knew it was never gonna be the same.
You've got ancestors inside of you that saw his face as close

as I'm sittin' 'cross from you. And that means theah's a part
of you that should sense it when the wind changes. But you
don't pay attention, Skid, so I gotta tell ya. And tell those
brothers of yours too. Start askin' your mauda to tell you
who the hell y'all are, you heah me? I mean, just the odder
day y'all were knee-high to a grasshopper, but y'all grown up
now... it's time. Lord knows it's time. You don't know who
you are, and it's a shame."

What he was sayin' was pretty cool and deep and scary, but
I was more happy about him agreein' to let me help him with
the crawfishin' and such. So I was about to ask him 'bout
a salary package when Moms, she heard the talk and came
around the side of the house past the new well and water
tank. She stepped over the PVC pipe, leant on the rake in her
hand and called out to Pa askin' him how I did out on the
bayou.

"Boy's a nachural," he called back. "Gathered a whole pile
for you guys too. And if you don't mind I'd like to borrow his
help ag'in come next weekend."

"As long as you be tellin' him only about fishin', that's all
right."

"Oh yeah," he said, avoidin' her eyes and gruntin' as he
picked up the cooler. He walked past her towards his house.
"Matter of fact, I was tellin' him that to read and write and
speak good is a spell in itself. I told him to study that grammar and those mathematics and cast a spell on the world that
way."

And I just wished that old man hadn't said a word about all
that. Valerie Beaumont is no fool.

Twelve

Backhoe Benet moved out of the swamp in a hurry. That was before Christmas, right after he came there one last time with some guys in one of those new GMC trucks. He went inside his house and came back out with the dried-up sunflowers and threw them out into the yard. Then he took down the curtains himself and dropped them on the floor and just stood there lookin' out over the train tracks and past the sinkhole. He went for Medusa and put her in the passenger seat of the GMC and drove away. The guys took sledgehammers and a tractor and demolished the house, which was wood and glass anyway. A flatbed came and scraped up the junk and they all left with it.

When they were drivin' out, the wind picked up and you could smell dead leaves and damp earth. That winter was bitter cold. How cold? So cold I wore all those acid-wash, denim hand-me-down jackets without feelin' bad about it. How cold? We hardly got snow so far South, but that winter there was a seven-minute snow flurry and we needed serious heatin'. So Tony, he got nerdy and built us a heater out of a wood stove, steel sheets and some bricks Pops left behind. I think Pops helped him by calling through on the CB, but I couldn't be sure. For one thing Valerie Beaumont was turnin' that thing off more regularly. Pops' voice would come over on the frequency. He'd say, "Break, break, Lady T-Rex," and she'd say, "Oh, gimme a break indeed." Well, I guess Pops was out of the hospital and was tryin' to follow up on that note he sent to Moms.

Yeah, he sent her a note. See, when Pa Campbell brought that whiskey bottle back to Moms that night, the old fella didn't even know he was being my pops' little postman. Cos that Pops is real sneaky. He used the rolled-up photo to hide a note that he wrote to Moms. So when she broke that bottle that night and said she was gonna put back her photo where it came from, she found some paper rolled up real neat inside the photo. We all got a hold of it and read it one night while she was sleepin'. And it was a shocker. Her blood pressure went up and the whole place smelt like green tea and garlic for days.

Dearest Valerie,

I've done you wrong. I lied to you sixteen years. I am so sorry, but the time has come to speak the truth, because a greater evil is coming. The land we have been living on, that you and our children still occupy, is not ours. Our land titles are lies. The money we put together sixteen years ago did not purchase a piece of the wetlands. It was invested in Benet's attempts to find oil or gas. I only wanted to make a better life for our children and I went ahead and did foolish things.

Benet is never satisfied. He still wants money. And now he also wants blood. The land you are living on belongs to him only. I am afraid he is ready to do something desperate. Please let us make arrangements to relocate as soon as possible.

I love and care for you,

Alrick

Well, my mother, she read it and bawled. Then she stomped outside in the night with a storm lantern and a shovel and buried the PVC pipe. For seven days we held hands around the table when she prayed for courage. And like I told you, that makes me scared as hell. Moms started goin' and sittin' with Ma and Pa Campbell on their porch for hours. When we watched them, we'd just see them noddin' and pointin' and gesticulatin', but I couldn't for the life of me make out what those ol' people were sayin'.

Nineteen Eighty-six. Well, the changes were happenin' fast. Pa Campbell gave us a beat-up pirogue and Moms', well, she was learnin' to shoot.

One day I heard her around the back with Pa Campbell churnin' out bullets from the old .270 rifle, and I said, "Yeah, that's my momma." By spring we were catchin' bass and panfish and crawfish out on the bayou instead of standin' on the banks and wishin' we could. Valerie Beaumont said it was about time we got our feet wet. We didn't mind, even though Tony had to learn to keep quiet out on the water and Doug had to park his dainty white tennis shoes and Frico had to lay down his paintin' sometimes and grab a trap or fishin' pole. I had to learn to stop tryin' to tell all of them what to do like I knew it all just because I went out crawfishin' with Pa Campbell a few times.

Now, us learnin' to live off the land couldn't have come at a better time. Some people in the city were shuttin' down shop and those who worked for them were headin' out to Dallas and Atlanta to find jobs. We came home from school every day and practised our fishin' and packed shrimp and crawfish. Pa showed us how to scoop silt from the bayou floor and pour it into the garden, at the root of whatever greens he was growin'. Man, that mud stunk to highest heaven.

"Aww. Smell dat? Dat right theah is rich nutrishun for dose greens right theah! You know, I heard the Mayans or dose Aztecs I think, yeah, they use to do dat. Pour the swamp floor or river bed on all dat corn and cassava. They had to grow things fas', cos... they had people to feed!"

One day in the middle of our enterprisin' and history lesson, Belly rode into L-Island and just up and said he'd be leavin' after summer to continue middle school in Atlanta. Tall Horse sent for him – God knows I don't know my uncle-in-law's real name – and there was no time for debatin': it was just time to move. It was a weird time, cos almost on cue here comes Marlon the Fading Child Star with the same story. He was leavin' for some place in New York called Rochester, cos he would be closer to big auditions and more opportunities for TV commercials. Well, Frico took a break from paintin' critters and he sketched a design for a costume that Marlon could do his auditions in, and Marlon's grandma, she got to sewin' it for him, even though his grades didn't budge upwards. Now, even though it wasn't a magic suit or nothin' (Frico drew it with his right hand), I was a little surprised at how easy it was for *other people* to get this guy to draw stuff – so I just felt mad that week.

I was mad at my pops too. That letter only showed that Alrick Beaumont was a coward who couldn't come into the swamps and man up and tell Moms to her face about the whole thing. Even though, with her new shooting skills, maybe he really shouldn't. Apart from that, that letter mentioned nothin' about all them seals he buried in the earth – hundreds prob'ly. Then again, maybe she knew, and that's why we were holdin' hands around the table all the time. Now, I'll tell you who wasn't a coward: Frico Beaumont. One school mornin', he was brushin' his teeth, and since I was thinkin' about the suit he just up and drew for ol' Marls, I just stepped into the bathroom and stood behind him and glared at the guy in the mirror.

"I got somethin' for you to do for *me*, Frico."

That freckle-face boy just looked at me in the mirror all blank and started brushing his tongue and letting all the toothpaste suds fall out – all the time he knows he's disgustin'. He told me to hold his nasty toothbrush while he cupped both hands to rinse his mouth cos the tank was runnin' low again. I repeated myself.

"Said I got somethin' for you to do for me, Frico."

Rinse. Gargle. Spit.

"And what you can do for me is put my toothbrush down and get the hell out. You gonna watch me floss too?"

He snapped a thread off his T-shirt and wrapped it around his fingers. I tried to sound reasonable.

"Look, we ain't had words about Broadway and Squash, but we need to."

"Go ahead, have words. This should be interesting."

"I know you did it."

"You *think* I did it. You imagine that I do lots of things. You should be careful with that. That's why momma took you to see that shrink lady."

"That lady doctor is none of y'all business. And by the way that was not because of anything I was thinkin'. It was because your friend Suzy Wilson got me into trouble and all that. I used to *think* things those days. These days, I *know*."

"Uh-huh, you know? Why? Cos these days you are the Prophet Beaumont? I thought the only thing you believed in was money."

"Sure I believe in money, like Doug does. I believe in *you* too." That sounded crappy as soon as I said it. He stuck his finger into his mouth and made that fake-vomit sound that girls do when they think you're a creep – well, at least that's what Marlon told me.

"Look, we got things to do, and instead of usin' those powers, you're just markin' time around here."

"Don't know what you're talkin' about. You're mistaken."

"I'm talkin' about the earthquake and the sinkhole and all the stories I heard about you since I was born."

He wasn't lookin' at me any more. He pulled on both ends of the flossin' thread. Something flicked off and stuck to the mirror.

I realized this boy wasn't budgin'. So I got real menacin' and husky in my voice, like they do on those interrogations that come halfway through every cop show.

"I'll tell you what will be a mistake, Fricozoid. Not doin' what I say when I say it. Cos I got the drop on you, y'hear me?" I was thinkin' I would use some cool police phrases too.

He just laughed.

"Wait, wait... wow. Ha. You got the drop. On me..."

He used one finger to tap his chest, while he smirked at me in the mirror. Then he went from amused to bored, but I wasn't goin' to leave without makin' my point.

"Frico, I heard you say 'shhh' up in that tree, but I'm prepared to do the opposite if we don't come to an understandin' right now."

To be honest, at that point I knew I pushed too far – and by any measure I was being too big for my britches, as Pops would say. But Frico didn't grab for my throat like I expected him to. Instead he just stood in the mirror, took up the toothpaste and squeezed a bit on his fingertip. Then he started draggin' his finger around and sketchin' on the glass with the toothpaste. Meanwhile he's doin' it, he's talkin' real calm.

"See Skid... maybe I said 'shhh' up in that tree so you would shut up and not scream like a girl again, and let ol' man Benet see us and start blazin' bullets – cos maybe he thought it was Calvin climbin' a tree or some Loogaroo or something. Or maybe I did it so you can keep your mouth shut, period – especially to Belly and Marlon and Harry T about all this rubbish – you got that?" He moved from in front of the mirror and pointed.

"Aww now Skid... look what you done gone and did to yourself."

I looked and – would you believe it? – that bastard sketched a perfect image of my face on the mirror with the toothpaste. And then the guy added pimples! Lots of them. I grabbed my face. I was ready at this point to back off and fight another day, but he pushed past me and was walkin' out the door when he said: "I will sketch that every mornin' and find somewhere to add one more spot until you promise to shut the hell up. Even if it's on your scalp. You got that?"

* * *

I got obsessed with mirrors after that. Had one in my pocket, lookin' out for a bad complexion every hour on the hour. Then I started hoggin' the ol' dresser mirror inside of our shack as well. Now, come to think of it, I know I never told you anything much about the inside of our one-room swamp shack. That's because a man can't describe what he can't see. But since Pops moved out with his stuff, we did some spring cleanin' and threw out more junk – and, frankly, our house was in better shape. Inside at least. There were pale patches on the floor, squares and rectangles where appliances used to sit, pale wood undisturbed for years and years. We took out some of the furniture. It wasn't much, just four iron chairs and a formica table with wooden legs, three beds – or, rather, two beds and a cot – and a big, tangerine fake-leather armchair behind the door.

We decided not to move the heavy stuff, like Moms' display case with all the fine china that's never used, and the stuff that was hooked up to Pops' power sources, like the fridge and CB, cos he wasn't around to fix anythin' if it went haywire. The old record changer that some poor soul had brought in to get fixed was still there. They'd left a Justin Wilson Cajun comedy record in it, but the changer played real slow, so ol' Justin's jokes took too long to hit the punchline. Pops' workbench was still in the far corner of the room, with yellowin' electronic magazines hangin' over it from shelves like an overstuffed Po' Boy sandwich. Moms took down each shelf herself and put them out in the yard for the mosquito fires. Tony snuck half of them back inside.

The job to clean the floor went to me and Fricozoid. Moms went into an old shippin' barrel and took out a few ounces of some red powder, and we mixed it with water and washed the wood floors with it until it was blood red. Then we started on the porch. She called the red powder "annatto". We called it "weird". She was grinnin' and sayin' she "hadn't seen a floor so pretty since…" – and when she trailed off, I got brave and finished her sentence: "Since San Tainos?" Well, right then she just stopped and stared ahead right across to Pa Campbell's place. And he just turned himself around in his wheelchair and slid inside his house and locked the door behind him.

She put up some new white curtains after we painted the inside of the house with this aquamarine flat emulsion that we found in Pops' left-behind belongin's. "It's time things got a little more permanent round here."

That night the mosquito fire was a huge camp-style blaze fuelled by some of Pops' old magazines. When the light from it was brightest and made the trees and their shadows elastic, Moms started a show-and-tell. Dozens of jars and old clothes and albums and some knick-knacks later, we had heard all about San Tainos – just like that. She said our Pops didn't want us to grow up confused, so she didn't tell us much, but we were older now. She made it fun, better than many teachers I've had – playin' all the parts in the drama of when the sun was young and the Caribbean gods created San Tainos by breakin' off pieces of Peru and draggin' them up the Central American Walkway and hurlin' them into the sea right off the coast of Mexico to make steppin' stones into the Greater Antilles. This was a road of escape from other tribes, who raided Taino villages like it was a hobby. Well, some of the Taino people went on ahead into Jamaica, Cuba, Puerto Rico and Hispaniola, but others stopped to rest a while on those steppin' stones – and the breeze was so cool they fell asleep and had sweet dreams for centuries. When they woke up, Columbus was knockin' on their door with a nightmare. But after a while some of them found refuge from the ol' Spanish sword by escapin' in the dead of night with some runaway slaves that the Spanish called Cimarrónes. Them and the Cimarrónes took to the mountains to live high up inside a cooled-down volcano cone on the north of the island. And up inside that big burner, the Spanish didn't even know where they were at first. That group of people recognized the volcano as a *zemi*, a god in itself, since it was apparently the one who saved them from the invaders. They called the mountain Bik'ua.

Moms spoke that legend like it was all true, stoppin' a few times to get the glisten out of her eyes. Well, even though I was all of twelve goin' on thirteen at the time, I felt brand-new again, like I was just born, like back in the day when ol' Pa Campbell used to hang out with me and tell me cool stories.

I don't know 'bout my brothers, but before all these revelations there were questions deep behind the ol' Skid skull. To me it was like you're at the bottom of a pool, so all you can hear is muffles from above and everybody below is speakin' in bubbles. Or you're watchin' a movie and some dude decides to drag a chair through the most important part of the dialogue.

So I guess that San Tainos place was hauntin' my head long before I heard about it. I tasted it in Valerie Beaumont's cooking, when the meal came out not quite Creole or Cajun but stopped somewhere in between, or was just completely different. I could hear it when she was navigatin' the corners of her American accent and she hit a syllable really hard, and somethin' else tumbled out from under her tongue. Her grammar always stood steady, but the sound changed, like that time in Principal Phillips' office. I heard it in my own voice, but only when I talked proper English and the kids at school looked at me weird. They said my accent kept changin' gears. Talk about goddamn sour grapes. I told them they needed to listen in English and go learn to spell words like 'colour' and 'honour' correctly. Of course, it was *me* who always got those words wrong in class. Life is not fair. Anyway, slowly I was realizin' that I was more San Tainos than New O'lins. Or maybe I was caught in between them, like Moms' cookin'.

"So when are we goin' there?"

Frico was askin' if we could ever visit the island, and she just smiled and looked off at nothin', starin' dead ahead with her palm under her chin, like she was watchin' reruns in her head.

"You can go there right now. If you can fly real fast like a hummingbird, go west-south-west. Keep your eyes open or you'll miss it. It's always under a cloud."

After that, when the fire was dyin' down, she didn't make it blaze again, and we knew she needed the shadows for a few seconds. There was a question-and-answer session after that, and I had a coupla things to ask – but I couldn't just jump into the hocus-pocus part of San Tainos and her natural-magic workin' and she and Captain Benet and all that, so I played smart.

"Did Pops like San Tainos?"

"Oh boy, that man *loved* the place."

"He used to come all the way there to see you?"

"Quite a bit... yes."

"By himself?"

At that point Moms, she just looked at me like she knew that I'd heard all about the conjurations and the grimoire seals and, worst of all, about her and Benet. The thought flashed in my head that I could twist her arm a bit and get her to influence Frico, but for three days after that she kept me so busy with chores every day after school I knew she was sendin' me a message.

By the way, I found out the reason that tamarind-tree conference room was so cool. It grew from tamarinds that my pops carried from San Tainos back in the day. He was eatin' some of that stuff and spat those seeds in the swamp years before we were born. He was still a coward, though.

Now, maybe it was cos Pa Campbell told me all these other stories, but I was diggin' this whole San Tainos thing. Like somebody found an old picture of me and blew the dust off it and handed it back to me. Moms bought shoots and seeds, and we started a garden. She was better at real food, like tomatoes, callaloo, peppers and corn than those flowers she wanted to plant. In the summer we boys tried our hand at dasheen and cassava. Those are like root foods and stuff. They taste much better than they sound, by the way.

We learnt about Taino words – that, like us, were only slightly changed or misinterpreted and hidden in plain sight. When we cooked outside on the "barbecue", when we rowed out to fish in a "canoe" and when Doug got in trouble for tryin' some chewin' "tobacco" that made him drowsy for hours, those were all Taino vocabulary.

Shortly after, I wanted my hair back in a topknot, like when we were little. I could have it like that at home at least. Moms didn't mind teasin' it into a knot and all, even though it was coarser now. She said we were on earth to gather up the pieces of our lives and make somethin' of ourselves. The African and the Cajun parts of us were easier to find, but the Taino took a little more diggin', cos the culture was almost buried along with many of the people. She said I should go dig at the library over in Algiers. Well, I did, and it turns out that in San Tainos' case, the Spaniards did those Tainos in with hard work and diseases – all the ones who didn't head for the hills, I mean. Meanwhile those who ran away to live with the Cimarrónes were sittin' pretty. The volcano had two massive cones up in the sky and inside one of them was a world by itself. There were lakes and rich soil and little crop farms and lots of birds comin' and goin'. Spanish soldiers tried three times to come up into those sky burners, but Bik'ua hid herself under a cloud, so they got confused and fell down ditches and stabbed each other and all that. The English came after a while and threw out the Spaniards, to put it nicely. Then they tried to make it up the mountain and got caught up in bloody clashes. But then the mountain started rumblin' and heatin' up, so the Cimarrónes slash Tainos called a truce and came down the volcano to meet them. This part was eerie, written by an English guy who travelled all that way just to write stuff down:

> The Tainos and Cimarrónes came down from the mist of those cones after generations, blinking eyes and straining ears. There was hardly any echo of Spanish and no trace of any Arawakan tongue, save that which stammered from their own lips. The streets were empty of their people and filled with brand-new, loud and fearsome contraptions.

Contraptions. Now, there's a word that sounds like the thing itself. I like those long-ago guys, though. They got words to shake ya. Anyway, after readin' that at the library, I told Moms about the volcano drawin' I did for that lady doctor back in the day. She said she saw it and she wasn't surprised. My Pops warned her never to tell us about San Tainos, but she would whisper Bik'ua's name in both ears when we were born.

"Stranger things have happened in our house. You didn't just draw that out of the blue."

So we settled in – and, honestly, it was like an adventure all over again. That is until some of the gloom and doom that Pa Campbell predicted walked up to our doorstep, literally. One mornin' Pa Campbell rapped on the window with his rifle, and when we went out, he shook as he pointed out some huge, grey footprints from one end of our front porch to the next. Whoever or whatever paid us a visit had walked barefoot and then tracked mud across the anatto-red floorboard to the front window. He pointed out that they were crouchin' as they walked, sometimes goin' down on all fours, and you could see that they had tipped up on their toes to look inside on us while we slept. Calvin's kids hadn't made a sound, so Doug was sayin' it's Pops, but Moms said her husband's foot is half that size: he'd never go barefoot, and the man she married didn't walk up the aisle on all fours.

After that she bought her own rifle. Bolt action. She blamed those parasites, the swamp rats, but I knew what she meant. Tony took sticks and old clothes and started trainin' Calvin's six kids. And that's when Moms gave Frico a job to paint some diagrams on the lower part of the house usin' that red-powder thing. He had to do it before nightfall each day and within seven days. Turns out that the red-anatto thing also wards off spirits.

Thirteen

Mai was mad at me cos I'd finally told her that we were the ones who sent Calvin over to the Benets' house that night a while back, and that's how the whole thing started. Doug and Tony made me swear not to say anythin' to anybody, but Mai wasn't just anybody. Well, as soon as I told her, that girl gave me a solid scoldin' about bein' more responsible and how I could have been killed. You shoulda seen her rockin' her head and hollerin' at me in Vietnamese and very good English. You believe that? You teach your girl English and she beats you over the head with it. After that, whenever I went to the Lam Lee Hahn, she talked to me like I was just a customer: "May I help you, sir?" or "Sorry sir, we don't have any brown rice." Worse than that, she stopped givin' me my lagniappe – that's like somethin' extra that you get in your groceries, just for shoppin'.

"*Lan-yap* is for people who deserve it. Have a good day."

And she would close the cash register and look away, like I wasn't there. Well, that kind of abuse just made her cuter.

So one evenin' after school I washed my face and spruced up my topknot and put on clean jeans and went over to Lam Lee Hahn. That day she wasn't mindin' the shop, so she was in the backyard. I didn't have to knock, cos by the time I walked up, their little butt-biting dog started hollerin'. Mai, she came around the side and saw me. She opened a small gate in the wooden fence and put one hand on her hip.

"May I help you sir?" Cute as hell.

"I didn't come to see you, I came to meet Kuan – that person you told me about that day at Al Dubois."

"Hmm. I see. Let me check if she's available."

She closed the gate again and walked away down a neat footpath that they had made from broken pieces of Vietnamese pottery. Seemed like every time someone dropped an expensive pot or a bottle, they just took the accident and made somethin' pretty. I trailed my eyes along that mosaic of deep-blue and red glass and yellow clay pieces and listened to her footsteps fadin', while a tall weepin' willow howled in the breeze. Meanwhile, the dog, he recognized me even though it'd been five long years since we danced cheek to cheek. So he decided to keep an eye on me until Mai got back. He put his paws under the fence and stuck his face between them and kept sniffin' the air and sneezin' when the dirt got sucked back up into his nose. Stupid dog. I tried to ignore him, so for the first time I really took a look at the Lam Lee Hahn property. You really couldn't tell it was a shop by just passing by in a train. It looked like one of those pagodas you'd see in a World Atlas. Well, not as fancy, but the colours were the same. And it looked like somethin' that grew out from the ground, rather than something constructed. There was a high red wooden fence at the front. Grapefruit trees were planted all along the length of it, and the bright-yellow fruit stood out against the flat red. Four tall wood columns divided the fence into sections. Rough dragon carvings curled around each column, with the dragons clawin' their way towards a blazin' gold ball at the top. A white sign with Vietnamese writin' hung right above the front doors. I couldn't tell if it said "Lam Lee Hahn", but it looked cool. The dog jumped up and wagged his tail. Mai came back to the small gate, opened it and stepped back to let me in.

"Come this way, sir."

She clapped her hands at the dog. He ran ahead of us growlin' over his dog shoulder. My hands went into my back pockets and covered both cheeks until he parked himself under a bush. We walked on the path, and suddenly I was in a completely different place in the world. The Lam Lee Hahn front yard and shop was nothin'. The backyard was an experience. Everywhere people walked around busy. Some were pickin' bitter melons and veggies from vines wrapped around wooden frames erected in the yard. Others were cookin' in aluminum pots, and behind them there were rice fields that stretched almost out to the mangroves in the pass.

Lam Lee Hahn was on L-Island, but a long fence separated them from us. I reckon their rice fields was in line with Pa Campbell's sugar cane on the other side of the red wooden fence, though. That fence went all the way around the property 'cept for the back, which faced the lake and the Gulf. I couldn't tell if the people in the rice field were men or women, cos they all had these huge cone-shaped straw hats on their heads. They all sang a Vietnamese song as they bent down and stuck little plants into the water. I didn't want to know the English lyrics, cos that would just spoil the sweetness of it. One guy was flooding the rice field with a desalination pump. Mai looked at my eyes and asked if I was excited. Well hell yes, I *was* excited... about all the money they must have been makin' in the swamps! But I wasn't going to say that last part. My moms taught me better than that. When I thought I'd seen everything, Mai, she walked away and motioned with her head for me to follow.

"Want to see where we grow the shrimp?"

Now look, these people had ponds – not small pools – ponds full of juicy shrimp and prawns and mud crabs. And beyond the ponds you could see the fishermen. Some takin' off in boats across the lake headed for the Gulf and others landin' and haulin' out big baskets of sea fish. Still others hauled produce into boats to take around the swamp and sell from what they called a Vietnamese "Floatin' Market".

Mai put her hands together and spoke to one of the men in Vietnamese, and he brought us some big ol' prawns that he roasted on an open fire. Mine was hot and burned my mouth. Mai laughed at me, and that's when I knew she wasn't mad any more. She grabbed my arm and, runnin', she pulled me into the buildin'. I couldn't see, on account of just jumpin' out of the light, so Mai led me through a long corridor, stoppin' as soon as we were safely in the dark to pull me towards her with both hands. My first kiss tasted like seafood with some shell in it.

We stood there winded, not from runnin', but from borrowin' each other's breath. I saw the white of her eyes close up. She had the softest stare – the kindest eyes – and she didn't know it. Then she told me to close mine. I waited for the second kiss, but she slapped me lightly on the cheek and said we were in a temple, for godssake. I chased her through the corridor. Up ahead there was light reflecting off a big brass gong, and the whole way down the hall there was this smell – extra sweet and warm, but sooty – like perfume on fire.

We walked into a dimly lit room with more dragons. But this time the dragons were carved into wooden walls of deep red, like dried roses. Those dragons had the same beautiful broken pieces of pottery for scales and eyes. Vietnamese words were everywhere, but I'm sure all of them said "silence".

"Quiet, now," Mai was whisperin'.

She took off her shoes and tiptoed across the floor. I did the same and followed her, happy that I was bandwagonin' Frico's clean, new sweat socks that didn't have holes in 'em. The perfume smell was stronger now. Incense. I really wanted to know what kind. I sniffed the air.

"What's that?"

Out of the dimness, a man's voice boomed: "Your nose!"

"Who's that?"

"Your ears!"

Mai sounded apologetic. "*Thay Samadh, tôi…*"

"Englis'!"

"Master Samadh. I didn't know you were in here."

"I know you not know I here."

It was the old Vietnamese man. That's the exact same voice I saw in his eyebrows. Funny how it made me think of a big block of cracked ice.

A lamp in the corner slowly became brighter.

He was seated on the floor in a pumpkin-coloured robe. It had a sparklin' embroidered collar that had all the colours of the mosaic walkway. The collar looped around his neck, curved down across his chest and disappeared under one arm. His eyes were closed, but he moved a string of big brown beads between his fingers, like he was learnin' to count.

"Skid, this is Master Samadh – Master Samadh…"

"Yes, I know, Skeed. What that name is… Englis'?"

I swallowed, wonderin' if the guy could see us with his eyes closed. "Yes, sir."

"Sounds funny… Skeed."

I think it was a good opportunity to use his phrase back on him. But when I said "Your ears", I realized it didn't make sense in the same way he said it. Mai looked at me and rolled her eyes and shrugged her shoulders and opened her palms and mouthed at me silently as if to say, "What the hell was that?"

Samadh opened his eyes and caught her mid-what-the-hell.

"Why ahh you here?" he asked me.

"I came to see Mai."

Mai rolled her eyes again. "He came to see Kuan Am, Master Sam."

"Ah! Then we do not keep Kuan Am waiting… Skeed."

"Skid." *Pause.*

"Yes." His eyes shut down again.

I wondered about his kung fu. All guys like him in the movies can fight kung fu. I asked Mai, and she said stupid questions are worse than kissin' in the temple.

We walked between two columns, and there in front of us, sittin' cross-legged under a slice of sunlight through the roof, was a big bronze statue, about seven feet tall. Fruits were laid out in bowls in front of it. The feet were covered in chrysanthemums – those fluffy yellow flowers with petals folding over each other. Orange tongues came up from candles and licked at the shadows in the room, revealin' family faces in gold frames. The photos were sittin' on two low tables to the right. Mai said one was of her father, who died when she was three. Around the pictures, burnin' incense sticks scribbled a strange language on thin air. A wooden screen with floral designs was folded out behind the statue, and you could see the red wall of the room and two paper lanterns through the cuts. Funny how a heavy wooden thing could look like lace – or as if it was crocheted instead of carved. Mai sat on a fancy carpet on the floor and rested back on her heels. I did the same, uncomfortably, and looked around.

"So where's Kuan?"

"Keep your voice down." She pointed at the bronze statue with her entire hand. "*This* is Kuan Am."

"*This* is Kuan?" I repeated out of disbelief.

"Yes. Kuan Am the Compassionate is very important goddess in Vietnam. We're Catholic now. But this was my family shrine-room statue when I was baby. She's beautiful, isn't she?"

I couldn't believe I washed my face and got dressed and braved her dragon dog to meet a *statue*. Mai was on a roll.

"In Asian custom, she's a person who – how you say in English? – oh, delays her own happiness to help other people. She tries to help everybody in the world, even if that's impossible. That's why she has so many hands." That's when I saw that Kuan Am had about twenty-eight arms, and I was happy she wasn't a flesh-and-blood person, cos the handshakin' alone would have taken us a little while.

"Kuan Am has a thousand arms."

I tried, but I couldn't make out the rest of them. All I saw was what looked like a vertical halo behind her. Then Mai really started whisperin'.

"Master Samadh was a monk in Vietnam. Now he's just homesick. So I'm happy the statue is here to remind him of it."

I asked her about her family, just to be polite.

"I was baby, but I hear Master Samadh helped my family leave Vietnam – and then, at the last minute, he decided to come here with us. I call him my grandpa sometimes, but he's not. And still, even though he isn't family, he did everything he could do for us."

I just shook my head. I knew a guy that could help many people with one left hand and he wasn't doin' nothin'.

"Kuan is very nice," I told her. And I meant it.

Then I felt somethin' in my pocket and remembered that I had picked the last tamarinds from the tree and taken them as a peace offerin' for Mai. She liked that kind of tangy thing more than I did. I told her I didn't have any more, cos Moms said we climbed that tamarind tree too often and shook off the little blossoms, so the tree can't catch a break. Right about when I was imitatin' Moms' voice sayin' "And it's a shame when something doesn't come to full fruit", Samadh told me to shut up.

"Shhh! *Ăn có nhai, nói có nghĩ!*" – or something like that.

"English!" Mai called out. I was happy she gave him a taste of his own medicine.

"Think today, speak tomorrow."

As soon as I heard the translation, I decided to go. I realized that was a recipe for gettin' you to shut up for your whole damn life.

"What time is it, Mai?"

"Time for leavin'!" Samadh was shoutin' now.

We walked back past him. I stopped at the door before steppin' out into the corridor and reached into my pocket. I was standin' in front of Mai, holdin' open one of her jeans pockets and droppin' the tamarinds in, when Samadh opened his eyes and caught me. The monk stood up so slowly he might as well have floated like the sweet smoke.

"What that is?"

"Uhm, your eyes?"

He ignored my comment, even though I know I used it perfectly, and he just floated closer, his hands behind him, his face set, his eyebrows cursin', his pumpkin-coloured robe sweepin' the floor.

Mai took the tamarinds from her pocket and held them out so he could see. Her hands shook a little. He stopped in front of us. He was tall as hell.

"Where you get these?" He spoke slowly as he took them from her hands while lookin' at me.

"From where I live... we have a tree."

"Then you have answered my prayers, Skeed." He cracked open the fruit. "Do you have more of these?"

"Yes, yes." I was relieved. "I can get you some."

"I need lots of it. How you say in English?"

"Tamarind."

"Ah, well, I need more... *tamring*... today."

"Sure. Of course. Gimme half an hour." Mai was tryin' to teach me something respectful in Vietnamese to say when talkin' to him, but I couldn't catch it. I always learn curse words first.

Anyway, Moms wasn't home yet, so I went in and did a raid on the tamarind preserves in the cupboard. We weren't using them anyway. Then, when I was walkin' back to Lam Lee Hahn, I thought to myself that maybe I should've taken all the seeds out, cos Mai, she might start a whole tamarind farm behind your back if you're not careful. You don't know that girl. Well, when I got back, Samadh was out of his robe and in his work clothes. I handed the goods to him and he looked at me over his glasses, like he knew there had been a heist of some sort. Maybe he was expectin' the fruits in their shells and fresh off the tree. Not stewed and in three marma-lade glass jars that looked suspect. He shrugged.

"How much?"

I was happy Mai wasn't there when he asked that, cos I liked her a lot, but she can really muck up negotiations.

"Hmm... let's see." I scratched my chin and counted on my fingers, startin' with my thumb, and I tried to sound real businesslike.

"Well, we have to include the hazard pay for the tree-climbin', plus labour charges for the reapin' and the shellin' and storage fees for the marmalade jars. Outside of that, the tree was damaged with a chainsaw recently, so..."

"Shree dollah!"

The monk was getting that look in his eyebrows again, so I decided that three bucks was OK. He told me that next time I should talk to Mai about money. Great.

He held the jars to his chest and hurried away down the corridor. I followed him, and he went back into that shrine room and sat on the ground. He opened the jar and scooped some tamarind paste out into his hand. Damn. That old monk was really goin' to sit there in the dark and eat all three bottles by himself. His stomach was goin' to be *so* bubbly. Well, that's what I was thinkin', until he bowed, then crawled over to Kuan Am and started rubbin' tamarind on the statue's face.

"What..."

"Shhh. Look more."

He took a dust cloth from his pocket and rubbed the face for about a minute. Well, when he moved that cloth, I had to cover my eyes. Kuan Am's bronze face had turned into pure glistenin' gold. The shaft of sunlight was bouncin' around the room from the statue. Samadh's eyes lit up.

"Tamring polish!" he said triumphantly, and tried to high-five me, but it's hard to do that when one guy is too tall and you are both stoopin' down and off-balance.

For the next few days after school I had a job helpin' Master Samadh polish the statue. Well, actually, all I did was hold the "tamring polish" open while he chanted and scrubbed the bronze clean. I reckon I had to demonstrate that I deserved the extra dollars I was goin' to make that week, so I pointed out that he missed a spot or two around the back of the statue. He shook his head.

"When you clean house, you clean perfec'. OK? Perfec'! But when clean statue, leave dark corners. To make perfec' places show more better."

Yeah, right. Nothin' like a little ancient wisdom to hide your arthritis. Anyway, by Thursday she was gleamin' bright, and the old man's English wasn't too rusty neither. All the fishermen who came into the shrine room said "Ahhh yehs!" and bowed down when they saw Kuan Am glistening under the slice of sun. Friday evenin', Master Samadh was outside and I was there sittin' in the dimness of the shrine room when I thought I'd look the statue over. I reckoned I could reach those spots he missed and surprise the old guy. Bad idea. Soon as I slapped on the tamarind and started rubbin' the halo thing at the back, a whole section of the halo just broke off Kuan Am and fell to the floor. The sound was sickenin'. I was dead. Immediately, in my head, I saw myself handin' all the money back to Mai to pay for damages. But Frico could fix this, easily. I just had to figure out a way to get him there, into that room and then make him do it...

Master Samadh must have been waitin' at the door. He stepped in and spoke softly.

"What's that?"

"I was... she... the statue... somethin' broke... Master Sam... I can fix it." It was the first time I called him "Master Sam", and it felt weird, but somehow I thought it was wise under the circumstances.

"Why did that happen, Skeed?"

"Cos I tried to clean it."

"Hm."

Maan, he could call me Skeed all day if he was goin' to be that calm about me breakin' beautiful Kuan Am. But as he sat on the floor and closed his eyes and cupped his hands together in his lap, I felt so terrible – I just wished he would get angry and chase me out of Lam Lee Hahn, instead of goin' into deep breathin' to keep himself calm. Well, while I was stoopin' there feelin' stupid with Valerie Beaumont's tamarind polish in one hand and the cleanin' cloth crumpled in the other, Mai's mother walked in. She bowed to Master Samadh, then took one look at the statue and spoke softly but firmly.

"Oh, that fell off again Master Sam? I don't know why after all these years we don't just leave that broken part on the floor, where it belongs. It makes too much noise when it falls off!"

And the old monk opened one eye, and he and his eyebrows laughed at me. Loudly. I didn't mind.

Mai walked with me to the train tracks. She was wearin' one of those cone-shaped straw hats to block the sun. It was so huge I could only see her mouth. 'Sam Pan hat' she called it. We stopped and looked across to where the Benets used to live. Flatbeds and tow trucks had come and hauled away the few remaining old cars from Backhoe's scrap-metal junkyard. I used to like those old, rustin' cars and junk. After school, when I walked into the swamp, as soon as I saw the cracked windshields and the old Esso gas-station sign, I knew I was home, although it was all just broken stuff collecting rainwater and makin' mosquitoes, and I had to be gettin' ready to run from Broadway and Squash. All that junk was there for so many years – I never thought the day would come when I would only see burnt-out rectangles and odd shapes on the nut grass, like those empty spaces inside my house where my father use to fit.

"What's happenin' to your face?" Mai was lookin' at my lower cheek, her eyes concerned. Damn that Frico.

I laughed it off. "I guess I turn thirteen this year!"

"Hmm. Guess I need to give your mother some things to balance you out... *Skeed*."

"Oh, please don't destroy my name like Master Sam. And don't gang up on me with my moms and all that balancin'-my-energy stuff."

"Too late." Mai stood on tiptoes. She took off the Sam Pan hat and put it on my head and laughed at me. Then she held my chin and smooched me right above where the pimples had started to show.

"What's that for? Lagniappe?"

"The hat or the kiss?"

"The last one."

She walked away with her hands in her Levi's pockets, then turned around and started walkin' backwards.

"Nah. *Lan-yap* is for customers, you're *mon petit chou*." And she broke off runnin', her ponytail bouncin', her lanky legs awkward in her blue jeans.

And when Mai stopped at her gate and smiled, she was even sweeter than when she got mad at me.

Fourteen

That night, the kisses were still makin' me feel giddy-headed. I sat with my mother on the makeshift bench at the back of the house, watchin' the sky and wonderin' if Mai was sleepin', or studyin' for cram school as usual. Moms hadn't made a fire, so the bugs were rovin' around in airborne gangs and stabbin' at people. Well, we were waitin' for the stars to come out, so we weren't budgin'. I slapped my palms together and made "mosquito sandwiches", as Pops used to put it.

Then, when the stars came out – *ooowee*. Sugar sprinkled on a purple plum. And that's what I should have said. Instead, I asked Moms if she didn't think it looked like God dropped a planet on heaven's glass floor and it smashed and all these tiny pieces were gonna sit there until somebody up there got a real bad splinter toe. Well, she just looked dead ahead and told me not to play with the Lord like that. I wanted to explain to her that I didn't mean any disrespect, but she just said it again and I got mad and asked her why the heck they paid for all those extra creative-writin' classes with Miss Halloway and sent us to a school with a strong Arts programme if I couldn't use my imagination any more. I said my pops would understand my imagination. She laughed and stared ahead and said, "Maybe you're right." Then she told me she wasn't tryin' to stop me usin' my imagination, but I was gettin' to be a teenager, so I needed to use it more responsibly and be careful of the things I imagined up.

"Now go on and imagine yourself ready for bed."

So the next mornin', just as the sun was comin' up over the Gulf – or as the orange lollipop started stickin' up out of God's blue jeans' back pocket – Moms announced that we all should go look for Pa Campbell, cos he had Parkinson's. Man, I didn't see that comin'. He got so wobbly, Tony drove him and Ma Campbell into town a few days before, and the doctors said it was so and it would only get worse. All that gas Pa used to pass was a sign, they said. Moms said we needed to look out for him, cos he's been a good neighbour to us. Tony gave him that leftover HF-1200 walkie-talkie and told him to put it beside his bed and holler on Channel 14 if we couldn't hear him across the fence. No need. Every time I lay in bed and heard him cryin' out all the way across the fence, I remember laughin' at him and his crazy beliefs and I felt bad. But I wondered why all his life he was so concerned about all those dark things when to me poverty was the scariest thing of all. I still wanted the day to come when, like Pops said, the swamp would move out from under us – when we would go to sleep and wake up in another part of town. Well, maybe not overnight, but over time. I heard Pa Campbell sayin' that "happy is in your heart". Yeah. Well, some money in your pocket might help, old man. If he wasn't puttin' aside money all these years, there's no way in hell he could have said that. I say money and power help with the happiness part. Whatever that power might be. Doug said the same thing in not so many words.

I mean, if I had powers, maan the things I'd do. I'd prob'ly have a superhero name and a costume with pockets to collect contributions and everything. But my brother, he didn't think like that. Instead he had his mind on a brand-new girlfriend. Yeah, some girl he met from his new school called Teesha Grey, who started comin' into the swamp all too regularly, sayin' she needed to do "research on endangered species" and all that. She and Frico were suddenly always out on the bayou in the pirogue. That boy didn't even like leavin' land, but all of a sudden he was a fisherman, paddlin' this girl around, shirtless and sweatin' bullets while she took pictures of birds.

Nice girl, though. Sweet-lookin', with dimples. And large hoop earrings. And short hair. I like short hair on a girl. Mai should've cut her hair short. Even though me and Mai were nothin' like Frico and Teesha. Not to mention Tony and Doug and their girlfriends. Damn, that Doug was sixteen and on the soccer team in high school, and so popular he always had girls' phone numbers fallin' out of his pockets, even though he didn't have no damn phone. Then he was so secretive, and that only made them more curious, so you'd be comin' from the train tracks after the school bus dropped you a mile up the road and you'd just see all kinds of high-school girls at the entrance of L-Island on a stake-out for Doug Beamount. Usually they wouldn't find him, cos I'd warn them not to follow me, and they'd prob'ly swear to themselves to come back for ever until they figured out exactly where he lived. Nobody believed Doug Beaumont – or anyone for that matter – lived in this swamp. Some nights, I swear, if I went out into the woods, I'd find girls behind trees waitin' for that boy. Tony was shy with girls, and we never even knew he had a girlfriend till they got real serious. She was a geek like him – and that's about all I can tell ya. They were both seniors and in the Science Club at LaVaughn High School, and now that he was drivin' Pa Campbell's truck and deliverin' stuff to Al Dubois's Fish and Seafood after school, he was in the city more often with her. Some weekends me and Frico, we'd find ourselves abandoned in the back of the truck along the crack in the map, while Tony and his mystery girl would be watchin' the sunset or walkin' on a levee or foggin' up the truck windows, includin' that rear window, so we couldn't even see nothin' from the back of truck. That was OK, cos even though the girl was sweet, I wouldn't want to see ol' Tony Beaumont gettin' domestic – no sir. One day those two rocked that van until I damn near got seasick. That's when I knew what Frico meant when he said they were just doing "physics and chemistry" all the time. Couldn't believe they went that far in a '57 Ford that smelt like Bengue's Balsam and dead gators, for godssake.

Now, even though those footprints that appeared on the porch caused Moms to make a rule that we had to get home before nightfall – and that really cramped everybody's style – she didn't stop this idea we came up with for a Southern outdoor shindig on L-Island. Even though I wish she did. It was to be an afternoon swamp party for all ages. Frico, he was cool with the idea. He was proud of the new diagrams he did on the house and wanted to show them off too. So we called up the crew, but we didn't have a tamarind-tree meetin', cos Tony and Doug and Moms were involved. Furthermore I don't think anybody wanted to stare at that sinkhole for more than the time it took to cross over the creek. It was bad enough that Pa kept whisperin' that ol' Backhoe shouldn't have left so soon. He reckoned the footprints on the porch belonged to the Benet boys, who dragged themselves out of the muddy hole every night. Two spirits walkin' around, lookin' for where their father went.

Well, soon as we started talkin', we knew we were all goin' to pass a good time at this shindig. It was a send-off for Marlon and Belly, but I guess it was kind of a declaration of independence for Moms and a dare to anything that wanted her to leave where she'd lived for nearly seventeen years. She made up her mind when she found out about the whole deal between Benet and Pops. The party guest list was like twenty people: Ma and Pa Campbell, Teesha Grey, Mai, four of Doug's female fans and whoever else was behind the trees, Tony's girl, who still had no name, Marls, Belly, Harry T, Peter Grant and his guitar, and any of their girlfriends with parents crazy enough to allow them to go to a Saturday-afternoon party in the swamp.

Then Moms got too neighbourly and said she was goin' to invite other people from farther up the tracks. Chain-smokin' Evin Levine, Miss Gladys and Chanice Devereaux and her girls were OK, but there were some new good-for-nothin' boys from up the bayou that she invited. Pa Campbell said that was a mistake, but that was after those boys rowed up and dragged one of their pirogues on land and filled it with party ice to use as a beer cooler. They brought their own six-packs and Moms regretted it, cos it wasn't that type of party. So we got rid of them real quick and they rowed back into the dark sittin' on the ice, still drinkin'.

Now, up to the plannin' meetin' we hadn't seen Harry T in a while since he got into scoutin'. That boy was one for a grand entrance, I tell ya. We could hear him comin' in from the train tracks with a cassette-player boom box strapped to the back of his bicycle playin' Doug E. Fresh featurin' MC Ricky D. He flew over the new footbridge, came blazin' around the corner, squeezed the brakes and sent dust flyin'. Everybody cheered, cos this guy had on the Ricky D sweatsuit and shades and everything. Then it seemed like Doug E. Fresh was the only cassette Harry T had brought, so we heard "La-Di-Da-Di" nearly all evenin', 'cept when we were tellin' ghost stories in broad daylight and Tony was tryin' to tell Cajun jokes like Pops. Only Pops can tell Cajun jokes like Pops. So after Moms rescued him and gave her welcome speech, we were diggin' in to the crawfish and potatoes and corn and sweet-potato pie when Doug, he brought out a piece of cardboard from Pa's truck, put it on the ground and started breakdancin' – or b-boyin', as we called it. That boy did a windmill and a headstand, and all his girl fans went crazy. Then all of a sudden everybody was tryin' to do the latest robot dances. They all succeeded in lookin' silly with all that mimickin' of machines. Maybe I was just jealous, cos I looked like a duck with wooden wings when I tried it. Tony jumped into the back of Pa's truck like it was a stage. He couldn't dance either, so he did a lame rap on the beat. It wasn't even lyrics. He just said "Sucker MCs!" and then went nuts.

"Dah to the dah-dah-dah to the dah-dit…"

Well, everybody started booin', until Harry T joined in the dah-dittin' and shouted that Tony was rappin' in Morse Code. Then suddenly Morse Code was cool and everybody wanted to know how to rap their names in Morse Code. Sigh. That party was full of nerds or sheep, I tell ya. It was a real blast though, and the whole time Mai sat beside me holdin' my hand until it got sweaty, but I wouldn't let go.

Of course durin' all that fun that hot girl Teesha Grey put Frico to work on the porch, sketchin' bird pictures from photos and labellin' them like it was a frickin' school day. He said he had to help her make flashcards to show younger kids some birds that had disappeared from the State years ago. Great. Real fun stuff.

Anyway, we didn't intend to take the party into nightfall, but when the batteries in Harry T's tape deck were callin' it quits (and Ma Campbell was thankin' the Mother of God), Fricozoid took a break from sketchin' birds and came down from the porch beatboxin', and the dancin' and rappin' continued. Ma Campbell went for Pa in his new wheelchair. The old man could walk, but only slowly and he was bent over. Pa Campbell started riffin' on his blues harmonica to the beat, and as easily as Frico did the beatbox, Peter Grant, that boy who busted his face at camp, started playin' jazz chords on his box guitar. The whole thing was fresh. Or *def*, or whatever Doug always says.

Somebody stopped the warblin' cassette player, and it was pretty much jazz 'n' blues and country and folk music from then on. Moms came down near the fire, and Pa put down his harmonica and started tappin' a drumbeat on the side of the truck, even though it was difficult for him. We all picked it up and clapped it – and Moms is in a free-flow skirt, and while she's dancin' we're trying to keep up with her moves. She was breathless, but she's tellin' us while dancin' that this is Bomba. Pa wheels over and shouts over the noise that Bomba is African and Spanish and Taino culture, and Moms learnt it on an island called Boriken when she went there. It was a little embarrassin', but she was pretty good.

When she got tired and went for a drink, Peter Grant and Pa Campbell were singin' 'Just a Closer Walk with Thee' and we were havin' a little church.

Well, ol' Marlon interrupted to say he didn't get why everybody got to rap and dance and beatbox and Bomba in the swamps without gettin' fined, and he still couldn't sing even at his own send-off. Of course Belly couldn't pass up the opportunity to tell him the fine he got was for "impersonating a singer", but since we wanted him to quit gripin', we'd let him sing one song. Well, he chose one of those corny camp songs that goes on for ever. You sing in rounds until you have a headache. But we all said OK, since he was bein' a mother hen about the whole thing.

"Ohhhhhhhh..." *Pause.* Take a deep breath. "The cow kicked Nelly in the belly in the barn, and the doctor said it wouldn't do no harm!"

Now, Southern people know you need to start that song real quiet, almost like a whisper, and then you get louder and louder like it's Super Bowl Sunday and the Saints just won on home turf, or until the old folks can't stand you – that's the idea. And when you get to the end of the first verse, which is pretty much singin' that same Nelly line four times, you get to the good part. You get to say: "Second verse! Same as the first! A little bit louder and a little bit worse!" – and it's very important to pause right there and really linger on the "Ohhhhhhhh" before you go back to the cow kickin' poor ol' Nelly and what the doctor said and all that. Now, we started in on that song at about sunset, and even when it was pitch black and we made a ragin' campfire, and Ma Campbell had wheeled Pa back into the house in a hurry and the other older folks had said goodbye, we were still shoutin' about Nelly in that swamp.

Well, lemme tell you, when we got to I think it was the fortieth verse or thereabouts and we were there lingerin' on the

"Ohhhhhhhh", those good-for-nothin' boys from down the bayou that Moms threw out of the party, they came back in bigger boats and jumped on land and ran up on us full tilt and doused the entire party with gallons of bayou water from a couple o' fish buckets. The girls got it in their hair and on their clothes and pretty much everybody swallowed some of it – especially Marlon, on account of the long "Ohhhhh-hhh". For the first few seconds we just sat there shocked and drippin' without sayin' a word. The boys moved in quickly, surroundin' us. Their guns came out. One finished dousin' the fire. Two others were roundin' up anybody who started runnin' and put them face down in the grass. Moms, who was sittin' on the porch, recognized the boys and jumped up and came towards us, then turned back to go grab her gun, but a tall shadow stepped up on the porch and blocked the door. Moms was pushed to the ground and right about that same time, a warnin' shot exploded in the air.

Fifteen

The sound of the gunshot came from out on bayou. We all forgot the thugs surroundin' us and looked in that direction. A bunch of birds lit out from where they were sleepin' in the swamp, and the crickets fell silent for a breath. Calvin's kids went and huddled behind the water tank.

"Dammit James! I told you not to come in heah no mo'!" Ma Campbell had wheeled Pa back out on his porch. He was shakin' and fuming like a gas leak.

The whisper went around the smouldering campfire: "Couyon". The very tall, pale man in the baseball jacket had the kind of moustache I'd been tryin' to get for ages. He rode the boat up on the grasses, cranked the shotgun, pointed it down and squeezed the trigger. There was a pop. Like a full stop before he even said a word. The copper shell pinged on the aluminum boat. A jagged tail rose above the edge of the boat, relaxed and fell again.

"Yep, that be the motherload right there," said James Jackson, pointing the rifle to the sky.

He stepped out of the boat loaded with six alligators that he had caught in the night with his gang. Monsters. All prob'ly over ten feet and just as ugly and menacin' as the guys standin' around us. He looked at us real scornful.

"Now, that… is how you hunt dinosaur elligadors with a point-two-seven-o rifle. And by the way, ol' man, don't talk to me like you's my Pa, cos you ain't. Oh, I borrowed your boat while you were just sittin' aroun' doin' nothin'. Knew you wouldn't mind." Pa grunted.

"Ma, your baby's here!" shouted James. "What's for dinner?" His boys laughed.

And that's how we were introduced, or reintroduced, to James "Couyon" Jackson, legendary Mississippi Murderer and Ma Campbell's part-time son. We immediately knew we were in deep trouble. He sent around one of the fish buckets.

"My apologies for the foul smell of dat receptacle, but um, feel free to deposit all your valuables in it."

"Now, ladies and gentlemen – and Pa Campbell... this heah meet'n' is hereby called to order. I'm James Jackson, and from my left to right are the members of my team. That right theah with the Smiff & Wess'n is Grizzly, my right hand, then that's Miercoles – cos I rescued him on a Wednesday when he was almost dead in a ditch – and up on the porch..." – he called out – "hey, Shotput, how's Mrs Beaumont treat'n' ya?"

Shotput, a large guy, just nodded. He had a shotgun pointed at Moms, who was now sittin' on a chair on the porch arguin' with him. We heard that Shotput was a star athlete who could have gone on to international games if he hadn't swung that iron ball and knocked his coach into a coma for tellin' him he was late for trainin'. Got two years for it before he joined up with Couyon's gang. Then there was another guy who just stood there with his gun holstered. I think he was instructed to do that cos, look, this was the first gangster I ever seen in bifocals, and prob'ly the last thing Couyon wanted was to get shot in a friendly fire accident.

"*Pierre*!" – that was the bifocals guy's name – "Escort all these fine shindiggin' folks, except for the Campbells and the Beaumonts, onto that there Beaumont porch and hold 'em theah. Anybody tries to run – well, you and Boogers could use the target practice." Boogers stepped up. He was the youngest in the gang, and I reckoned they called him that cos nobody ever got to see the end of his index finger.

Two of Doug's fans broke down and started hollerin' in fright. Couyon Jackson turned back to his audience and continued the one-man show-off. Pierre, blond as corn silk

and wiry and green as the stalk itself, he rounded up everybody and – can you believe it? – while he's walkin' them to
the porch, he's tellin' the girls things like "Come this way
please", "Watch your step" and all that. That boy had no
business bein' bad. Anyway, as I'm watchin' Mai and Marls
and Belly and all the girls walkin' up to the porch, I'm gettin'
concerned, cos those other thugs have different intentions towards the women. You could see the salivation and the swal-
lowin', and their eyes lookin' around for the darkest corner.
One guy pulled Frico up from the ground by the collar. Moms
stood up. Then she looked like she decided to stay put on
that porch to protect those girls that were walkin' up, and I
bet if that gang tried to throw her off she could make herself
as heavy as a mountain. Well, I'm trailin' behind the crowd
headin' for the porch and I can hear Moms already up there
threatenin' the gang with hellfire and sickness if they came
near any of the kids. They laughed, but they'd heard she was
a conjurer. So I was watchin' them back away, when Couyon,
he comes and collects me and Frico. He grabs us by the arms
and points to Ma Campbell's house with the gun barrel.

"You're missin' the best part, Beaumonts. Let's all go back
into my office."

Now I'm thinking: "OK, soon as we get into the house, Pa
Campbell's gonna grab a rifle and tell James, 'Stand down
soldier', and James and his boys, they'll take off and leave us
alone." See, Pa told me once that you need to understand a
disturbed guy like ol' James. He's the delusional type that says
things happened to him that never did, or the details didn't
quite go the way he described it. And if you talked down to him
without respectin' his delusion, then you're plumb out of luck.
So let's say he's got a gun pointed at you and he says he was in
WWI, then he *was* in WWI. Don't tell him he's too young to
have been there. That's gonna get you shot. Twice, in the head.
You gotta know that he really feels like he went to WWI, and
you got to let him cry and then tell him the War is over and hug

him a little bit so you can get the goddamn pistol out of his grip. But as we all got shoved into Ma's house, I realize we were behind the eight-ball. Ma and Pa were both being tied down to their bed, and there was a big can of gasoline on the floor.

"Now," said James, "it's gonna get hot as hell in here if I don't get some cooperation. First order of business is roll call. Please answer to your names when they're called. Let's go... Paw Campbell?"

Pa groaned. "Jesus."

"Nope, that name ain't on the register, Paw. And I'm the one doing the name-callin', not you. So let's go again. Paw Campbell?"

"Oh Lawd."

James trailed his finger down a make-believe register. "Nope, neither."

"For godssakes Pa, just play along!" hollered Ma Campbell beside him. Ma was annoyed enough already that she was still horizontal and starin' at the ceiling at the end of the day, when there was work to be completed. Well, soon ol' Couyon, he ditches the register that never existed and declares that he was done with watchin' Pa's "elligador and crawfish bidniss go to pieces, and therefore he was there to conduct a takeover to move the bidniss forward". Said he wanted to be on the cover of Fortune 500, and the old man had no vision.

Meanwhile, Pa Campbell's eyes kept drifting off to the space behind the door. Couyon saw it before I did. He reached around and snatched up Pa's rifle and said, "Ah, nothin' like a little more staff motivation."

"Aw, shit," said Pa, gettin' worried.

"Nope. No bathroom breaks yet, Paw. Now that we're all heah, let's begin again."

And James went through the purpose for the meetin' and marked the register again, only this time addin' the year, Nineteen Eighty-six. Now, as I looked around the room and saw

Ma and Pa and my brothers, I honestly started blamin' myself for this whole mess, until I realized that all was going to be all right. See, everything was going according to some divine plan. I didn't care about whatever CEO obsession Couyon Jackson was havin', even though he was talkin' about money. But I was thinking this situation is ideal. Soon Moms, being held out on that porch, is gonna say to hell with it and start conjurin' or – better yet, since she and Frico were prob'ly workin' together – they'll definitely see this as a crisis and sketch us the hell out of all this mess. So I was excited like it was Christmas and I got presents and I was going on a campin' trip all at the same time. This was show time. And Couyon Jackson didn't know the kind of Beaumont Retribution that was comin' to him.

"Now, ladies and gentlemen – Paw included – I, James Altamont Jackson, today in my capacity as the Human Resource Director and CEO of the New Campbells' Catcheries, will be conducting interviews to determine my Vice President of Operations."

Everybody groaned in a chorus, but me, I was almost impressed with James' speeches for a guy who walked out of the third grade. That was until I realized I had heard some of them before. He'd actually ripped off most of the dialogue from a few of those soap operas on Channel Twelve, where people are always taking over oil companies or wineries and vineyards and celebrating every single nothing with a glass of champagne.

With one hand still on the rifle, James reached into the toilet and yanked at the toilet-paper roll. He reeled the whole thing out into the livin' area and handed the end of it to me and said I should take the minutes. Tony told him he didn't need minutes in an interview. He said, "Shaddup, your interview is first. And you ain't off to a good start."

So of course my eldest brother is sittin' there lookin' at James Jackson and not cooperatin', and the CEO slash Human Resource Director slash Rigolets River Murderer now has two rifles and is not amused. But Tony isn't budgin'. And I see this waltz was turning into a wrestlin' match real quick, so I started blurting out loud.

"Mr Jackson, Tony is real good at electronics like his pops. He's almost out of high school and has a lot of ideas about the future of technology." Doug and Frico and Tony are lookin' at me like, "What the hell, fool?" But this is for their own good. I want them to cooperate while he's still in character and give Frico time to make his move. The last thing you want to do is give Crazy James Jackson reason to add more damn titles to his name and then let so many of his personalities get pissed off in a group. Then we would all be eaten by catfish over in the Rigolets. So I keep talkin' and I ask Couyon if he knew that they were inventing helicopters with tractor beams like the aliens use, and once the light hits you, you're frozen.

"Rubbish." He spat black liquid from his chewin' tobacco on Ma Campbell's floor. I didn't blame him, cos I didn't believe that one when Tony told me neither.

"Wait, there's some more!" I told him. And I blabbered on about how Tony predicted that in the future everybody in the world would travel thousands of miles in less than a second, just by walkin' through a door, and read two hundred books in an hour.

"Bullshit," said Jim. "Learnin' takes your whole life."

"Then we'll be able to learn much more in a lifetime," said Tony, soundin' real cool and controlled, even though he was biting the nails on his flat fingers. "Computers will make everything pos'ble. We'll even have photo maps of the whole Milky Way. So we can look down from satellites and see everywhere in our Galaxy, including the swamps and the L-shaped island and the house with the man holding people hostage."

So I see my big brother was trying to psych out ol' Couyon Jackson. And that wasn't part of the plan – at least not in my head. So James, he starts lookin' up and around. He's gettin' jumpy, so I hand the toilet paper off to Frico and I tell him to get to sketchin'. He looks at me wide-eyed as usual, and then says it doesn't even make sense, cos the paper is not ideal and he doesn't even have his pencils.

Now James, he sees I'm fidgety and talking to Frico, so he points the rifle at me and tells me I'm his secretary and I should go make him a cup of coffee. And – would you believe it? – in the middle of this crisis ol' Ma Campbell, tied up as she was, she starts doting on her boy James.

"Skid, maybe you should make Jim a coupla hush puppies too – poor boy must be hungry – that's why he's actin' up. You hungry Jim?"

"Damn right I am, Ma."

And that old lady is tied to the bed, but she's craning her neck to look into the kitchen so she can give me instructions on how to deep-fry hush-puppy biscuits for ol' James Couyon Jackson.

"Not too much buttermilk, now Skid", or "Mix them ingredients real good, or it'll upset his bowels. Yes, that's right – keep stirring, Skid, keep stirring."

Damn. I used to like Ma Campbell – up to that point.

So I'm deep-fryin' them hush puppies in a big ol' cast-iron skillet that must be older than Pa and Ma put together, while James is conducting his interviews, and I realize somethin's goin' on. For starters, Tony is not sayin' another word. Every time I dropped a hush puppy in the hot grease and it crackled up a bit I could hear Tony just hittin' the key on that HF-1200 walkie-talkie beside Pa Campbell's bed. *Dit. Dit. Dit. Dah Dah Dah. Dit. Dit. Dit.*

He did it about three times sittin' on the floor with his hands behind him. Then he dah-ditted some more – but hell if I could make out them words.

So I went ahead and brought the hush puppies to Couyon, and he's lookin' at me suspicious. He had good reason too, cos I'd heard a rumour that because he walked out of the third grade, James couldn't read too well – and that's why he ripped off speeches from movies. Hell, they said it was so bad that you could write his name on a slice of bread and he'd gobble it down like there was nothing different about it. So I had gone ahead and written "JAMES" on the dough of a hush puppy with a fork, and he guzzled it down like a hungry blind dog. After that, outside was completely dark, and I was wonderin' what's next and where was Moms in all of this and why the hell Frico wasn't sketchin'. Then Pa Campbell, on account of missin' his chill pills, he just started hollerin' at Jim.

"Now look, I really need to go. Are you done keepin' us all hostage, you S–O–B? Sorry, Ma."

And James said, "I'll keep ya-all ostrich for as long as I can."

And Pa said the word was "hostage", and James said: "No, it's ostrich, cos ostriches, they can't fly – and right now, right now I got your wings clipped." And Pa Campbell said, "Look it up – I ain't got taam with this shit, Couyon!" And Ma is tryin' to calm Pa down, but Pa is hollerin' harder.

"Woman, don't calm *me* down, calm your *son* down!"

Pa is losin' it, and Crazy James "Couyon" Altamont Jackson, he just whips around with flames in his eyes and puts one of the rifles in Pa's white-bearded mouth and pulls the damn trigger. And we all scream loud, cos we're waiting for it to rain brains in there, but there's a click and Pa is laughing still with the nozzle in his mouth – and I didn't even know there weren't no rounds in that other rifle Crazy James was swingin' about. Pa Campbell went ahead and emptied out the chamber when James appeared in the swamp. Then, all of a sudden, there was a thunderin' overhead. And the wind came. And I'm ready to shout hallelujah, cos the Great Beaumont Retribution had begun – but then a light comes through the window, and we all get down real flat on the floor, cos it became obvious that it was one of those new Coast Guard helicopters with a goddamn freeze-ray tractor beam light on it, and it's thunderin' right over the house and the whole swamp is as fluorescent as the comin' of the Lord. Then I hear Moms above the noise from all the way across the yard. She's chantin' "Jerusalem" and girls are screamin' and Couyon's whole gang is tryin' to get inside, and Couyon himself is tryin' to get outside, and before launchin' through the window he looks me in the eye me and says, "Next time not so much salt in the hush puppies, Skid Marks. That stuff will kill ya before I do."

Pa saw that the man was fixin' to escape. So he wrung himself free, reached up off the bed and grabbed Couyon, who was already halfway through the wooden window. Couyon spotted the turquoise ring Pa must have been hidin' all evenin' and, in three quick moves, he hit the old man in the face with the back of the rifle, spat on the hand that was holdin' him and easily slid that ring off Pa's finger before tumblin' out backwards into the darkness. Professional.

We all jumped up and burst through the door. And we see James running and the tractor beam from the helicopter looks like a big ol' broom the colour of lightning, and it's sweepin' away shadows left and right, searchin' for Couyon and his gang. He's behind the house when the chopper buzzes over the tin roof and the light swivels around and shines on that sucker through the trees, but it doesn't freeze him like Tony said it's supposed to. Damn. I couldn't believe it, but that bastard kept on running, and him and his boys, they dive straight into the bayou. And the police dogs and Calvin's kids and the Coast Guard and the City Police went in right after him – and Moms, she splashes in right after them as mad as hell with the rifle she retrieved from the house, and she's yellin': "Oi! Oonu try nuh come back 'roun me pickney dem again, y'hear bwoy?" Then she stops and she's standin' knee-deep in the bayou with the rifle on her hip pointin' up. The chopper is right above her head. There's a big circle on the water around her. The beam sweeps across her face and out into the bayou, and she's not droppin' the rifle like they're tellin' her over the loudspeaker. *Freeze frame.* Bad Ass Pam Grier with a Caribbean accent. And that's the first time I heard my moms speak San Tainos patois. It was like somethin' preserved in a jar, but that jar broke and the stuff flowed out strong and sharp and deadly like moonshine full of broken glass pieces.

And by the way, I swore that would be the last time I listened to any more of Tony Beaumont's predictions. To hell with freeze rays and teletransport and all that. Frico would change the world as we knew it, even though in that instance he didn't do a damn thing.

Sixteen

Well, after the Couyon Gang cleared out of L-Island, we realized they'd cleaned us out as well. Somewhere between the
time those boys were drinkin' beer out of the boat and the end
of James' ostrich-takin', they disconnected our four eighteen-
wheeler back-up batteries, tore down our thirty-foot CB antennae and dug up and sawed through the PVC pipe attached to
the well tank just to flood the place. Worst of all, they swiped
our big ol' 45-kW generator. I guess they couldn't get inside our
house on account of Frico's protection paintin', but they took
our electricity, so Moms had to stumble around in the dark to
get the rifle, especially since she couldn't find her way around
the house without Pops' clutter. After the drama and the police
takin' all the city kids home to their finger-pointin' parents,
Moms just went inside quietly, and we followed her. We could
hear her searching under the cupboard for ever. When she finally emerged, she struck a match and lit this old kerosene lamp
that I'd never seen. It was huge with a glass base and a cord
wick in it. A jagged flame jumped up, and black smoke spirited
off the edges. She put a lampshade over the flame and it settled
down a bit. "Home Sweet Home" was printed on the shade in
letters that were curly like the smoke. All this time she's hummin' a hymn. She broke the stanza to say: "I guess we can see a
lot more stars now, boys."

Yeah right. I wasn't goin' outside *ever again*. Her face
looked tired by lamplight. Doug brought her some tea. The
KeroGas stove was about the only thing that still worked.
Our sink was piled high with gummy pots and pans from
the shindig. In the sad lighting, the CB radio sat cold. Those
neon-red digital numbers and lights that would greet you in

the dark when you woke up at night and those voices from the static of some far-off American highway were all gone. I guess we all felt more foolish than afraid, and across Moms' brows you could see her thinkin' that she'd made a mistake – or a couple of 'em. She was barely thirty-eight years old, and she was fixin' to go grey any day. But this episode wasn't over by a long shot.

Harry T turned up next morning when Moms was still sleepin'. That's how early it was. The guy had pedalled in the half-darkness all the way into the mist of the swamp. Crazy. We heard a tappin' at the window, then a copy of a gossip tabloid, *Télépathie*, was slapped against the louvres. Even through the frosted glass you could read the headline: "SHIN-DIG SEVENTEEN: DARING RESCUE IN SWAMP". We tumbled out onto the front porch, and below the headlines there was a photo of a chopper and the story of the whole drama. Well, at least their version of it. They said it was around midnight that Couyon hijacked the party. Hogwash. They said we were all tied down to beds and tortured. Bullshit. They didn't even mention the Morse code or Moms' runnin' after the gang and the police tellin' her to stand down. Hell, it wasn't even seventeen of us.

They had a very eerie picture of our house in it, all painted up and lookin' spooky. They "reported" that supernatural elements from the swamp were takin' over the city. Man. Only one thing was true in that whole fake story, and that's the fact that the police caught Shotput and Boogers the same night they dived in the bayou. Shotput gave himself up to let Couyon get away, but that Boogers guy prob'ly got caught cos he was swimmin' with one hand up his nose.

Well, we couldn't believe what we were readin', and I'm sure Belly felt the same way, but we couldn't say for sure cos Aunt Bevlene, she was packin' him up and gettin' him ready to be shipped off to Atlanta like a bat out of hell as soon as those stories started flyin' around. Poor guy begged her to let him "touch the swamp again one last time", but she said "over my dead body" and sent him off. And she was smart too, cos pretty soon we were all catchin' hell at school in the city.

Doug said after that night his girl fans' parents forbid them to come into the swamps. And all of the fans that didn't come to the shindig, well they saw the papers and just couldn't believe that the Great Doug Beaumont lived in a one-room, run-down shack in the swamps. So, pretty soon he wasn't cool any more, especially after he busted a guy's lip for callin' Moms a witch and the coach put him on the team bench for the whole soccer season.

Now, over at Long Lake Free Gospel Church, one Sunday after the rumours caught on, we got an hour-and-a-half sermon dedicated to us and our witchcraft. Of course, even though they didn't call any names, everybody kept lookin' over at us, shakin' their heads and fannin'.

Moms had more serious problems to think about uninformed sermons and gossip columns. She seemed more concerned that she wasn't hearin' from our pops even in all this excitement.

Pa Campbell reassured her that he was still gonna be lookin' out for her, so she needn't worry. As if. Then, changing subject, he started bragging from his wheelchair.

"Matter of fact, Valerie, as soon as Couyon got up out o' my house dat night, I wriggled myself free and, in the middle of the hollerin' and the helicopter and the barkin', I took a shot in the dark. Ma got free and grabbed the barrel to save her son, but even in the noise, I know the sound of a bullet findin' flesh, I tell ya dat."

Ma Campbell wasn't worried, cos she said most days Pa didn't even remember who was in the mirror, much less what happened that night. And maybe she was right, cos apart from them catchin' Boogers and Shotput, there was no report of any of them finding Couyon or any of his gang killed or injured.

Moms was looking for ways she could secure her family. What she wanted was money from Pops, and for a few months that wasn't forthcomin'. We also needed him to come put some things back in place after Couyon cleaned us out. So Doug and Tony drove around and went lookin' for him in New O'lins at all his usual hangouts, includin' Copper Stills Bar on Bourbon Street, but no one said they saw him.

That pretty much meant we were on our own, so Tony, he took over and put some makeshift things in place. He sent me and Frico under the house to get some car batteries and a car alternator that he salvaged from Benet's junkyard. Well, after Frico dragged out the first battery, he brushed off his hands and he was done. I had to crawl on my belly to pull out the other four, one by one. Then Tony, he sent me back for the car alternator, and at the time I had no idea what I was lookin' for.

"It looks like a turbine!" Tony was shoutin' from inside the house through the floorboards above my head.

"A whaaat?"

"A motor kind-of-a."

"A what?"

I heard them all laughin' through the floor. "Skid, just bring out anythin' you've never seen before."

So I brought out this metal cylinder with a grill around it, three huge eggs and a strange rectangular card the size of a driver's licence. The card had been down in the dirt for a while, but it was covered with Scotch tape, so you could still see that it had weird markings on it, like those yellow envelopes somebody dashed into the yard. Moms was worried that an alligator had laid eggs under our house, cos it meant the bayou was risin' again and under the house was gettin' swampy. Frico and Doug were debatin' whether I should have touched the eggs or not, as I told 'em there must be about forty more. They said mother gators can count, so she'd come lookin'. And since I smelt like her kids now, and my face was lookin' as rough as her babies, she'd come hug me in my bed at night. Jerks.

Meanwhile, Tony was makin' use of the car alternator. He hooked it up to the batteries and mumbled about "regulators" and "rpm" and "groundin' wires" and blah, blah, blah, and said he'd give us at least some "low-voltage electricity" by nightfall. So that night, when we were lookin' at the card with the weird markings in Tony's fluorescent light, Moms went over to Pa Campbell and then came back and snatched up that card from in front of us and went back over to Pa – and when she finally returned, her face was dark again. I thought it had something to do with the old Cajun tale that an alligator under your house means someone's goin' to die – but it wasn't that. She held up the taped-up card.

"This is a seal that your father planted. I'm not goin' to go into what that means, but they're all over the yard. Now, don't none of you go searchin' for them. But if you *do* see anything that looks like this, don't take it in here. Just let me know where it is and I'll come get it. Understand?"

We nodded. I felt a "Let's Hold Hands and Pray" comin' on. After the prayer, I looked down at the kitchen table disappointed. I thought the seal was some kind of disc that was all metally and shiny and carved like some of the golden-dragon decorations over at Lam Lee Hahn. I thought that when you found them, they would glow like in the cartoons – but no. Just plain ol' paper. Pa Campbell said to shuddup about cartoons and never to underestimate the seals' power. Then Moms bought a coupla chickens, and prayed over every one of them, and let them loose in the yard and threw buckets of water on the ground so the chickens would start diggin' and scratchin'. And everyday you'd see her checkin' around the house to see if any of the seals had come up.

"That won't stop it, Valerie, it's too late! They're too many buried over theah," Pa called out one evenin' from his porch.

Moms didn't answer until Ma Campbell stuck her head through a wooden window and asked: "Too many berries over where?" and "What won't stop what?"

Moms answered without lookin' around.

"Tryin' to get these yard fowls to stop diggin' up the yard, Ma!"

"So why'd you buy them in the first place, chile? Lawd, Val, that's what free-range chickens do, they dig! For the life of me... you young people! Tell her, Pa."

"I told her, Ma. I told her."

"Well, tell her again!"

And Pa, he cleared his throat and glanced back at Ma Campbell, who was over his shoulder, and then hollered out:

"That won't stop Valerie! There're too many chickens over there. And lots of chickens means lots of diggin', gurl!"

And Ma was satisfied and closed the window again, mumblin' that she taught us all the common sense in the world until she was sick of it – and what the hell were we gonna do when she was dead and gone.

Seventeen

Well, for the rest of that year we got so isolated and paranoid I swore trees were people. Even when there were no reporters or curious campers comin' to look at the scene of the "most intense hostage situation in the State's history", I was seein' shadows. Then again, it was weird how L-Island was suddenly empty. Everybody stopped comin' 'cept for that girl Teesha Grey, who still had "wildlife research" to do. She even tried gettin' an interview with *Télépathie* to "get the word out" about protectin' the environment and buildin' a refuge for endangered species and all that. Man, those gossip reporters just backed away from her real slow, like some kids at school who thought we were evil. Now, I thought she was really just hangin' around spying on Frico, and I wanted to catch her in a lie. So I asked her how much more research she was gonna need to do.

"Well now, let's see, we have about ten thousand species of birds in all… and about another hundred or so that are extinct. So… I'm, like, on number *one* of my ten thousand – one hundred birds. How does that grab ya?"

She was a feisty one, that girl. And I liked that a lot. But I couldn't let her get in the way. That Frico needed leadership, and she had his talent headed in the wrong direction with all her damn birds and what not. She didn't have a clue about half of what this boy could do. If she did, she wouldn't be wastin' his time when there were dreams to fulfil and money to be made.

Speakin' of which… Apart from the bad publicity that stupid gang gave us, they also cost me some dough. See, I was plannin' to ask all the shindig supporters for a modest contribution of a quarter each, 'round about the same time James rode up shootin' gators – gators he left behind to stink to high heaven in the next-day sun.

So, anyway, I lost that money, and Samadh only needed so much tamarind polish and no more. So I was runnin' out of the usual options. I reckon I could always hunt down the Couyon Gang in hopes of getting the hundred-thousand-dollar reward, but that would take me until I was thirty, especially with no Frico-sketchin' support.

And Lord knows I tried to get him to help me go after ol' James Jackson, but there was no convincin' Frico after he said no. But I know for a fact that he was doing some sketching behind my back, the bastard. That Teesha Grey girl he was talkin' to, just kept getting cuter and cuter all the time. That's how I knew. And what pissed me off was the fact that she thought he sketched her because she was pretty. But I knew she was pretty *because* he sketched her. Soon she had a cute little nose, fuller breasts and a butt with a mind of its own. You shoulda seen that thing. *Freeze frame.*

Now look, it wasn't like I was jealous or nothing – but hell, I'd made an investment a few years back, so I thought that I needed to get my Snickers' worth at least.

So I see her braggin' one day by the school, and I just rolled up on the bicycle that Belly left with me, and I told her she owed me money. Well, she started actin' up in front of her friends, so I just pulled her aside and told her the whole damn story about the sketchin', and then I demanded some money again. Of course she didn't believe me, and she told Frico that his little brother's crazy like ol' Mississippi murderer James Jackson.

So I'm up in the house doing dishes and, of course, here comes Frico chargin' in through the screen door shoutin' about what I told Teesha Grey. So I told him we're business partners and he was givin' away the sketchin' services for free. But he denied it and said she was pretty from before.

And I said: "Yeah, *pretty* dumb."

And maan, it was on. He punched me in the face. Now I don't believe you should punch your brother square in the face. That's the family face you're messin' with. So I recovered and hit him hard with my elbow, but he was stronger than me. So he grabbed a hold of me, but I had my head in his belly, so I pushed him into that glass display case with all of Moms' fine china in it. There was a horrible crash, and splinters and broken crockery was everywhere, and the fightin' suddenly stopped, cos now we had to make up a damn good excuse to tell Valerie Beaumont why her display case was broken and her crockery all smashed up. Then I remembered that this guy could fix anything by sketchin'. So I hit him again, with a gravy dish this time. So after he knocked me out cold for hittin' him with the gravy dish, he woke me up and told me to hold still so he could sketch my face back good and proper, and then I had to hold the mirror so he could sketch himself. Then he sketched the display case real quick. But when Moms came home and we were sittin' there smilin' like Cheshire cats, she took one look into the glass display case and said:

"OK, where's my gravy dish? That's not my gravy dish. The pink flowers are supposed to be on the side, not around the rim – so where is it?" And Frico just sat there cool as a creek and told her that I broke it and then I went and borrowed one from Ma Campbell, cos I was so sure she wouldn't notice.

"And I told him to tell you he broke it, but this little boy of yours is stubborn and *pretty* dumb."

That's how I realized the guy deliberately sketched that gravy dish different just to set me up. But I couldn't say nothing about the sketchin', of course, cos that would just sound like nonsense – and furthermore, his story was the bomb.

Well, after that, him and ol' Teesha Grey broke up, but I don't think it was my fault. She probably got too caught up with the environment and all those birds instead of him. So, soon after, she wasn't so pretty no more. Things wasn't pretty between me and Frico after that neither. I think that was the beginning of us growin' apart. It wasn't just because of a fight about some girl: I think it was just that he prob'ly felt like he really couldn't trust me to keep my mouth shut any more. And you can't sketch a relationship back the way it was: you gotta work on it in other ways, you know.

Of course, I didn't see Harry much any more neither. I figured him and Frico started hangin' out. Me and Harry were still cool, but it wasn't the same – especially after that evenin' he zoomed into the swamp with an Air Force recruitment book and said he was goin' to be in the Armed Forces when he left school. To me, he just sounded like that wannabe teen idol Marlon Rodgers. So I wasn't even thinkin' straight before I opened my mouth. Or maybe I was just envious. Everybody seemed to know what they wanted to do. But me, I'd spent so long on this swamp dream that all I'd done with my life was write a stupid ten-dollar poem.

"You don't even know who you are, Harry. And you want to go lose that identity you're still workin' on... in the military?"

Man, I remember he had a cold drink in his hand and one foot on the bicycle pedal. And he just wasn't thirsty any more and emptied the can on the ground and sat there balancin' on the bicycle and holdin' the recruitment book under his arm. Then, when he was crushin' the can, he started out loud:

"Well, look, we didn't all get the opportunity to know our father, Skid Beaumont. So consider yourself frickin' lucky. And you know what? Maybe I don't know who I am, but you don't know neither. You're supposed to be my friend, man. I stand up for you when people talk about your cheese-grater face behind your back. I went with you to Gentilly, and I even went along with that dumb sketchin' plan you talked about that summer when we were kids. You're a real jerk, man."

Well, I repeated everything he said word for word just to mock him. But I left out the "cheese-grater face" part, cos that kicked me in the bells a little bit. And he just sucked his teeth and pushed off and rode away over the footbridge just as the sun was rollin' out a tattered gold carpet across the bayou. I called out:

"Man, that boy Harry Tobias is so dramatic! Say something sad and then ride off into the sunset, won't ya? Too much TV, I tell you!"

I thought he'd turn back, but he just stopped and let go of one handlebar and flipped me the bird without lookin' back. And you shouldn't say anything more to a person after they flip you the bird. Besides, one fight for the month was enough.

Well, it seemed like I ticked everybody off that year 'cept Doug, but by the following year Doug had his own crew, and even though I'd be fourteen right before the fall, bigger boys don't like new teens comin' around. So that's when I started hangin' out with Peter. Yeah, the same music-playin' Peter Grant that busted his face open at camp.

Eighteen

Well, Peter Grant, he didn't live near the swamp. He lived close to Armstrong Park. We could only hang out a bit on weekends when I didn't have work to do. Now, he's Irish-American, but he always liked tellin' people: "Yeah, me, Skid and Frico, we're all brothers." That guy had a deep respect for Frico's artistic skills even before the camp accident, and after Frico fixed his face, Peter had a new kinda reverence for the guy. So no matter how mad I got about anything my brother did, he was always on Frico's side. He would answer everything I said with: "Yeah, I hear you, but he got serious talent, man."

Peter Grant was a genius too. He started playing jazz by ear from when he was eight, he said. Now, we started hangin' out cos his father picked him up from school in a big eighteen-wheeler truck nearly every day. He said it used to be fun in elementary school, but it was gettin' cheesy in middle school. Well, hell I didn't mind climbin' up in a truck from school – I didn't care if kids laughed and said we climbed up so high we got a nosebleed or whatever. So we made it cool again, especially after Mr Grant slapped some fire decals on that custom rig and flung two exhaust pipes up in the air and sprayed the whole thing metallic purple.

He had two eighteen-wheelers, but he called this one the "family car". Ol' Mr G was cool enough to make me hitch a ride into the swamp from school most days. Peter would ride with us, even though after the shindig Mr G was a bit cagey about lettin' Peter come into L-Island by himself. Well, Peter's mom, she was a sweet lady, but kind of a worrywart, so Peter made every excuse to avoid his house. So that left us lookin' like two bums who lived on the street. To make it worse, Peter got a little keyboard that used batteries and we used to go into Armstrong Park or head over to Jackson Square and sit around playin' mostly Oscar Peterson stuff. Well, actually, he played, I just sat around and gave girls the eye. And if somebody ever came up and dropped a coin in the Casio keyboard box, that boy Peter would get mad and ask them if it looked like he was street-performin' for tips. Hell, I told him to just play music and let me worry about all that annoyin' money. One time an older, big-belly guy playin' a trombone, he saw us makin' money and told us we'd better play along with him, like we were his band, or he'd have to chase us out. So he had to chase us out. That was the first time we went over to Jackson Square – and I saw this artist guy sketchin' lovers. Now, they were payin' him to make them look ugly. So I went home and told Frico I had a brand-new business idea.

I sat down near to him on the floor beside the bed, and I said: "Frico, I saw a guy today gettin' paid to make people look bad on paper. So just imagine. We could sketch some of those not-so-pretty tourist people over at Mardi Gras, reduce some spare-tyre gut and love handles and stuff, make them look all handsome, and they pay us a coupla bucks. We can do the advertisin' ourselves. I could be the pitchman at fairs and exhibitions across the country, and Peter can play music and sing like one of them real ol'-time attractions."

Well, he just sighed and looked at me with his eyes all tired. And all I could hear was crickets and frogs far away in the damn swamp. And since I knew that he was always lookin' at Art and Photography schools, I kept goin': "Frico, you could sketch and get to save money... for school."

"I can get money or a scholarship for school, fool... That ain't the problem."

The problem, I was thinkin', was that he was scared. Yep, Frico was scared. I thought he wasn't scared of nothin' – especially with these powers he got from God, or God knows where – but God bless a damn duck, he was scared as hell.

He always said – and when he did, he sounded real artsy -fartsy – he wasn't so good at drawin' the human form. See, Frico liked to draw landscapes and animals and Teesha Grey's birds and nice buildin's. Those he drew real good. But he hated drawing people. Even though in reality he was good at it. So before he could even answer, I flipped it and said: "Fine, you're afraid you'll draw somebody all screwed up. But supposin' they need to be drawn all screwed up?" I could think of a coupla people who deserved it, damn it – or at least one guy: that same ol' James Jackson. One year after the shindig that Couyon guy was back to snatchin' clothes off people's clothes lines like he forgot he was the CEO of some place in his head. So I told Frico that maybe we could tell reporters some big lie to bait ol' James Jackson – and when he comes back into the swamp, Frico could draw him without arms or legs or somethin'. Then, when he's rollin' around on the ground, we nab him quick and collect the re-ward money.

"Where do you come up with this bull? And by the way, didn't I tell you to stop talkin' to people about all this stuff?"

And that was the end of the conversation right there. If he was goin' to be as dismissive as that, then I wouldn't ask him anything any more. Except to stop the pimples. For one whole year I rushed into the bathroom every mornin' to try and stop him from sketchin' me on the mirror, but I'd always be too late. It was like the guy slept in there.

But, seriously, I couldn't see why tellin' Peter Grant was a problem. I thought Peter would be the first to say he believed in Frico's powers, but the first time I stopped by his house, he suddenly didn't seem to have a clue. Now, first of all this boy lived in a mansion – at least compared to our one-room shack in the swamp. Peter's house wasn't like one of those historic houses that all look alike. Naw, the Grants' house was a mansion fixer-upper. White Lions on black-marble columns greeted you at the front. Then there was a veranda with black-and-white tiles. It had three bedrooms, a guest room and helpers' quarters. Kitchen counters went on for ever, and there was a huge gas range and a fridge with ice comin' out the side, clink-clink into your glass. Man. Two carved bannisters led upstairs, but one staircase was blocked off. That was to accommodate a Hammond B3 church organ. Yes, a real, live church organ that when Peter held down the keys and stepped on the pedals his whole family jumped up and praised the Lord or cursed the Devil.

Anyway, like I was sayin', about the first time I went to the house, I saw the Frico face sketch in Peter's room. It was done such a long time ago it was faded, and the blood that got onto it was deep brown. I asked him about that night. He said he didn't remember much, cos he lost consciousness, but the nurse woke him up with smellin' salts and then Frico gave him the drawin' he had done.

"Do you remember me holdin' up a flashlight to your face?"

"No, not really man. Why?"

"How long ago was this camp accident?"

"Two, three years?"

"Five."

"OK, and?"

"And do you remember how you got hurt?"

"One second I was running beside the stupid bus, and then next thing I tripped and hit my face on a rock in the road."

"Maybe you were lookin' at Donna Milleaux in the bus. She was cute."

"Donna Milleaux was not cute."

"Cute enough to make you fall hard and bust your face up."

"Back to the point, Skid."

"Yes. Now, don't you think it's strange that there's not even one scar on your face from that accident? Think about it."

"Good genes, I guess."

"Good genes, bad memory. A miracle happened that night, man."

"I dunno. Like I said, I can't remember."

"Well, you got to."

"Yeah – as soon as you tell me what you're getting at, I'll try."

"Just look at your face in the mirror, remember the accident and try to find a scar, then we'll talk."

The whole way into the swamp, Peter was checkin' his face in the rear-view mirror, until his old man told him to stop makin' him nervous.

"Dad, remember that camp injury?"

"Can't forget. You chased some girl called Dora Miller until she hit you in the face with a rock. I must've paid for the stitches. Waidamminit... did you get any stitches?"

"No."

He fixed his cap on his head and looked sideways at Peter while drivin', just like Pa Campbell did all the time.

"Come to think of it, you came home properly patched up, really. We sent the nurse a thank-you note and everything."

"Good genes and a good nurse, I guess."

I looked straight ahead, smilin'. "Man, I got some things to tell you, Peter Grant."

That same evenin', Moms was cookin' up a storm with so much skill she made it look like kung fu or like she had more limbs than the rest of us.

I watched her from the bed. In our swamp shack, you see everything just by turning your head – and that made me think of the Grant Mansion and the fact that you could actually be inside that big house the whole darn day and no one would know. I was feelin' so triumphant that day I wasn't even afraid of ol' Frico and his nonsense. So I rolled over to the edge of the bed and looked down on him. "Why don't you just sketch us all a bigger house right here in the swamp and we can all live in it?"

And as soon as I said it, I knew it was the dumbest suggestion he ever heard. But he just said: "It don't work that way,

Skid. I told you this before and so did Momma. You can only work on what you already got."

And that was the first time Frico Beaumont didn't flat out deny that he could do magic. So I knew we were makin' progress.

Nineteen

Now, don't judge me for what I'm about to tell you. But I reckoned I shouldn't let all that progress go to waste. So let's just say I strongly encouraged my brother to do some sketchin' for his own good. I knew he was all bent out of shape with the Teesha Grey breakup, so me and Doug, we tried to cheer him up by playin' soccer with him on the porch.

See, we'd made this wooden ramp for Pa Campbell's wheelchair. Just a gentle slope from the porch down to the ground, with rails, so Ma Campbell could wheel the old man back home easily when he started gettin' too rowdy. So what we would do, we would run up the slope with the soccer ball, and as soon as we got to where the ramp met the porch, we'd drop that ball and kick it before it hit the floorboards. Well, when it was ol' Fricozoid's turn to kick, he backed off and jogged a little bit, then ran full tilt from way out in the yard and up the ramp and he dropped the ball and gave one hell of a kick – and kicked the edge of the porch instead of the ball and broke his big toe. *Freeze frame.*

Now, to be honest I knew that Frico wasn't wearin' his glasses, and I really should have pointed that out to the guy and insisted that he go and get them like Moms said we should, but he was havin' so much fun... I just couldn't. As a matter of fact I went hid them under the kitchen sink so he'd definitely forget. I also knew that the porch was slightly higher since Pa Campbell last raised it, but I was thinking: what's a inch gonna do?

So when he was laid up in the house for days, nursin' his toe, I came home one evening from school and climbed into the bed beside him, and I said to him real smooth, like the

Devil to Jesus in the wilderness: "Why don't you sketch your big ol' toe all good and better, just to see what happens?"

And when he cleared his throat and started makin' excuses as usual, I pulled out a Snickers bar and five dollars and fetched pencil and paper before he did it, even though it was for his own good. Well, he said he didn't have any appetite, on account of losin' his girl, so he only took the money and the pencil and paper, and of course the next day we were playing ball again. Moms said he'd just been pretendin' to hurt himself that whole time so he could cut school. That evenin' Frico comes around to the old car seat under the shady spot at the corner of the house.

"Hey Skid, I been thinkin'. It's time your face cleared up."

I didn't show it, but I wanted to do cartwheels. I was tired of talkin' to people with my face turned away, and the teasin' at school was gettin' unbearable. I looked like a reverse raccoon. The only clear skin were the circles around my eyes. Everything else was darker and scarred. Worse than all that, I had had enough of Moms' blood-purgin' bitter cerasee tea in my gut and aloe-vera slime on my face – not to mention that cleansin' bar that smelt like wood glue. So this was goin' to be double bonus. More sketchin' and a healin'. Hallelujah!

Then, when Fricozoid added the fine print, I started gettin' suspicious.

"You gotta help me out, though. I need you to go out into the yard and fetch one of those big fat branches we use for firewood and drag it back here. Then, when Moms ain't lookin', go into the bathroom and give the toothpaste sketch I just did on the mirror a good wallop, and that should do it."

"Say what? Ain't that goin' break it?"

"Yes, and? See, you gotta break the image for this to work, Skid. Destroy what you are and start all over. Anyway, lemme know if you're interested."

He sighed and started walkin' away, and even though I knew he was bein' dramatic like Harry T, I grabbed his arm.

"No. OK… I'll go do it. Where's Moms?"

"Cookin' catfish outside. Go, go, go."

I ran with my head down and my fingers scrapin' ground like I was on a real mission again. Matter of fact, this was the first mission Frico and me were gonna undertake in a while.

He called out after me: "Make sure that branch's gotta big knot at the end of it."

Well, I dragged that stick inside and lined up the mirror and put my back into it and swung like I was at the World Series and – wham. No sooner had I smashed a spider web into the middle of the mirror and that God-awful toothpaste sketch, I heard Fricozoid right outside the door, callin' out: "Momma, Skid's done gone crazy. He's messin' with the bathroom mirror again."

I ditched the stick and came out with my palms open in the silent what-the-hell kind of way that I learnt from Mai.

Frico was leanin' against the door jamb, pretendin' to clean his fingernails with a pencil. Moms was wadin' through the chickens in the front yard, stormin' inside from the porch.

Frico used the few seconds before she got close.

"That's payback for the porch football, Skid. You know I needed my glasses. I found them under the frickin' kitchen sink. Didn't you think I'd know?"

Anyway, if I was superstitious, I'd say that my seven years of bad luck for breakin' the mirror started immediately. I look past Moms, and there was a policeman at the doorstep. A few others were out in the yard. Doug and Tony stood around watchin' them. Moms saw the bathroom mirror in pieces and didn't even blink. She went back outside. The cops wanted to look around. Well, I'd welcome the city police instead of gossip reporters any day, but they didn't have good news for us either. One of them, a detective, he looked up under our house with a flashlight. He took a scoop on a long stick and carefully picked out a few things, including another alligator egg. Then he pulled off his rubber gloves and looked Moms squarely in the face.

"We've been investigating since you came in and asked us to look into his disappearance. Your husband is now officially missing, Mrs Beaumont. And I gotta tell ya, we're fearing the worst."

The cop smelt like rubber and asphalt and concrete, if you can smell all that at once. And he wasn't usin' any fancy cop phrases.

A lady officer came around the corner of the house with a pair of Caterpillar work boots in her hand. They were waterlogged and swollen, and the leather looked rotten enough. Duckweed and water bugs were all over them. Three of Calvin's teenage kids sniffed them and then slinked away, uninterested.

"We found these in the water. Did they belong to your husband, Mrs Beaumont?"

Deep breath. "Yes, they *do*."

"Are you sure?"

Moms reached into her apron with one hand. The other hand started pointin'.

"Look here, officer. See those scuff marks on the toes? Those are from my two last kids learning to stand and walk on the front of their daddy's shoes when he came home from work. See those heels all slantin' and broken down – with pebbles up in the grooves? That's from him runnin' in here half-drunk every night to tell me some wild dreams o' his. See those tracks on the bottom? I can trace those footprints from here all the way to Gentilly when he goes stomping down some young gal's front yard, so yeah, uh-huh, I'm sure. I threw those boots out the goddamn house every day, twice a day, so of course I'm sure! And inside those boots is where he hid his damn cigarettes every time he fell off the wagon... like I'm fixin' to do... right now."

She pulled out a box of cigarettes and some restaurant souvenir matches from the apron, and in a flash she was a smoker again. I'd heard about it, but I'd never seen her do it.

Funny how the first part of a fresh-lit cigarette almost smells like some delicious thing roastin'. Then, when you get to the middle, it's stiflin'. The smoke floated up and gave away the sunlight splinterin' through the treetops. The lady cop put the boots on the nut grass.

"Mrs Beaumont, we found body parts inside the boots. We'll have to analyse it carefully, but—"

Moms dragged the cig harder to numb the sharpness of that statement.

"Not in front of my kids, please. Tony, everybody inside."

He dropped his voice. "I'm sorry. We just don't think that with the gators—"

"Detective. Please be kind enough to desist from telling me all the gory details until my children are out of earshot, thank you."

When my moms was tryin' to hold herself together, she spoke proper English. Broken English is only for laughter or anger.

By the time the cops left with the boots in a bag, Ma Campbell was leanin' halfway out of her window, strainin' her neck to get the drama.

"Valerie! Valerie! What the poh-lice want now?"

"Nothin' Ma. Same Shindig questioning."

"Heh? Ain't they done with all that? You know, I reckon those cops got a big crush on ya, and they usin' all kinds of excuses to come round heah."

"Uh-huh. Yeah, Ma, maybe." She sucked her teeth.

"Good thing you got that spider of yours to chase ol' Mr Officer Muffet away!"

Moms pretended she didn't hear that last part. That Mr Muffet joke was somethin' Pops started sayin' to Moms after I was born, I heard. He'd joke with her before he left early for work.

"Now, Val, don't you open the door for no strangers today. And if any Mr Muffet comes by trying to sit on my tuffet, well… now you got eight legs and eight eyes to scare him away."

I liked thinkin' of me and my brothers as one big black-widow spider that scared things away, but I don't believe Moms saw it that way or found raisin' four kids in a swamp funny at all.

None of us breathed easily for the five minutes or so that Moms was speakin' to the police and Ma Campbell. I just remember being in a daze sittin' on the bed lookin' at my cheekbones, cos they were the only thing I could recognize from my mangled image in the dresser mirror. Mangled: that's how I felt. A crazy mosaic. Shattered, all over the place. And those pieces wouldn't even fall out so I could start again. Maan, I couldn't even destroy somethin' properly. Moms walked into the house, fire first, smoke trailin'. She sat down at the kitchen table and took a last drag, squintin'. The corners of her eyes showed brand-new crow's feet that she prob'ly got five minutes before. She crushed out the cigarette in a shallow tomato-paste can, waved away the last of the reluctant smoke and set the can at her feet.

"Y'all get in here."

We stepped into the kitchen area. She looked at all of us, one at a time, for the longest time. Then she told us to get closer, like what she had to tell us was a secret.

Now, between what she said and the details that Tony filled in later on, here's what happened – and it ain't pretty.

The police believed that somebody had been under our house the night of the shindig. Somebody had been diggin' for somethin' and dug up dozens of alligator eggs instead. Soon mother alligator, she came by to check on her kids, and was so alarmed by the hollerin' and the helicopter, she dashed under the house, and her mouth just fell wide open when she came face to face with a certain Alrick Beaumont, who made a run – or, more specifically – a crawl for it. But Pops was no match for the speed of the gator, especially with the bayou shoreline almost up under our house and all that extra mud. He prob'ly tried to get vertical, and he made it to the water eventually, but long and short, they found one of my pops' legs from the knee down floatin' under a patch of marsh grass out in the bayou. The rest of him was nowhere to be found, and they thought there was a slim chance he might still be alive.

I don't know if they were puttin' us on to make us feel better, but they said he might have used his other steel-toe Caterpillar boot to clobber the gator quite a bit, so the lizard took off and left the leg alone. Great, but when they pulled that decomposing leg from the water, it had a bullet hole through the trousers and didn't make us very confident. My pops had been shot through that leg before the gator took it off. The police would have to do the whole ballistics testin' of the bullet and all that to see if it was a cop bullet or gang bullet that got him.

Now, if my pops was alive, he'd have a hell of a lot of questions to answer about his possible involvement with the Couyon Gang. Why was he on the scene? Was he their lookout guy? Was he trying to break into the house from underneath it? Well, we could answer all those questions for 'em right away. First of all, my pops had too much pride to be led by James Jackson, even though his ambitions were crazier than Couyon himself. Secondly, we could bet that Alrick Beaumont had snuck into L-Island from God knows where and was obviously diggin' for seals that night – and prob'ly just chose the wrongest time to do it. I mean, the guy is the master of bad timing and poor judgement, and I hoped I didn't get those genes. He wasn't involved in anything but a bad deal with Backhoe Benet – and it ruined his whole life.

Twenty

Speak of the Devil, not more than two days after the police came, Benet appeared in the swamp all gussied up in a white felt hat and smellin' just like that city cop.

I saw him comin', but I wasn't goin' to tell Moms. I was goin' to crawl up under the bed and lissen. Tony and Doug were off in the pirogue, settin' a big ol' trot line to catch more catfish, and Frico was with them. Benet strode up to the door and knocked loudly. Moms moves the curtain, sees him, makes the sign of the cross, takes a deep breath and opens the door. She steps out onto the porch and closes it behind her. I go to the window where I can see her, but not him.

"How can I help you, Cap'n?"

"Hello, Val. Let me... get to the point. I came to tell yew... two things. The first is... I'm sorry for yer loss."

"Well, that seems quite previous of you, Cap'n. The police don't think—"

He laughed softly, and when she stopped he dropped his voice even lower.

"And yew think the police know anythin', Val? Who do you think told them about the body parts? How do you think the Coast Guard swarmed in here when yew was all shindiggin' over my sons' cold bodies? Look, I know what goes on in this swamp. I been here for ever. And from the looks of it, ain't nowhere for an injured man to hide... from the sixteen gators in this section of the bayou – not countin' their gator friends who come by to visit. See, the cops like ta say things... all fancy, so yew feel better, Val. But I'm-a tell you like it is, in plain black and white. Alrick was a good man. He tried his best. Sorry for yer loss."

Pause. Cigarette smoke floatin' up and collidin' in slow motion with the underside of the porch's tin roof. Weird how Backhoe sounded like Broadway. Or was it the other way around? I was happy I spoke more like Moms. In English, I mean. My pops, he is brilliant, but he talks country.

Anyway, she had her other arm folded over the one that held the cig. She puffed again and sent a choo-choo-train blast to the ceilin'.

"I think that brings you to your second point, Cap'n."

Backhoe sighed heavily. I imagined him adjustin' his hat, like in the movies.

"Val, we go way back, so... we should be able to help each odder out. I knew when yer boys were born... every single one of 'em. So, look, I found a place for you in the city. You and yer boys can go there... whenever you want. Just pack up and go. If it makes you feel better, yer welcome to pay me rent... but yew need to get your sons and get out of this swamp, Valerie. It's time."

"Well, thanks for your concern and your offer, Mr Benet, but me and my boys'll be around here just a while longer. We waited so many years now, so a few more won't hurt nothin'."

I heard him step towards her on the porch, and the angry blood in my ears drowned everythin' else out. But by the time I busted open to the front door to take the guy on myself, I saw that Tony, Doug and Frico were already standin' side by side in the yard starin' down ol' Backhoe. The Beaumont Black Widow, all eight legs and eight eyes, was in full effect, and we got this guy surrounded. It looked like Doug and Tony were gettin' ready to send that five-foot alligator gar they caught flyin' any second, so I was happy when Moms spoke up, cos that was our dinner.

"I think our front porch is a little too crowded, Mr Benet. Now I know this is your land... heard about that only recently – but it's still my house, so thanks for stoppin' by."

Well, ol' Backhoe, he just smiled and stepped heavily down the three steps and walked with his hand in his pocket in the direction of his Lincoln Town Car that was parked far up near the tracks. He looked into the trees and the sky that was darkenin' a little, and a little breeze tugged at the hem of his white trousers when he stopped a little ways off. He spun around.

"Two things Valerie. One... it looks like it's gonna rain soon. Yew might wanna think about catchin' your drinkin' water from the heav'ns... instead of pullin' it up from hell. And two... what makes you think this is still my place?"

PART THREE

Can anything be sadder than work left unfinished?
– Christina Rossetti

Twenty-One

After that I decided to run away. It all started when I had an argument with my mother, and it still makes me cringe for some of the things I said.

She was cleanin' a channel catfish on a washstand out in the yard, cos two days after Benet came by, the water in the kitchen comin' from the well turned brown and smelt. We went back to haulin' from the lake. Even though it was brackish, it was cleaner. Anyway, I was sittin' on a stool behind her, keepin' her company. She was workin' with this long fillet knife. While she filleted the fish, she wagged a cig in one side of her mouth and used the other side to say that with the absence of our pops she was hopin' we could all work more closely together.

I told her I agreed with that, especially if it meant Frico would pitch in and do some house chores as well. Well, she got defensive right away and said that wasn't the point she was tryin' to make, and I should let her finish. So I shut up and she said prob'ly us all workin' together to make things better was just wishful thinkin' anyway, cos my eldest brother Tony, he had told her he was movin' out of the swamp. Damn. That was as shockin' as the fact that Pops had come face to face with a gator under the house, so I asked her for details.

She tightened her lips around the cigarette and said I should ask Tony himself for the full story, but the little she knew so far was that he found a room-mate and was goin' to live out in New O'lins. Said she could do the drivin' to deliver to Al Dubois, even though she told Tony he could still do that to make money. Well Tony, he had other plans. He knew he could get a merit scholarship, but wanted to find a job first. A

199

city job. Moms had been savin' what she could, cos even with a scholarship it wasn't goin' to be easy. But the money wasn't what bothered her. Him leavin' first was just not how she expected it was going to be. I guess she always thought that we were goin' to tough it out in the swamp a little more, and stick together until we made enough money and then we'd all just rise up together one day and leave real soon. And that would have been sweet, but those days everythin' was happenin' in pieces.

"Maybe that's just his way of dealin' with his father disappearing, so…"

I interrupted her and told her not to worry about it. It was just that we were growing up, and the edge of the swamp was getting too small for all of us. Then with a big smile on my face I dropped my voice and told her that some major expansion was about to take place.

Well, the first thing I should have learnt by the time I was fourteen is never tell a woman not to worry. See, they're not tellin' you their feelin's so that you can bust open your shirt and show your costume and swoop down and save them. Naw, women don't necessarily need you to reassure them or fix nothin'. They're just workin' things out for themselves – or, better yet, they prob'ly got it all figured out by the time they're talkin' to you. You're just the sounding board for the solution they came up with. Second thing is, if you can't explain what the hell you mean by "major expansion", then don't say anythin'.

So she asked me what that meant, as if she thought I heard somethin' on the news or whatever, cos they were always debatin' that whole development thing since it stopped in the Seventies – but of course you know I was talkin' about Frico finally makin' Pops' dream come true. Well, she looked at me blank – like a no-light-goin'-off-in-her-head kind of blank. And that's when I realized that me and Moms never ever really had a real conversation about all this magic stuff, even though I had convinced myself that the woman knew what was goin' on with ol' Fricozoid.

Well, now. You shoulda seen Skid Beaumont back-pedallin' like he was on a unicycle goin' down the wrong side of the highway. Cos this lady wanted to know what I meant. I hemmed and hawed and coughed and scratched my head and played with Calvin's kids.

"Out with it, Skid."

Pause. And those yard fowls, they just kept walkin' back and forth past us, caw-cawin' in the empty conversation space. One mother hen in particular, she was leadin' a trail of chickens like yellow lint balls across the backyard – cluckin' and diggin' at nothin'.

Moms kept cuttin' the catfish right below the head bone and then slicin' against the middle bone all the way to the tail. She flipped over the fillet and slid the knife up under the flesh and took off the skin. And that catfish was me bein' skinned alive – and I was dead meat, cos you don't back-pedal on ol' Valerie Beaumont. She was the oncomin' traffic, and I couldn't find the brakes again.

So I put on my sincerest voice and couraged up and told her the whole plan and all that I believed about Frico from the beginnin' since I was three years old. I told what I thought about the blue light over the crib. I told her all that Pa said about the Archangel and his six wings, and about her Caribbean mixed magic. I told her about the cat and the shorts and the plum tree and Peter Grant's face and how hot Teesha Grey was lookin'. And somewhere in the back of my brain, somethin' commonsensical and logical is tellin' me to shut the hell up, but I'm trippin' down those verbal stairs again.

So my words, my words are just runnin' when I tell her how I thought that now, any day now, Frico was goin' to use his God-given sketchin' to bring the city thunderin' into the swamp, and there would be a great day of celebration and shindiggin' and crawfish-eatin'. We would bead up all the cypress trees like it was Mardi Gras – and all those flowers Pops saw in his vision, they would bloom, and we'd all walk around feelin' brand-new and beautiful, and she and Pops would dance even though he'd have only one foot, and the sky would be blue and full of popcorn clouds like the ones down in San Tainos when she was young. Well, there I was breathless, and she turned around and looked at me real sad, like that lady doctor once did.

I was still sittin' on the stool when she hugged me – but I didn't need a hug: I needed her to believe me. And the chickens were still walkin' around and clawin' and cluckin', and the swamp was sinkin'. And in my head I knew my father was dead – dead like his dreams – and I hated him for it.

So I had my face in her apron and I just let it all out. I felt it was full time to purge myself of all the bitterness and annoyance caused by people who didn't believe. So I told her I knew by the look on her face that she thought I was a fool for thinkin' all that, but at least I wasn't a hypocrite like her, cos she could talk about the damn nonsense about Jerusalem and those silly legends of San Tainos and be all emotional, but I wasn't allowed to believe in my brother's gift. I told her she was lyin' if she said they weren't conjurers, cos I knew that she and Frico chased my pops out of the swamps and then put that red wash on the house. That's why he had nowhere to run from that stinkin' gator. And him losin' his leg didn't matter anyhow, cos she already cussed him and made him into half-a-man even before that gator got to him.

Well, my sweet mother she just pulled back and slapped my face hard with her raw-catfish hand. Then she drew her breath and touched my cheek as if she wanted to pull the slap back off of it. When she realized she couldn't, she held on to my whole head and started whispering again: "Jerusalem, Jerusalem." And I gotta tell you, she slapped me so hard the world shook. Right there somewhere between my mad rantin' and when she raised her hand and brought it down, I just felt the ground shake and heard the house begin to shuffle like God was cuttin' the deck and dealin' the cards again. The whole place started shake-shakin' like hell, just like Sinkhole Night up in that tamarind tree. The shakin' got heavier and the moss hangin' on the trees was whippin' back and forth. Birds darted around, confused. Calvin's kids were howlin'. The yard fowls quarrelled and took off in all different directions – earthbound birds flappin' their wings and wishin' at the sky. I heard the low rumble and watched the water in the bayou sloshin' up against the banks and ripplin' like soup in a movin' bowl. Then it just stopped.

"There now – we're all OK. I'm sorry. Now, you go on and wash that catfish with a lemon for me, I'll be back."

And I heard Moms rummagin' in the dresser drawer, searchin' through the years for that sweet lady doctor's business card. Not even my mother understood.

So that very day I decided to take off. Maybe I could end up followin' Master Sam for the rest of my life. Or I could head north and go join Couyon's gang. I know they needed replacements. I'd only use them to help me find the rest of my pops – even if he was just a bunch of bleached bones on a muddy river bank somewhere. At least the man would be free from the cage that kept him closed up inside himself. Cos now he could fly. Well, if he was heaven-bound, at least.

So right after some afternoon rain, when Moms was out front still discussin' the latest earthquake with Ma, Pa, Mai's mother, some fishermen and every gossip that came up from the east side of the swamp, me and my backpack, we slid out.

I walked along the banks of the bayou for cover, thinkin' that as far as I was concerned that day's tremor started right where Moms and I stood. Now she was out there coverin' up her earthquake-conjuration from everybody. I stopped at the tamarind tree to load up on refreshments. But once I shimmied up into those branches and got near-soaked with rainwater from the leaves, I gotta tell ya, all the way across the bayou I could smell that wicked woman Valerie Beaumont conjurin' up some Cajun French slash Caribbean slash Creole cookin' – no, not just cookin': *cuisine*.

And I just said "Hell, no" and came back, and she told me to wash my hands, and I sat down and gobbled up a feast like that young Prodigal Son fella. And while I was there half-asleep after the meal, she took a galvanized-tin washtub and drew a bush bath with tamarind leaves and Florida Water and eucalyptus and a jungle of other horrible stuff in it. She told me to strip down and get in. Now. Said she couldn't find that lady doctor's card, and she was thinkin' perhaps what I need-ed was a more spiritual cleansin' from whatever somebody put on me to mess with my mind.

So it was either the washtub or a baptism in the creek. Valerie Beaumont washed my face with herbal soap and dried it. Then, when she started up with Psalm 37 and anointed my head with olive oil, I swear my whole body went numb in that washtub like I was frozen. But when my brothers came around the corner of the house laughin' and sayin' they were goin' to call Mai to come and see, I let them know my middle finger was still workin'.

Now, I *did* get to run away after all, but with my mother's permission. She told me that what I needed was friends – friends like my brothers had – and other things to occupy my mind. So I got to stay over at Peter Grant's house in the city for the 4th of July weekend. Another way Moms kept me occupied was by puttin' me permanently on dog-food and chicken-feedin' duties. She said there was a lot to be learnt from the animals. Well, when I didn't learn anything, she gave me a notebook to write a full report of what was happening on the TV news that I'd see at the Grants every single night I stayed there.

Now, that's a bunch of goddamn stress if you ask me, and I still don't know how people watch the news every day. It was during one of those depressin' newscasts that I said to myself:

"Skid, maybe Frico just doesn't have the willpower to change the world from what it is" and: "Skid, maybe you don't have the power to convince him". I was ready to give up, no lie. But that point of view changed that same weekend.

See, I discovered the music of the marchin' band and somethin' else in the process. Peter was the drum major slash music director for his high-school marchin' band, so I hung out with him at an Independence Day celebration in Jackson Square. Man, it seemed like everybody was at this one celebration. If someone owed you money and you hadn't seen them in a while, this was the place to find the bastards. It was like a fairground with uniforms and instruments and brass bands and different beats. You couldn't help but do everything to a beat. But this wasn't some ol' French or English military marchin' music or just jazz or the blues. No siree. Peter especially, he had his band playin' stuff from Cyndi Lauper and Culture Club.

Maan, I couldn't hold still when they started playin'. Boom-boom-boom-dut-dut. And it made you want to be an idiot all day shoutin' cool stuff like those drum majors: "To the ready! Atten-hut! Horns up, Slooow March!" – even though you know that if you were really the drum major, the field would just look like crap. I'm serious. These things are so much fun they make you want to do stuff you know you *cannot* do. Like start plannin' your own jazz funeral. Like, what you'd want them to play behind your casket when they're walkin' through the streets of New O'lins, second-linin' and dancin' and all that stuff. OK, maybe that's just me. I'm creative like that, and maybe that's why Moms tries to police my imagination so much.

So anyway, they brought the parade to a halt on the field. They stood still without a sound, and all you could see was this wave of blue helmets, feather plumes, brass instruments and the Red, White and Blue flutterin' there in the breeze – and even the sweet silence made you want to cheer in anticipation.

Then they decided to spice it up a little, so the guys in Peter's drumline started up again. Boom-boom-boom-dut-dut – and these sweet cheerleaders, they came tumblin' out of nowhere in their itty-bitty skirts and tall white boots and glittery make-up, and they were flashing their pompons and shakin' all over, and you just didn't know where to focus, cos everything looked so damn good all at once.

Anyway, this troupe of girls, they start chantin' "Whatchoo want? Whatchoo want? What-what-what-whatchoo want?" and doing some moves that they know are gettin' people like me all bothered. Now Peter, he's leadin' the band, but he's lookin' over the crowd at me and usin' his mouth to point at somethin' to his far left. Maan, don't do that – don't point with your head or your mouth. You got ten fingers and you're kissin' at what you want me to see?

Anyway, I finally figured out that he wanted me to look at one particular cheerleader. This was his new girlfriend he said he wanted me to meet. Not bad. I showed him a thumbs-up when they were tossin' her in the air. They held her up on a pyramid while the band did a drum roll and she bent one of her legs till she was almost touching the back of her head with it. And her leg was tanned and so toned from all those backflips. And time stands stills. This girl is gorgeous. She's not ultra-slim like a model. She's got meat on her bones, but she's flexible enough to do her own stunts. Maan, if I could sketch, every woman would have meat on their bones.

Suddenly she flips in the air and lands in her team members' hands again. She curls her leg one more time and she looks happy even though she's so bent out of shape, and the guys are playing Boom-boom-dut and the horns are screamin' and I'm movin' through the crowd, tryin' to get a closer look at this hot cheerleader who I have to remind myself is my best friend's girl. Then she dismounts, and the crowd goes crazy, and she is smilin' and her lips are glossy and her chin is all pointy and she brushes some of the curls from her face in slow motion. *Super slow motion. And – freeze frame.*

Would you believe it? That cheerleader is Suzy Wilson. And I'm head over heels in love with her.

I must have zoned out the music and the people, cos I didn't even see when the crowd walked away. And Peter walks up to me holdin' Suzy at the waist, and her body is tight and firm and she's still breathin' heavy on account of all those stunts. She isn't sayin' much 'cept, "Hi, Skid. How've you been?" No exclamation mark, no italics, nothin'.

There's somethin' new about Suzy. She's not yappin', and even her eyes have a different kind of light in them. Her skin is softer, her chest heaves higher, and there are these cute drops of sweat on her upper lip that I saw somewhere before. Suzy's wearin' see-through lipgloss, and her pout is a pink hibiscus bloomin' around every word. Sparkly green dust glistens on her cheeks and her neck to match her eyes. I get cold drinks and straws for the both of them, but I make sure hers is really cold, cos I remember she likes restin' the bottle against her neck and her chest, and that should make wonderful things happen now that she's older. Peter doesn't have a clue. Anyway, he realizes we know each other, and he's over the moon. We sit and talk a bit. She didn't go back to Canada. She went to Slidell for a while. Then she says:

"Skid is the guy I was tellin' you about."

And they laugh at the same time in an inside-joke kind of a way, and then they talk a little bit of French and laugh some more. Now, that's worse than pointin' with your kisser.

Anyway, Suzy, she wraps herself around the straw, sips her drink and puts her head on Peter's uniformed shoulder. She looks up with her teeth bitin' the tip – man, for some reason that was hot – and she's lookin' at me while talkin' to Peter.

"Tell Skid what I told you about him."

"Oh man, seriously?"

"C'mon! He'll find it funny. Plus it was years ago."

Peter was sheepish at first, but he made a drama out of it like a newscast. It turns out that when Suzy met Peter she told him there was only one boy she ever really liked: Skid Beaumont. Damn. And she wanted me to sing for her, but I wouldn't, cos I was a bit of a jerk. And she couldn't stand her aunt Miss Fiola – and that's why she got jealous and told ol' Screwdriver Phillips when I did the thrust-and-grind thing. And she knew about my pops fixin' her aunt's stereo.

Well, man, life is a brick, and I felt like a bug. Imagine: the finest girl in Armstrong Park is telling me she used to like me, and I was too blind to see it at the time. If I had made her yap without tunin' her out, then I would have known the whole time that she was tryin' to tell me somethin'. Damn.

So, right as I was addin' losin' Suzy to my list of favourite failures, she started yappin' about Frico and how talented he was – and I began to feel better, cos it made me remember clearly why I couldn't deal with her yappin' in the first place. Then she said there was a State of Louisiana Art Fair Competition comin' up in three weeks, and she thought Frico would do very well in it. That SLAF Competition was every two years, and artists from all over Louisiana submitted work for prizes and all. Ho-hum. My ears were noddin' off when she said: "First prize, five grand. This year's theme is 'New Orleans 2020: a vision of tomorrow'."

We—ell now, that just made mad bells go off in my head like three Spanish weddings in the same church at the same time. I jumped on the Beast and rode off to get a flyer so fast I had to come back and ask Suzy where I could get information on the competition on a 4th of July weekend. She took one from her tote bag and wrote a note to Frico on the back. I couldn't wait to tell ol' Fricozoid we could make five grand drawin' the New O'lins of the future. That was it! Money and Pops' dream in one. I discovered the way to make it happen – and it was so simple all along. That Suzy wasn't just hot: she was brilliant. But she was my best friend's girl. Furthermore, I could see Mai and me in the future, in a city that was about to finally wake up and sweep into the swamps and surprise people like Moms who, for some reason, didn't believe me.

Twenty-Two

When I rolled into the swamp on the Beast that Sunday mornin', everybody was crowdin' the creek – at the same spot where Broadway and Squash went into the earth.

Everybody from L-Island was there, people from farther downswamp and all of the Lam Lee Hahn fishermen with their Sam Pan hats hangin' down their backs like a turtle shell.

I had the one Mai gave me on my head. They all looked up when I rounded the mangrove, and I felt a little silly, so I dropped it down my back as well.

But my hat was the least. Pa Campbell had been wheeled halfway across the new footbridge built a little ways off from the sinkhole. People were listenin' to him speak.

I dropped the bicycle and went down the slope to stand beside Moms and Frico.

"It's a sign! It's a *sign*. I keep tellin' you people dat this place is 'bout to be cleansed!"

People looked sheepish. Some half-smiled – nervous laughs.

Chanice Devereaux and her girls were the first to leave. Then Evin Levine bummed a cigarette from Moms, tipped his hat and took off. His dog stuck around playin' with Calvin's kids, before dartin' off to follow him over the bridge. But Pa was just gettin' warmed up.

"We should've known when we saw that snow last winter. Snow? In Louisiana? It was a sign. It snowed for about *seven* minutes right heah in these swamps! If you went to take a piss you'd miss it. Do you know what dat was?"

"You tell us Pa!" Miss Gladys was eggin' him on so she could have proper gossip for the east side of the swamp.

"Dat was God throwin' salt over her shoulder, is what dat was."

They respected the old man, but this wasn't the Pa Campbell they knew.

Ma Campbell patted his shoulder. She'd given him his fair share of time to embarrass himself, but she really didn't want him to start rattlin' off about—

"Seals and spells and yellow letters! They're all over this place! Picked some up myself a'ready! I tell you the wrath of the gods of every religion is on us! They gave us a garden and we ruined it. Furdermore, dose two teenagers who died in dat dere hole, theah spirits are thirsty. And all that waada, won't quench it! Ha! But you wait! There will be more tears than rain in these parts. So run away, greedy men and women. Take your greed with you!"

The whole time he's glarin' at Mai's mother and the fishermen, who he thought was his major competition in the business that he no longer ran. You could see that Parkinson's wasn't Pa's only problem. He was just plain losin' it. Ma Campbell grabbed the chair handles and spun the old man around. In the sharp turn he caught my eye and started screamin' at me.

"Skid! You ol' Jonah! I told you, and you told *no one*? Now see the sign! Ha!"

A cold streak did a dash from my head to my bells. Last thing I wanted was to look like I was part of Pa Campbell's demented rantin', especially in front of Mai. As his chair rolled back into the mornin' mist and the crowd dissolved from the banks of the creek, I saw it. The sign. The creek, the whole, entire creek that fed the bayou in front of our house since we were born, was now pouring down into the sinkhole where the Benet boys died. The full flow of the water was literally disappearin' into the hole and makin' a hollow sound.

The riverbed beyond the sinkhole was emptied, but still wet, and some poor minnows were marooned on smooth river stones, still flappin' their gills. This happened overnight. It was like our little river lost its way in the dark.

"That last earthquake must have caused it. Don't get too close."

Moms was tryin' to sound like Tony. He was a city boy by then. This was the first time we wouldn't hear the scientific chapter and verse of why this happened. I would have to try and figure it out. Frico wasn't interested in fallin' in, so he held on to a tree on the bank and leant over to look into the hole. Moms got hysterical. And for the first time I heard that boy stand up to Valerie Beaumont and tell her to relax. After all, I was nearly fifteen, and he was a year and more older than me.

Moms lit a breakfast cigarette and walked away, turnin' back twice when she saw Frico holdin' on to the tree with one hand and me holdin' on to his other arm and reachin' over further to look down into this strange thing. The water was way down in the sinkhole now. You couldn't see the surface once the creek poured in. Frico spoke between grunts.

"I hear this happened in Florida one time."

"Yeah?"

"Yeah, the ground swallowed up a whole river."

"After an earthquake?"

"Hm. Don't know, but..."

"By the way, on Sinkhole Night, and the last earthquake, all that shakin' started out in the yard – under Moms' feet."

He sucked his teeth. I felt his grip loosen.

"Pull me up."

I waited till I was completely vertical again before I challenged him.

"I'm tellin' you. I was there. Outside with her. Just last week."

"This is goin' to starve the bayou that gives us all the catfish and crawfish you scarf down. Why would *momma* do that?"

"Ha-ha. I notice you ain't sayin' she couldn't. You're just sayin' she *didn't*. Big difference."

"Big deal."

He was gettin' that tired look in his eyes again. I felt the Art Fair flyer in my pocket and changed the subject. He threw pebbles in the hole like he'd rather be doin' somethin' else, while he listened to me talk about the Fair.

"Some of these things are bogus, so you can't guarantee me winnin' the five grand. But I'll do it. Sounds like fun. Just get me a coupla things."

CHARCOAL
6 BLUE PENCILS
SHARPENER
CONSTRUCTION PAPER
ALL-PURPOSE GLUE
1 DRAWING PEN
GEOMETRY SET
LARGE ERASER
T-SQUARE
FRENCH CURVE
COCA-COLA
SNICKERS
PISTACHIOS

Damn. Didn't see that superstar backstage list comin'. So I went in to ask Doug to up-front the money on the project. He was out at the sinkhole earlier, but went back into the house in a hurry.

"I got nothin', Skid. And you shouldn't be fixin' to spend anythin' on foolishness now. These are serious times and this swamp ain't what it used to be. See that hole this mornin'? Well, that was my cue to come back in here and start crunchin' numbers. See how much we need to get on up outta this hellhole."

I could have told him that Moms been savin' from our runnin' Pa Campbell's catch-and-sell seafood business, but he was in one of those moods. So I borrowed a few chickens from the yard and sold them to the Lam Lee Hahn Floatin' Market when Moms wasn't lookin'. One of the younger Vietnamese fishermen pretended he didn't understand English. I wasn't barterin'. I needed cash.

Three days later we waited two hours for Tony to drive into the swamp on his first visit since movin' out to New O'lins. He said he'd take us into the city and show us around and help us shop for art supplies for the project even though I didn't bother lettin' him in on the secret agenda behind the whole thing. Doug said he'd come along. Now Tony was behavin' like a big shot. He had his friend's ride, a Honda Accord, and was playin' that Tears for Fears song about rulin' the world. The car came down the slope, but he didn't get out. He had white shoes on.

"What the hell? Where's the creek?"

"Long story," Doug told him. "You can hear it on the way."

"How's Momma?"

"She's at work. Let's go."

"Dang, this place looks different."

"You been gone only a month man, just stop."

"Yeah and look how y'all made it go to waste, dang."

"Just drive."

Tony smelt like the city: English Leather and cement. There was also somethin' else in the air there. Somethin' burnin'. And it wasn't just the asphalt and rubber. I couldn't tell what it was. I just knew that the swamp and the city smelt different. Anyway, it was Tony's girl's new car, I figured, what with the red pumps and leg warmers behind the driver's seat, the purple-hair Troll hangin' on the rearview and the stacks of Photo Romance magazines we had to share the back seat with. But the sound system was his idea, no doubt.

We told him about the quake and the creek and waited for his take on it again, but he was too busy bellowin' out the chorus of the song to explain anythin' to us. He was yappin' about city things like parallel parkin' and mergin' into traffic. He wanted to take a road trip to Silicon Valley with a group of his former high-school friends. His pals took and developed photos of the road trips he'd been on with them since he left the swamp: Silicon Valley, California, palm trees everywhere. New York. A rash of buildin's and the Empire State in the middle, stabbin' the sky like a big ol' syringe. Construction happenin' on every corner. Peter Grant said tourists go to Manhattan just to take pictures of the advertising. Then there was a picture of this flood of taxis rushin' past a cathedral. All that yellow made the world look like I borrowed Backhoe's 1960s San Tainos sunshades.

"Hey we should take a road trip! The Great Beaumont Escape."

I didn't say anything. The last "Beaumont whatever-it-was" left me pissed off. Suddenly, Tony shoved a camera at Frico.

"Happy Birthday when it comes!"

The camera was second-hand, but Frico's eyes bugged out and a big ol' grin flashed across his face. Seein' the guy actually smile was a rare thing. The camera had a long lens on it and a filter and everything. Frico turned the lens into the sky and took a couple of shots just as we zoomed under the massive first overpass. City-boy Tony chaperoned us to places where we could get the stuff from Frico's list: bookstore, corner store and then to the library to get a photocopy of a map of New O'lins.

We stopped at a diner somewhere along the Mississippi. Through the window I could see cranes hundreds of feet high reachin' down and offloadin' containers from ships on the khaki-coloured river. I kept askin' Tony questions, but he was shushin' me all the time, cos some infomercial-type message was on the diner TV about that same thing Pa Campbell blabbered about: natural-gas extraction in the swamps. They had guys in pristine white shirts talkin' into the camera. They had on white helmets with little green logos on them. There was always a fresh, grassy field and pretty blue sky behind them. But in the background there'd also be a metal tower in every scene. Tony said the tower was a drillin' rig for gas or oil. I didn't have nothin' to say, so I told him that if they were gonna be diggin' around, I hoped they'd find some of the grimoire seals that Pops planted in the ground.

Tony stopped watchin' TV.

"Seals? We should be more concerned about the fracking and the chemicals they must be dumping around there. It's time for everybody to leave that swamp."

I agreed with him. But sometimes he sounded as crazy as ol' Pa Campbell with his science mumbo-jumbo. Sure the swamp was lookin' shabby, and everything looked contaminated, but he had no right to talk, since he's the one who bailed out and left us there.

Then, sittin' beside him in his slick city clothes, it came to me: Tony Beaumont hated lookin' and feelin' like a swamp boy. And I kinda felt the same way sometimes. I mean, even though we went to school in the city and hung out around it, we were still *aliens* to New O'lins. Take our shoes, for example. They were a dead giveaway. While everybody in the diner, includin' Tony, was in white Nikes or Adidas or whatever, we had on some strange waterproof, half-muddy footwear that they wear on boats, for godssake. The kind of boots that don't go with T-shirts. To prove my point, two punks looked across at us from their table and snickered. And I just lost it.

"See you in the swamps... soon!" I shouted across the table. And it was a really dumb thing to say – and I really meant the whole entire city, but in their ears it sounded like some kind of threat. So one of them, the one who looked like his parents gave him everything, including a big ol' overbite, he said he was goin' to call a cop, so we left our lunch in a hurry.

Tony couldn't wait to drop us all off back in the mud, and this time he stopped all the way up at the train tracks just because we made him hurry his lunch at one of the "best hangout spots in town". Well, when we came down the slopes with our hands full of drawin' paper, we saw a squad car and wondered if those punks had gotten them to follow us. But then we saw Pa Campbell out in the yard cussin' at the officers. He was wavin' his arms and tryin' to roll over them with his wheelchair. His old TV set was out in the yard sittin' in the dirt. He'd gone nuts and shot the thing full of holes. Said it was now dangerous to watch TV, cos no one's tellin' the truth any more, especially the news. He screamed at the officer that they shouldn't take his rifle, cos it was on "Condition One" since the shindig.

"I need that rifle! One bullet can buy you some extra breathin' out in dese parts dese days. Out heah's becomin' worse than the city! I tell my wife, we need to be on Condition One, like it's Beirut! Cocked, locked and ready to rock! Smell that air, officers. That's death's bad breath. I – need – my – rifle!"

Man, I hated to see him like that. But when the cop said they were takin' his rifle and ammunition to undergo tests and they wanted to question him about his friendship with Alrick Beaumont, it all fell into place for us, all at once. Pa cussed and frothed at the mouth. The cops took his gun and left him alone, cos he looked insane. Then he stared into the sky with his usual cataract stare. One shaky arm shot out from beside him and went up to heaven, pointin'. He let out a yell that made your bones rattle. We looked up, and the clouds were curdled milk. Now that was depressin', but not scary.

"Look! *Look!*" We all strained to see what Pa was pointin' at. He leapt from the chair as Ma was pullin' it backwards. He landed in the dirt and crawled towards the house frantically, lookin' over his shoulder in horror. The officers looked up, their fingers twitchin' beside their side arms. Then we saw it. A thing flying. Emerging from the clouds. A majestic sky creature comin' at us from the north. It was a spirit, an animal and a machine in one. It was black and then gunmetal-grey when the sun came through the clouds and hit it, but the skin gave off no glisten. The creature slid over our heads without a sound. Dark wings two hundred feet wide, body seventy feet long, Frico guessed. Bigger than an archangel, I thought. Doug looked for jets. There were none behind it. All we saw was the shadow of the thing running along the ground towards us like a liquid. I felt cold when it hit us. The shadow seemed to rustle through Pa Campbell's sugar cane and slip into the bayou. It disappeared among the trees out in the water, and in seconds the creature itself was a dot over the Gulf.

The cops had helped Pa Campbell to his feet, and Ma had just calmed him down, when the creature came back at us, swoopin' down lower this time. It was so low you felt a hum in your chest. The monster dipped towards the trees. We saw the massive wings, and what looked like two eyes and a mouth. We waited for claws to come out. This was a chargin' blackbird, an angry eagle, a stingray – and then somethin' else.

"It's a *bat*!" Pa was lookin' out from behind his fingers now.

He leapt from the chair again and tried to wrangle the rifle from the officer's grasp, but failed. He was face down in the dirt when the monster dropped in on top of us again. The shadow swallowed both houses, their backyards, part of the bayou and all the people on the ground. When the thing zoomed overhead, all the trees bent over backwards. Our clothes fluttered. Tin roofs rattled. We saw that the monster had a smooth underbelly, and it whistled as it went by. And that smell, that strange city smell was trailin' behind it.

Ma Campbell couldn't raise the man up by herself, so she lay on the ground, holdin' his face and grimacin' at the madness in her husband's eyes. The officers were busy cheerin' as the thing flew away. We Beaumonts all looked towards the train tracks instead of followin' the beast into the sky. Secretly, we wanted to know that Tony had seen those wings on his way back into the city. We wanted him to turn that car around and come runnin' back to explain this shape our eyes had never seen. But the train tracks were quiet, 'cept for a willow tree out at the very edge of L-Island, still writhin' in the wind, like a tail that lost its lizard.

Then those cops stood there high-fivin' about this thing, while Pa was still gaggin' on what he just saw. They argued about what they thought it was, and one even said he saw *another* UFO before, over in California. But like Backhoe Benet said, the police don't know anything. That was no UFO. And if Tony didn't come back and say what that thing was… and if it looked like a bat and flew like a bat, then a bat it was goin' to be. And any kind of bat in the daylight is a bad, bad sign.

Ma Campbell cried all night. We heard her above the low thunder that complained over the Gulf but never fulfilled the wonderful threat of rain. It was as if the wing of that thing got snagged on some black thunderhead clouds and dragged them in over our heads. We waited for the beatdown. In the flicker of blue lightning over the ocean, I swear I could see all the way to the edge of the world – the curve of that glass bowl they keeps us in.

Moms got up and took a piece of rope and made a clothes line inside of the shack. Then she threw a bedsheet over it and pulled that sheet all the way across the room, separatin' herself from us boys. We heard sobbin', but we dared not ask her about what was already becomin' quite clear. Pa Campbell's bullet had found his friend's leg when he took that shot in the dark at the shindig.

And that night after we saw the big ol' day bat, Frico started the drawin' for the competition, sittin' at Alrick Beaumont's desk. We had two weeks to do it. And even with all the strange goings-on, I was as excited as a hen layin' multi-coloured eggs. I saw when Frico took up the T-square, like a cross. He laid the head flush against the work table. His breathin' became shallow. He dusted the drawing paper with a bit of cornmeal for cleanliness. And when he raised the blue pencil and drew a line with his left hand, I stopped my breath for a beat. That was the Beaumont line in the sand, the end of an error, the startin' point of the fulfilment of a lesser-known prophecy. And it was right on time too, cos you could see it was happenin' on the night when the darkness had just gotten deeper in the room.

Twenty-Three

That summer was full of cicadas. And suffocatin' heat. And Pa Campbell mumblin' nonsense under his breath. But I was happy. It must have been ninety-six degrees under the trees, but I was cool as ever. I could feel a celebration comin' on, like the one that was happenin' in the city. Yep, round about that time, the Pope was in the New O'lins on a ten-day visit. Welcome banners were everywhere. People lined the streets. Even those who weren't Catholic came out to see the cool popemobile rollin' from the French Quarter to the Super-dome. I heard that some people cried when the shadow of the vehicle passed over them and laughed when the Pope tried on a sparkly Mardi-Gras mask with big, purple-and-yellow feathers on it. Ma Campbell couldn't contain herself. She came back into the swamp wearin' a white rosary tangled up in all her usual hoodoo talismans, sayin' that the Papa's visit was the best thing she ever saw happen to New O'lins. It didn't matter that she had only gone to the lakefront mass with Mai's mother for a couple of hours.

Pa stayed with us while she was gone. It was awkward. Moms fed him boiled vegetables and dandelion tea. She kept him cool and made sure he took his meds. You could see she wanted to ask him things about the shootin', but you really shouldn't do like the police and try to interrogate a person who's sick and tired – even if it's about your family.

Anyway, to be honest, it was as if Ma Campbell had stayed out the whole ten days. One day was a long time to sit on the porch with Pa Campbell those days. I kept myself busy by movin' his wheelchair from time to time, playin' hide-and-seek with the sun. But I couldn't ask him anything, and all his stories had dried up. At least he made me know he was alive every hour with a few ramblin' sentences, or maybe a shudder every so often.

"Skid. Those bugs. After a couple years or so, they come up out of the goddamn ground. They shake the grave dirt off themselves. Then they break their own backs open and come on out with a new body. And they leave theah carcasses behind, like a shell, just standin' there still, clutchin' a tree and starin' at nothin'. Meanwhile the new body grows red eyes and green wings and flies away like they don't know that other dead guy."

I didn't know all that about cicadas at the time – I thought it was only crabs that did that – but I wasn't goin' to ask him anything more. Even though I'm not nearly as superstitious as him, I felt it in my bones that Pa Campbell was fixin' to be a bad omen on Frico's work. That's why this whole time I never told him anything about it. I knew where he was goin' with this insect story, so I tried to change the subject.

"That cloth... what is it?"

"Cherokee. Beadwork and cotton. About sixty years old, this one."

I looked over at the cloth and then followed the plait of his white hair down his shoulder to the place on his finger where that turquoise ring used to be.

"Are you..."

"Not a single Cherokee bone is in my body, kid. I'm Cajun."

Then he turned to me shakin', more cataracky than ever.

I did a drum roll in my head, cos I knew he was just warmin' up. Then he brought in the violins.

"I spent my woman-chasin' years also chasin' tribes across the Americas: from Delaware to the Rockies to Ecuador and Peru into Tierra del Fuego, where the world ends. I hopped around the Caribbean: San Tainos, Puerto Rico, Jamaica, Haiti. Sat in volcanoes and caves and in the rain and listened.

I heard different languages, but the same voice, from the people befo' my eyes and from dose long dead and gone. So I marked myself with a symbol from every tribe. Because they were all the truth. Then, I left my heart all over the place like lost luggage, kid. I went nuts. And I'm so glad I did."

Oh man. Guess I asked for it. I thought that was the end of it, but right before nightfall he brought up the Benet boys again.

"Those two boys. They had Taino in them. From their mother. So when they died, they went to *Coay Bay*. The place for spirits. Know what that means?"

I didn't really care what that meant. Especially at night. Five minutes passed. Maybe he forgot his train of thought.

"That means... That means right now they're comin' back around this place after the sun disappears, like bats, lookin' for fruits to eat!"

Aw, man—

"You got to know them different, kid. You can tell an Op'a – dat's a spirit – you can tell 'em different from a live human. If they have a face and a navel, they're a live human. If not, you're screwed. Likewise every mornin' you get up, check for your goddamn face and your navel!"

He snickered.

Well, that old man knew he ruined my night with that Taino Op'a story. See, even though my pops used to tell me all kinds of Cajun junk and Pa himself had a couple crazy beliefs, there was nothin' was as scary as the idea that there was somethin' lookin' like a human bein', walkin' around like a human bein', but without a face to *identify* them as a human bein'. Hell, no.

So when I saw the Mitsubishi Montero pull up with Ma Campbell inside it, I couldn't wait to roll Pa gently off our porch – no lie. Mai waved at me from the back seat. I didn't know she had gone to the city. I'd have to have a word with her about that. She didn't smile, but maybe she was just tired after bein' among thousands of people at that lakefront mass.

Everything was weird, anyways. Not even the Montero had the usual wet tyres, on account of having no creek to drive through. It got weirder. That night I had a dream about Mai. She was in a church. She was walkin' up the aisle with a white veil over her face, carryin' a bouquet of water lilies. I was excited and waitin' at the altar for her. Then, when I looked, I saw that her white veil was turnin' black all of a sudden, like some invisible hand was pourin' ink on top of her head. I tried callin' out to her. But you know that inside most nightmares they don't allow shoutin'. And that girl, she just walked up and told me to be still and stood there happy with her bright eyes shinin' under the black veil like it was all OK. I could feel everything she was feelin', and it was beautiful. Like between us there was a new, secret language that had no words in it. And when it was time for me to put the ring on her, she raised her hand, and I saw that she had fourteen fingers, seven on each hand, fully formed with bones and everything.

"It's OK, Skid, I just want to help," she said, and smiled.

And I jumped up out of the bed and landed on the wood floor of the swamp shack fully vertical, wide awake and walkin' towards Frico. He stopped sketchin' the city and looked over at me.

"Hey, easy there, man. You really got time for a bad dream? I thought you were supposed to be helpin' me with this."

I sat back down on the bed and held my head in my hands. Moms stirred in her sleep and told us to quiet down. I got Frico a Coke and told him the dream.

"Frankly, dreamin' 'bout marriage means death, Skid – ask Momma. And funeral means marriage. So go dream about your girlfriend's funeral, and you should be fine."

He was being a jerk as usual, but he knew he could get away with it, especially now. On any other occasion I woulda gone to war with him in the middle of the night for sayin' that about Mai, the same way he knocked me out over Teesha Grey. But it would be a new day soon. No time for all that.

Frico turned up the lamp, and I saw the sketches. Oowee. Brilliant. He was workin' on the New O'lins map. But he'd also done a few close-up buildin' sketches based on some black-and-white photos he took in the city. He also took photos of the swamp. But when I asked him what the swamp photos were for he said:

"Just for reference."

Well, I didn't like that kind of short answer. It made me wonder if he was seein' through my whole plan. But I didn't sweat it. Frico Beaumont was finally goin' through with the plan. Even though he didn't know it. And even though I wasn't even goin' to give him a dime. Well not before we won that five grand, at least.

Anyway, this boy was not just an artist, he was a frickin' *architect*. His sketches showed he was clearin' land. He was movin' highways and sailin' them over into the swamp. There was a library and post office and a train station.

Then, when I thought he was done, he took the construction paper and glue and colours from his paints and built a wicked scale model of L-Island. Lam Lee Hahn was as big as a Walmart, and an all-inclusive hotel called The Beaumont Resort stretched from the bayou to the edge of the coast. Prime beach-front property, raised above sea level. Frico measured elevation and distance on the map. One inch equals just over a mile and a half in real life. Damn, that's some stuff I didn't even think about. Well, just when I thought we were on our way to winnin' this New O'lins 2020 hands down, Miss Teesha Grey, she appeared in the swamp the night before the competition. Aw, man. Frico would have ignored her I think, but she came there with some guy. The dude was obviously drivin' his dad's car, and she asked him for a ride into the swamp just to make Frico feel jealous. Well, that wuss Frico fell for it and went outside to talk to her. They were out there for two full hours – holdin' hands. Then when they started kissin', the poor sucker in the car honked the horn and Moms stuck her head out and said it was time Teesha headed home. I was ticked off that, with just hours to go, he'd gone off and left the future unfinished. Your girl is sweet, man, but makin' up can wait – c'mon now.

The next day Tony was late again. Said he had to get his hair cut. Anyway, he turned up for us in canvas shoes and a Miami Vice sports jacket in the hot sun. I looked down at my dirty boots and went and changed into my new Chuck Taylors that Moms said was only for back-to-school.

Tony took us to the library in Algiers where the judgin' would take place. Well, the long and short is: we didn't get the five grand. We placed second. *Second.* Can you believe that? Some kid from Plaquemines took it home. Got beaten by one or two lousy points. But Moms, she was proud as ever. She got a big ol' picture frame made with a compartment for each sketch, and she put those second-place drawin's in it and put it up where our few visitors could see it.

That stuff was so cool I can't believe we didn't win. Anyway, what really mattered was that the thing was now written in stone, so to speak – so any day now...

But every day after that was like a summer solstice. *Long.* I twisted and turned on the bed all night listenin' to that aquamarine paint crack and curl off the wood inside the shack.

Nights weren't easy on Moms neither, 'specially since my pops' disappearance. Worryin' about Tony livin' in the city and his road-trippin' only made it worse. Many times she would just sit straight up in her bed and throw punches with her eyes still closed. Damn near clobbered me a few times when I tried to wake her up.

Shattered nerves – that's what the doctor said. He recommended Moms drop some of her workin' hours in the city. Mai's mother recommended ginseng and rest. Ma Campbell anointed her with some water blessed at the lakefront mass.

Pa Campbell said it was too late. He said it was clear that the Op'as of Broadway and Squash had finally entered into our house. He stared out at the lake from his chair.

"Captain Backhoe should have seen to it. Those boys needed a traditional Taino burial, in a cave. Or at least a Cimarrón-style wake. He shoulda put nails in those feet and tied their big toes together. He shoulda leant up their beds on the wall and burned some frankincense."

That did it. I was never gonna sleep again, so I decided to have a nightwatch like we did back in the day. That good ol' tamarind tree would be my lookout point to see any evidence of the city advancin'.

Well, I was up there every single night and didn't see nothin' except that one night when I heard a rumble and saw lights, but it was a stupid freight train makin' fun of me. So I climbed down and ran beside it and flung rocks and cursed it until it disappeared like a snake in the dark.

Then one evenin' before sunset a bunch of guys came into the swamp in an official-lookin' eighteen-wheeler. They stopped over on the Benet side of the tracks. They had a huge sign, some equipment and no time to waste. Big steel pipes came out of the back of the eighteen-wheeler. They laid the pipes on the ground and started joinin' them together like they were buildin' the bottom of some kind of scaffoldin'.

Over the next few days they put up a chain-link fence and then dropped the sign behind it. I told Frico about the goings-on, and said that we should go check out the sign and everything, but he was busy writin' love letters to Teesha Grey. Yeah, love letters. Now, don't get excited, cos look, I went ahead and read one of those things with a flashlight under the bed when everyone was asleep. Damn, that boy should learn to spell. But really the love letter wasn't nothin' hot and nasty or anythin'. More about *birds* than pretty words. That girl had my brother by the bells, I tell ya. You could see he was tryin' to show interest in her environmental stuff. Her birthday was comin' up, and he bought her a Hallmark card and everythin', and he was taking his time to find the right words. Aww, sweet. So far he'd gotten to the "Dear Teesha" part. Pathetic.

Anyway, I didn't bother Doug neither, cos he was busy calculatin' how much fish and shrimp we'd have to sell to give Pa his share and still have money to leave the swamp.

But soon I didn't have to call anybody's attention to the fact that we had real trouble in the swamp. Our part of the bayou was dying. The water in front of our house was low and stagnant just like the Benet side had always been. Moms banned us from goin' anywhere near the water, not even to set a trot line or a pot. She said the summer days of jumpin' off the roof into the bayou were over. And if we were fishin' or swimmin', it was to be in the lake towards the Gulf or further east in the swamp. Soon Al Dubois came callin', sayin' he wasn't seein' much swamp seafood comin' in, and he had customers. So we were up a creek. We could always find somethin' to feed ourselves, but hell, we had a client to satisfy.

But by the end of August we had bigger problems than supplyin' Al Dubois. Those men came back in the eighteen-wheeler. They crossed over the train tracks and marched into L-Island. We tried to talk to them, but they tramped past us like they owned the place. They put on yellow rubber suits with the same logo from that TV ad in the diner and waded into the mud and water in front of our house. They got stuck a coupla times, and one of them had a paddle lookin' around for gators. I was expectin' them to drop into a sinkhole any minute, but finally, after lots of curse words, they stopped in waist-deep water and together they pressed a long cylinder deep into the mud and then pulled it out. Bubbles came up from the bayou floor. The men looked at the bottom of the cylinder and chatted back and forth for a few minutes about what they saw. The way they hurried away I knew it was somethin' important. Doug walked after them and asked why they were there.

"We don't know why *you're* still here," is what one of them told him, like a jerk. Moms tried to contact Benet, but he had gone to Europe, she heard.

Just before we went back to school, it seemed like the whole swamp was shrivellin'.The ground around us cracked into uneven mud tiles. Raw salt glistened on the soil. We were in the middle of a summer drought and with the death of our creek, it was gettin' worse.

We weren't the only ones who saw it. Every day from up in the tree I could see Mai's mother, directin' fishermen over at Lam Lee Hahn. They were in a hurry. Just reapin' shrimp and cullin' crabs. The boats of the Floatin' Market were on land, and there was no cookin' going on. I told myself they were gettin' ready for a Vietnamese holiday or somethin'. I decided to go get dressed and ask Mai, but when I got into our house the whole damn room was full of chickens. Chicken crap was on Pops' workbench, on the bed, and a couple o' hens were goin' wild, jumpin' off the fridge and the stove. Outside, Calvin's kids barked like crazy. Doug and Frico were standin' on top of the workbench holding the broom and a mop like spears.

"Stay still, Skid. Look in the back doorway."

A twelve-foot alligator was more than halfway into our house, and she meant business. Doug said it came up Pa Campbell's wheelchair ramp, but that would mean she'd walked through the house once before front to back, while we were sleepin'. Shivers. This was one hungry mother – and maybe the same one that took my father's leg. She looked the part – but that critter also looked so desperate I felt sorry for her. She hissed and took a step inside. A cluckin' hen dropped her wings and moved between her chicks and the seven-hundred-pound pair of scissors. I could see more gators convergin' on the back porch and out in the mud, like a serious alligator mafia meetin' was goin' down.

Now, Moms for some annoyin' reason always put away the rifle when she went to work, even though Doug is responsible

231

and a good shot. What's worse, Frico's sketchin' material was on the bed – on the other side of the room. I wasn't sure what he could do in this situation if he had them, anyway. So we just looked at each other and lit out through the front door. Yessir, we surrendered our house to those lizards without even discussin' it. And all we heard from outside was snappin' and cacklin' and stumblin' around. We alerted Ma. She couldn't come over. Pa Campbell was really ill, she said. We ran around the back of our house and tried to lure the monsters out from a safe distance.

Then Frico pointed. "That's why."

We turned around, and the water in the bayou was razor-sharp, reptiles everywhere as usual. But around them, dead fish and dead frogs by the score. Bluegill, catfish, bass all floatin' belly up. Some of our chickens were keeled over in the same spot where they went to drink. The gators were all bunched up in one spot, uninterested in all that dead meat and lookin' a little sick themselves.

"Somethin's wrong."

We stood there, shocked, as if we just landed on a nasty planet. Turkey vultures swooped down and dipped into the slime, bobbin' their heads up and down like they knew somethin' we didn't. The chickens got out of the house and ran off. The gator came out and splashed back into the sludge. They all jostled against each other, mud-covered. Then one big-head male, he grudgin'ly snapped at a dead fish, and a war began. Those killers churned the muddy water into brown butter. When the struggle stopped, we saw that the sludge continued boilin'. Tiny bubbles, by the thousands, came up to the surface.

When Moms came home and we showed her the bubbles with a flashlight, she just turned on her heels.

"We can't sleep here tonight."

As if beddin' down on Ma Campbell's floor was any better than sleepin' with a gator. But it wasn't about being safe from the lizards. The bubbles in the muddy water was the trouble. It was gas. And whatever kind of gas it was, it had killed off nearly all the fish and was forcin' the gators out.

The followin' mornin' we hopped onto our landing with T-shirts over our noses, just in time to see one of them big beasts havin' breakfast. He was a terrible-lookin' thing. A cranky machine with dark-green, corrugated steel skin on his back. He might as well have been put together with rivets.

Then all that body armour just trailed off and turned into the chainsaw tail, slicin' through the surface of the brown slime. Maan, that critter raised up his head slowly, like two clasped hands with teeth between them, ready to grab whatever God would give. We didn't see that the bastard was actually after somethin' until he rushed out of the slime and snapped up one of Calvin's kids, the one with the white patch on his foot like a sock – my favourite. The puppy had fallen asleep under the house, much too close to the edge.

We clapped and cussed loudly. But that gator had clamped down solid. He was reversin' with the dog's head in his snout, and the poor back legs were powerless to do anythin' but walk with the lizard. Then, almost as if waitin' to make sure that we saw, the gator paused, adjusted his jaws around the poor puppy, and flung himself into a death roll. Everythin' went red and bubbly.

Twenty-Four

Close to the end of summer, we officially moved in with Ma and Pa Campbell and gave up livin' in our house for good. It was a breeze. No, really. Too much breeze. Ma kept the large wooden windows open all day for "fresh air", so the wind from the lake would come through and disturb everything you were tryin' to do. We got used to it though. What Moms couldn't get used to was us growin' up so suddenly. It had been a while since I really looked at my face properly, what with the smashed mirror at our house and all. Now, in Ma Campbell's old-people magnifyin' mirror, I realized I was gettin' a moustache. A real one. And some fuzz was stickin' out my chin too. Typical goofy-lookin' teenager – but at least my pimples were all gone. It was about time too, cos Lord knows I was tired of that old woman Ma Campbell hollerin' out every mornin' "Did ya do it? Did ya do it yet, Skid?" Now, the "it" she was referrin' to was her "acne remedy". I couldn't even tell my mother about it. That old woman called me one mornin' and told me to catch my own pee in my hand, mid-stream, and wash my face with it while it was still warm. 'The hell. Said she guaranteed my face would clear up in one week tops. Yah. I never answered her about all that crazy advice. And it didn't work anyway, so whatever.

More beards gathered around the table at Ma and Pa. Breakfast was meagre on account of the lack of fishin' and more mouths to feed from one pot. But we made do. It was the only time we held hands around a table and I didn't feel afraid. Ma Campbell prayed for about five minutes. Meanwhile I'm holdin' Pa Campbell's hand flat on the table and it's shakin' so much I wonder if he's doin' it himself. Meanwhile,

Calvin's kids kept walkin' in and out of the house during breakfast, like they used to do at my house when we were ea-tin'. That ticked off the old lady, who thought that everythin' with four legs except a table and a chair needed to stay the hell outside. Moms on the other hand saw dogs and pets as fam-ily. She had this notebook where she kept notes, recipes and dates. She wrote down the date that the gator killed one of the puppies. When six of her yard fowls disappeared (on the Floating Market), she wrote that down too, even though with all her conjurin' she couldn't tell where they went. Come to think of it, maybe it was because we were all gettin' older why she always talked to the chickens and the puppies, cos they still had the baby energy inside of 'em. She always said the four children she had are somewhere else, and the men before her at the table are impostors with facial hair and arm sweat.

Well, after breakfast, Peter Grant popped into the swamps. One of his old man's spotters was drivin' the truck. It was the Saturday before the new semester, so I thought he just wanted to say what he was plannin' to do on the first day of school. He brought Suzy Wilson. Moms asked me how I could have visitors over when I don't even have decent water for them to drink. The water was just an excuse. Moms had taken one look at Suzy Wilson and saw Fiola Lambert's face. The whole time we were on the porch, Valerie Beaumont didn't sit down. And Suzy prob'ly felt it. Moms just kept starin' at the girl, and I was glad that Suzy and me hadn't become an item back at Long Lake Elementary. Cos maybe by the time we grew up and got to the altar, she would be Flawless Fiola in the flesh. And Moms would probably have to gouge the bride's eyes out.

Anyway, Peter came by to tell me there was a lot of talk in the city about the swamplands. People were movin' out of some places and into New O'lins. Well, we knew that already. We'd seen strange activity, and I knew we couldn't stay, but I reckoned Frico's spell would kick in and the city would be ad-vancin' before we even budged. Of course, I decided against tellin' Peter and Suzy that Frico's art-competition entry was really a conjuration. And I didn't bother mentionin' anything more about Frico's powers, period. If Peter Grant of all people didn't think that face-fixin' incident was a miracle, then so be it. I was done tryin' to convince people. They'd prob'ly just talk about it in French in front of my face and be all sceptical – so, no.

Soon Suzy starts feelin' sick, so the spotter guy revved up the truck and they drove out. Peter told me before he left that if we needed anythin' or needed to bug out of the swamps real quick I should just let him know and he'd have his old man get a truck there in a hurry, no problem. The boy is cool. Anyway, they couldn't leave soon enough, cos that bein' the final summer weekend we had lots to do – and then some.

Moms wanted us to move the few remainin' things that were in our house over to Pa Campbell's place. Now, their place was bigger, so I could see how the stuff could fit, but that was still too many people in one house.

Well Moms, she cleared that up right quick. "Ma and Pa are leaving."

"Leavin' to go where?"

"The city."

"But, those cops. They told him to stay put…"

"Those cops can come throw his dead body in jail if he stays here. He's very sick, and whatever is bubblin' out of that bayou isn't helping. It isn't helpin' any of us, as a matter of fact. So these are the last days here, Skid. For all of us."

She got that right. But I was still wonderin' what was takin' the city so long to move. So while me and Doug and Frico hauled things out of the house and over to Ma and Pa, I mulled the conjuration over in my head until I dropped Moms' "Home Sweet Home" lampshade halfway across the yard and it smashed into pieces. Frico walks up behind me, stoops down and hands the lampshade back to me, perfect, all in one piece. And he keeps walkin' like nothing happened.

Pause. Now, let me make this clear, real quick. Simple occurrences like Frico fixin' that lampshade perfectly before anyone even knew it got broke is what made me a believer. I never thought that we'd "fall asleep in the swamp and wake up in the city" like Pops said when he was half drunk. I didn't think the city would just pop up in the swamps in ten seconds the way I saw it in my head up in that tamarind tree when I was a kid. No, that wouldn't make sense. I was old enough to know that any kind of development was goin' to take town-plannin' and land-surveyin' and meetin's and contracts and mobilizin' people and machinery and all that yawn. But I knew the power of a good spell too. I'd seen Moms conjurin' in my house since I was born. She called on powers that turned back floods from our door or made our swamp shack stand still in a storm. Powers that cooled down a fever and chased away shadows that were sent for us. I saw Valerie Beaumont use rocks to make a circle in the yard, and she stepped into it and prayed in the rain and blue skies came back, for godssake. I used to think that this was ordinary, but thanks to Pa Campbell, I realized these were workin's that turned impossible things into somethin' as doable as dishes. So before any man moved a muscle or a machine, that was where it would all begin: in my house.

That same afternoon, I saw Mai's mother on the porch talkin' to Moms. She had brought some bougainvillea plants in Vietnamese pots and some jasmine tea for Moms' nerves. She showed Moms how to brew a cup. They looked out at the swamp and sipped and talked low about whether bitter melons and cerasee are really the same thing, and what plants can survive the salt. Then they talked about raisin' boys and girls and argued about which one was more difficult. Then they jawed about how humans are all from one place but we broke into tribes and now we have to find our way back together.

Well, after you go that deep, there's really nothin' else to say, so Mai's mother bowed to Moms. Moms hugged her.

Mai's mother didn't know what to do with her hands durin' the hug. Then I saw the fishermen comin' up from the lake in boats so silently. They had baskets draped on their shoulders. Mud crabs, about two dozen, were tied in them. Buckets of shrimp and dried fish. Large aquatic containers and chicken wire. The fishermen scurried around, and in an hour they took the chicken wire and boards and transformed the house we used to live in into a crab crawl. That's a kind of coop for keepin' crabs just like chickens. You tend to them and feed them fruits and greens till they're big and juicy and clean. One of the fishermen, that guy I sold the chickens to, he gave us a lesson in perfect English about how to grow the live mud crabs they brought for us. It wasn't safe to eat from the water any more. Now we had food for days. All we needed was rain for our gardens before they all went brown.

Then those men and women in their Sam Pan hats, they stood at the edge of our dead part of the bayou and made the sign of the cross on their chest and waded out. Some distracted the gator with food, while the others did their best to rake in as many of those dead things and passed them along in a line. We stepped in to help, but they refused. We lit one dead fish, and it burned bright blue. The fishermen dug a deep hole and buried the rest.

Twice the rain clouds came over and twice we took shelter almost sure it would be pourin' in minutes. The fishermen and women just kept workin' and lookin' up while lightning crackled everywhere. And when they were done, they just bowed and disappeared back into the water.

Twenty-Five

Moms came runnin' up from the lake after seein' the fisher-men off.

"Quick, hide!"

Tony had appeared in the swamp. He was walkin' down the slope from the train tracks. She was up for playin' jokes, even when she was tired. And who better to play one on than ol' Tony Beaumont?

Hell, last time we saw that guy, he was screechin' out of L-Island like it was almost midnight, and he was drivin' some-thin' that used to be a pumpkin. We hid beside Pa Campbell's house and watched ol' Tony Beaumont walk into L-Island with his pretty girlfriend on his arm. She was clingin' to him and lookin' all around. It must have looked like some cursed forest with all the dried-up waters and the witherin' trees. He stepped up on the porch of our house. He knocked and wait-ed. When no one answered the door, he opened it and saw chicken wire and two dozen huge, helluva mud crabs crawlin' around inside the Beaumont house, where people used to be. We could hear the door slam and Doug shouted out: "Ow!" from behind the house, the way he thought a crab would prob'ly say it. Man, you shoulda seen the sheer terror on Tony's face. Now he'd have some explainin' to do. Imagine takin' your girl to meet your whole family and – boom – your girl thinks your folks are some big ol' nasty mud crabs in a godforsaken swamp somewhere. You could see superstition givin' his logic a good ass-whoopin'. He wiped his brow and told his girl to sit on the porch for a second. He ran over to Ma Campbell and she was ready for him. That old lady just opened that door and grabbed her cheeks and looked ever so worrisome, and before he could say a word she beat him to it.

"Oh my Laaawd! Tony. You're so late!"

"What? Why? What happened?"

"Your mother and your siblin's... oh my Laaawd."

"Ma. Seriously... what!?"

"Well, don't get testy with me young man, I ain't the first-born who ran off and caused this whole calamity! Come in-side, quick!"

She looked this way and that way and pulled him inside with absolute terror in her eyes. This woman was a classic. I bet she was almost a Hollywood actress back in the day.

And when he came in and looked around and saw our fur-niture in the Campbell's place and no sign of us and Pa just sittin' there shakin', he couldn't even sit down.

Ma is lovin' every minute of this, cos she always thought the boy was too uppity and know-it-all. So she poured herself some tea and sat down and made him sweat some more bul-lets before she began.

"Those Vietnamese, Tony. They're good at everythin'. They got people who came to this country and made the best of things. Those Vietnamese fishermen over at Lam Lee Hahn, they went deep-sea-fishin' in the Gulf and they invented a new net that went so deep it caught them a nasty old mermaid."

"A what?"

"Listen, Tony, keep calm. You want some tea?"

"No, Ma. I need an explanation!"

"OK. Well, they went and caught themselves a nasty old mermaid – or a Melusine, or like what you'd call a Sirène or whatever. Those ones that sing and lure sailors to get all ship-wrecked. Well, she told them she was seven hun'erd years old and used to be French royalty, but she got cursed. Anyway, she wanted to know if they knew a conjurer in these parts who could change her back. And those fishermen were afraid o' her... so they brought her here."

"Why?"

"You mother can do stuff, Tony. I know you caught up in all your learnin' and whadeva, but you gotta make some room in theah for the natural runnin's of this earth, y'hear?"

Pa Campbell chimed in from starin' at nothin'. "Oh, yes."

"Anyway, your poor momma changed her back right quick. Right in front of us she became a beautiful dame again. Then she demanded the first-born son for a husban'. Well, your poor mother, she tried to pass off Douglas as the firstborn. Now Doug, he liked how she came up from the water – wet, naked, hefty bosom and all – so he was ready to go back into the Gulf with her. But when you're seven hun'erd years old, you cain't be fooled easy! So she smelt Douglas up and down and all around. Then she just turned aside and asked for you by name."

"By name?"

"Oh yeeesss," said Pa.

Ma lapped up the support.

"Yessir! Anthony Beaumont! Heard it with my own ears! And then, when Valerie confessed to tryin' to trick her, she just walked out the door headed for the lake, and when she got to the very edge she sang out loud, "*Ruine! Ruine! Ruine!*" – which is like "Doom! Doom! Doom!" in French. Then she looked straight into our eyes, folded her arms over her breasts, fell into the lake backwards and disappeared. She put a spell on this whole place. Me an' Pa, we old crabs already, so we couldn't be changed any further. But your sweet mother and brothers... they're so innocent. And you're so late!"

Well, I wish I could see his face, but by that time Frico and Moms and Doug, they're fightin' for the same peephole and pushed me aside, so I have to be dependin' on descriptions. Doug, he said Tony is fixin' to go crazy in about ten seconds, so we hurried back across to the crab crawl and sat on the porch right as Ma Campbell is tellin' him to shout out "Sorry!" and "Amen!" and turn around three times to break the curse. Well, if he did, none of us can tell, cos by that time we were busy meetin' his girlfriend on what used to be our porch, and she was lookin' as bewildered as ever, but fine nonetheless.

You shoulda seen the look of relief on this boy's face when he came back over there and saw us on that porch with just two legs each and no claws or beady eyes. Man, we just hung over the porch and had a good laugh at ol' Mr Logical while he took off his coat and sat down and wiped his brow and put his head in his hands and asked for some camomile and ginger tea to calm his nerves. And right in the middle of all that fun that's when the weather decided to go dark on us.

We were all inside watchin' Pa, silently laughin' at Tony and lookin' at his girl, when we smelt the earth outside being cooled. Delicious rain rappin' on the tin roof like someone arrivin' late at a closed door.

"Aw shit," said Tony in his fancy white shoes.

Moms stepped in with pots and pans and a look on her face that was more relief than excitement.

"Action, stations!"

We knew that meant we needed to hurry and set the containers to catch rain water. I grabbed a bucket and told Moms I would stick it under the run-off from the roof of the crab crawl. She told me to hurry and get back before it was a real downpour, but I had other plans. See, I thought I'd do somethin' romantic and run across to Mai in the rain, and she'd have a towel for me to dry my hair that would be all curly once the water soaked it, and we'd eat prawns and laugh. So I lit out and set the bucket at the crab crawl and took off my shoes. I was about to run out in the rain when I saw that ol' Fricozoid had left his glasses on the porch ledge. I hesitated, cos I remembered last time he put a spell on me over these specs, so I wanted to run back and give them to him, but then I'd be caught by Moms and my romantic mission would be off.

So I'm there contemplatin' while the rain was comin' down. I put on Frico's glasses to mock the guy, and I had to grab on to the porch to steady myself. Not because they're bifocals, but because it was as if my eyes, my eyes were opened and I could see *everything* that the Sketcher saw. The dying swamp was a different world. A wonderful world. Nut grass wasn't nut grass any more. Cypress and oaks were giant trees in their prime. No Spanish moss. Just over the porch the bayou was perfect and clear and ripplin' and full of water hyacinths again. I turned around and the shacks were new and the rain-drops on the roofs had turned into petals – thousands of pet-als floatin' down instead of fallin' hard. The broken creek was complete again – our tamarind tree was in bloom. Mai was walkin' across the footbridge in her Vietnamese *ao dai* dress, coloured petals slidin' off her red bamboo umbrella. I couldn't wait to see what she looked like up close, so I ran out in the floral rain, and the grass was misty and as soft as ever.

I met her just as she stepped off the bridge, and she was perfect. She twirls her umbrella, and that pretty Vietnamese song with no translation is playin' from the sky.

I swear that wearin' Frico's glasses is the best wagonin' I ever did. When we get to the crab-crawl porch, I run through the streams pourin' off the roof and try to help her up the steps. But she stops out in the rain and she's not movin'. So I whip the glasses off and put them back on the porch ledge. When I look up, she's standin' there lookin' sad, in a white top and blue Levi's. The red umbrella is cold steel, and the Vi-etnamese song drowns in the water whippin' the metal roof.

"What's the problem? Come on up."

She caught herself, but she stayed out in the rain. She tried to smile.

"Did you like the *lan-yap*? The men brought enough for a lot of weeks."

"Uhm, yes, we have a huge crab crawl now."

"Uh-huh. I heard. Did they tell you how to feed them?"

"They told us everything. So... with all that lan-yap, does that mean I'm a real customer now and not your *petit chou* any more?"

"Uh-huh. I have to go," she says.

"OK, I'll come with you."

"No you can't. I mean, my mother says we're leaving. Leaving the swamp."

I stepped down towards her. She took one step back, farther into the rain.

"Well, we're all leavin'. Even Ma and Pa are leavin' tomorrow, but we'll stay in touch, right? What about the shop — where are you movin' to... the city?"

"Closer to it. But you don't understand, Skid. I want to help..."

I tried to interrupt to tell her the dream, but she counter-interrupted me.

"Listen, Skid. The whole swamp is turning upside down. The earthquakes are increasing. We have sinkholes in our shrimp ponds now. We don't want to wait until one opens under the house."

"I know what's causin' the earthquakes, Mai."

"I don't really care, Skid. I'm trying to tell you something!" She never got so annoyed with me before, so I shut it.

"This swamp, this business, I want more than that. Or maybe less. I want to help people in different way. I need to be where people are dedicated to something big. So I've decided to become a postulant."

"A what?"

"It's the first step to becoming a nun."

"A nun?... You're sixteen!"

"It's not for another two years, but I want to start preparing myself now. So..."

"So we can't be friends?"

"Yes, friends. But only that."

"Oh."

Pause. The red wooden fence behind her is covered in bougainvillea. It's the time of year for it, and durin' a drought they come out in a rash. The bushes have more flowers than leaves, and all together they look like a white wave. I look around, and the swamp is once again a bowl of poison gumbo garnished with those bougainvillea white lies on the Lam Lee Hahn fence. The streams of rain running off the roof have become bars between Mai and me. They might as well have been a solid steel cage set in concrete. My breath is stuck in my throat again. It's hard to talk between these goddamn bars.

"What about you and me goin' to the San Tainos volcano and to Vietnam when we're eighteen? What about you showin' me the Great Mekong River that runs from the top of the world?"

She sighed. I had never seen her sigh.

"Those were promises that I will not be able to keep, and I'm sorry, but this is what I want to do with my life."

"I thought you wanted to be a businesswoman, like your mother."

"I do what my mother tells me. If I'm good at it, it's because she taught me to watch and listen well. She also told me not to fool myself. That's why I am doing this. I hope you understand."

"No... I don't."

"Look, it's kind of your fault, Skid."

"My fault... what?"

"Do you know when I made this decision?"

"When I turned my back, obviously."

"I decided this after you told me something you said no one else believes. When you told me about your brother, I saw it in your eyes how much you believe in what he can do. You believe that he can fix broken things in a much bigger way than your pops, who just repaired radios and TVs. It doesn't even matter if it's true. What is important to me is how deeply you believe it. Everybody else wish they were a star or maybe take trips to some place or had a lot of money. But I wish I had what I saw in your eyes and heard in your voice. Somethin' to believe in as *desperately* as you believe in your brother. I have to go and look for it, so I want you to let me go find it. And please believe in me too."

Yes, I did tell Mai about Frico and the whole sketchin' thing. But I didn't even know she was listenin' between tendin' to the shop and studyin'. But now there she was tellin' me she wanted to believe like that. That was the closest anybody came to givin' it a chance to be true.

So that was the beautiful breakup. She wouldn't let me hug her. She wouldn't know what to do with her hands.

She gave me a pen and said she had no paper, but I should write down her new address. I wrote it into the porch rail between two flower pots. 113 Meadow Vale, off Gregorian. Then she gave me her phone number.

"You gotta call first."

And I just laughed and wondered when I would ever have a phone.

"And ask for Francine. That's my American name."

"Francine" looked at me for a long time, and I knew she was in love, but she turned and left me anyway. Her T-shirt was shorter, the skin of her back glowin' and smooth as a river stone, with two dimples I used to call "hug handles". But you shouldn't think of a nun that way. Funny, she wasn't even my type when I met her. Now, walkin' over the footbridge as if on wheels and hikin' up the slope, Mai was almost perfect, like the English she now spoke, and I knew I would never see her again. I decided this. That address was the inscription on a gravestone.

Master Sam was waitin' for her at the train tracks with another red umbrella. He had on a red robe with neck embroidery, but the rain made the lower part of his dress look darker, like someone dipped him in blood. He looked in my direction, took her by the shoulder, and then those umbrellas just disappeared behind the mangroves.

When I got back, I was soaked. I made sure to walk slow through the showers, cos rain and tears, they look alike. Well, Moms, she was mad and told me I didn't listen when she spoke, and one day I'd get into big trouble for it. She said all this in front of Tony's girl, who was about twenty. Didn't matter, I'd taken a break from older women. And Vietnamese ones too.

Anyway, poor Tony couldn't even get to the car out at the tracks. I remember his girlfriend wanted to get back to her college dorm, and she needed to make a call to her dad. That expensive hand-held phone in her bag was as big as a damn buildin', but she couldn't get no signal out there behind God's back. Ma Campbell said she once heard they don't work well in the rainy weather, but on account of that lovely mermaid story, I think they should have that old woman hooked up to a lie detector all day long.

Twenty-Six

Now, don't you let that clock fool you. It drags your days through the mud, but races off your years when you're not lookin'. So don't be surprised when there's a wrinkle at the corner of your smile and a strip of grey where a milk moustache used to be. My pops said that time should stop when you step into your house, so we never had a clock. But, hell, we weren't livin' at our house no more, so we needed to get used to that big monstrosity of a grandfather clock over at Ma and Pa Campbell's. Now, *there's* one miserable machine to measure your life with. Forget the chimes – the tickin' drove you crazy long before you got there. And those hands, those three hands didn't help you do anything. They were only there to point out your limits, man.

It also didn't help that the thing was so "classic" that it looked like Dracula's vertical casket, no lie – but Ma Campbell, she was proud of that piece of funeral-home furniture. Said it was a "gen'wine Victorian Mellard" – which sounded quite uppity for a woman who would eat the fried skin off anything.

"When you git-a yourself a gen'wine Mellard, you hold it for as long as you can, even if it's brok'n."

That thing didn't even know it was broken. It still ran, but it never showed the right time. Well, for me, it didn't need to. I already knew that on one hand I was runnin' out of it, and felt like it was goin' too slow on the other. Ma and Pa Campbell were packed and waitin' for family to come all the way from Arizona. They hoped the police would come back and say all was fine with the ballistic report, cos they didn't want to look like they was runnin'. Moms had sold off nearly

251

all of Pa's goats, and they split the money. We handed off most of the mud crabs to Al Dubois for some more dough, even though they were a gift from Lam Lee Hahn. But there was no way we could eat all that crab in a coupla days. Evin Levine had taken three of Calvin's kids, and we told Pa and Ma to take one and we'd keep the other. The chickens were all dead, 'cept for one dethroned rooster that walked around, tail feathers droopin', wonderin' where his women went. We killed him and sprinkled the blood around the house, cos Ma said demons were advancin' on the place. Pa mumbled that the demons dropped down out of the big ol' day bat when it flew over the swamp. Never mind the fact that it was all over the news what the creature really was.

B2 BOMBER. FIRST-TIME FLIGHT. BRAND-NEW STEALTH PLANE. LATEST WEAPON IN THE WORLD. MISSION TRAINING EXERCISE.

Well, we could ignore Pa and his stories, but nobody was arguing with Ma about her beliefs any more. And if you came home and found a big ol' turkey vulture pacin' back and forth across your dinner table, like a preacher – with his nasty ol' wings spread above his half-rotten head – you wouldn't argue neither. You'd just ask her where she wanted that blood sprinkled. The moon was deep orange for four nights in a row after we chased that vulture out. Strange.

But the strangest thing of all was that everybody started experiencin' things. Suzy Wilson felt like she was underwater drownin' and gaspin' for air, and that's why she had to leave that day. Tony said the place felt stuffy, like there was a plastic bag over your life. Moms began to see things... like her husband's shadow slidin' up the stairs onto the porch. But she'd look up and that shadow wouldn't be attached to a man.

Well, like I said, Ma Campbell, she had the remedy for all that: blood sacrifice. She wanted to kill a goat, but the last goat kid, he escaped with the chain around his neck, and at night we could hear him runnin' through the goddamn bush, that chain rattlin' like a Rollin' Calf. Now, that's supposed to be a ghost slash bull with fiery eyes and smokin' nostrils – mostly bull, if you ask me. So instead of helpin' the situation, this stupid billy-goat was runnin' around the swamp at night, makin' people wet themselves.

Ma Campbell drained out all the rooster blood around the house, dipped the rooster in hot water, sloughed off the thick feathers and singed away the finer ones over a fire, before turnin' him into dinner. She put the candle of the Blessed Virgin against the mirror "to double the light in the room". We burned frankincense and put a large brass crucifix in the doorway. The shadow fell across the porch. The last of the blessed lake water was sprinkled to keep spirits out. But we also had to keep an eye on the gators that wandered across the front yard at night, preferrin' the brackishness in the lake over the gas bubbles in the dead pond. Mai's mother had said some people somewhere in Africa saw bubbles in a lake and thought it was nothin' until the entire lake rose up one night, swallowed up the village and burned everybody to the bones. I thought of Frico sketchin' a levee around the house, but to me, the real repairs had already been done. Now it was just a matter of time.

Bein' at school only made the waitin' worse. The first week after we packed and moved everything, it was pain all over, like I was arm-wrestlin' with Kuan Am. Man, my brain was dead tired too. Most days at school, I just sat lookin' out the window, wonderin' about life and listenin' to that piano in my head that kept hittin' one key all day. When I glanced around in the classroom, all those kids looked like they knew where they were goin' – or at least like they were OK with not knowin'. Maybe I was takin' myself too seriously, but I wasn't baby Beaumont any more. I would be sixteen in a month. And these brothers of mine, they set the bar real high for me. I was smart, I guess, but no genius – and I wasn't athletic. I wasn't a comedian, and I definitely can't dance. And it sucks when all your teachers already taught your genius brothers. You're screwed to suffer a life of comparisons, I'll tell you that. Long and short – I had to do somethin' big.

This event *had* to happen. But behind the glass window of Schoolroom 2E, with water runnin' down the windows and drippin' off everythin' and dirty clouds drapin' themselves over the world, you'd think God dropped his cleanin' cloth on top of the globe and went off to take care of somethin' else.

Now just to keep an eye on things in the city, I started bikin' it all the way home after hangin' out with Peter Grant. It took me an hour every day, but that way I could watch for any development all the way from the city to the swamp. Moms didn't like the idea. Said it was dangerous.

One evening, I came home to see that they'd taken down the Lam Lee Hahn fence. Sittin' on the crab-crawl porch, away from the bayou, I could see farther up the creek now that the fence was gone. It's weird how small a piece of land looks when you take stuff off it. Like once you move things, you say: "Now, how did they fit all that into that space?"

I could see the ponds left open and empty, and there was a sorry-lookin' wooden boat, beached far off on the lakeshore. When it got grey in the swamp, you couldn't tell the true distance between things. I was tempted to take a stroll on the other side but there were the sinkholes. I didn't want to discover one by accident. Worse than anythin' else, that place was haunted by Mai.

When breeze came across the yard from the Lam Lee Hahn side, Mai was in it: her smell – the same incense that was burning in the corridor that day I kissed her and met Master Samadh. *Nag Champa* was the name of it. The scent was still strong, even though no one was over there. That's prob'ly because there was a big frangipani tree in full bloom right beside where the fence was. They would use those frangipani flowers to make Nag Champa. To this day, I can't go near a frangipani tree without whippin' my head all around lookin' for that lanky Vietnamese girl.

"Soak your memories in a song or the scent of a woman," Pops always said. "Those things preserve them for ever." Corny as ever, that coward.

But it was true. And I knew that when I sat there and breathed in, I was just punishin' myself. And I could just hear Master Sam's warning in my head: "Your nose, your nose!" But I couldn't help it. The only thing that rescued me from missin' Mai was the reality of the swamp in those last few days. That place dryin' up was no trick of my smellin' or my sight or anything. That was the real stench of rottin' rivers and dyin' trees.

Usually I just got mad and blamed Frico, cos he could fix all this stuff with a pencil. But I told myself that this place was so low it could only get better, and any day now would be the new beginning.

Moms was makin' movin' arrangements. Aunt Bevlene said we could stay with her on Honey Drop Drive until we got a place, since she had an extra room now. Moms was goin' to help her get the place ready, but by that Thursday evenin' we realized that we should have been gone long ago.

Ma Campbell found a bunch of stuff under her house that Pa didn't even remember stashin' away. He'd started stockpilin' things before the shindig: petrol, canned goods, medicine, batteries, a sand filter and other doomsday supplies that we could easily sell off to Evin Levine. But by the time we got to the bottom of that army crate, we came upon the worst thing. Two sheets of bright yellow paper, both sayin' the same thing:

State of Louisiana
30 DAYS NOTICE TO VACATE

It had a fancy logo on it from some firm in Tennessee. It said that company was the new owner, our lease was up and we should have been off the land from the first week of August. Hell, we didn't even know we had a lease. Moms trusted Pops with everything, and that was crazy. The notice said some other things that all simply meant we were trespassers overnight. So Benet was also a coward. He sold the land out from under us, so someone else could give us the bad news and the ol' heave-ho. There was no reason to stay anyway, but we were officially out of time, and the notice said Moms and the Campbells could be arrested.

Ma was patient with Pa when he admitted that he rolled around one day in his wheelchair and collected the yellow signs off the doors with a stick. He hid them when no one was lookin', but only because he thought it was a scare tactic from Pops or Backhoe Benet again. Moms said he must've been damn drunk – and he shouldn't be drinkin' in his condition. Pa Campbell told her not to talk about him like he wasn't there, especially when she was shelterin' under his goddamn roof.

Well, after that it got pretty uncomfortable, and Moms, she went and packed some more things into boxes. Everything 'cept toothbrushes, man. She was ready. When that moon slid up over the trees that Thursday night, it looked big and amber, like lookin' through the bottom of a tumbler with whiskey in it – and seriously, we all felt drunk. That heaviness was in the air. In the mornin' the dead bayou was boiling. The brown sludge had begun to blow single bubbles, huge twelve-inch-wide domes that took one minute to pop open. We put hankies over our faces and decided not to go so close again.

Moms would try to contact the company or the City Council to get an explanation. She said any one of us who thought this meant school was out for the day was makin' a mistake. It was better to be out of the swamp for more hours of the day anyway. Well, by the time I got to school I had a headache. I couldn't tell if it was the bubbles or the eviction notice, or because I realized I'd left my already overdue assignment. Damn thing had been packed away in a box. Thanks, Valerie. Well, that just sounded like a classic whopper to the whole class, and they put me in the Hall of Fame for stupid homework excuses. I had to stay back and complete the thing, worst of all on a Friday evenin'. Afterwards, I pedalled to Peter Grant's place, and he told his old man I didn't want to ride into the swamp too late that day. So Mr G, he said he'd help me out. He musta been tired of obligin' me, but he was too cool to show it.

Well, look. That day, he didn't have to take me whole way. When we got closer to the New O'lins city limits, there was a "DETOUR" sign up ahead. Mr Grant honk-honked at the guys with flags, but they wouldn't come talk to him. So he sighed and said he would drive around, but that would be miles if we went through Michoud then right up along the coast to get me into the swamp from the east side. So I told him it was OK, I could just walk in. Peter said, "Hell, no," and was insisting – and when his old man started backin' up the tractor trailer to turn it around, I saw this puff of black smoke. Nothin' unusual. Just a puff of black smoke a little way off near that first overpass when you're comin' out of the swamps. Then there was another one and another one and then one more, like a smoke signal.

Peter's old man was about to rev the engine when I heard a distant rattle and a rumble and a whistle in the air. Maan, that tractor trailer was suddenly too slow for me. I grabbed my bicycle from behind the seats, flung it outside. You shoulda seen me jumpin' outta that tractor trailer – damn near broke both legs. Peter shouted somethin'. The word "crazy" was in it – the rest was all bubbles under water.

I stood up on the Beast and pumped the pedals and didn't look back. Up a slope – down a slope – up a slope – round a bend – down a steep grade, and then – bam – goose pimples. Cos, maaan... I see machines. *Freeze frame.* Big, beautiful, tangerine, heavy-duty machines. *Freeze frame.* Everywhere

I turn, there are cement-churnin' trucks and excavators and front loaders with their claws in the air. And massive bottom-dumper trucks and cranes that look like ladders stretchin' to the sky with wreckin' balls swingin' on the end of them. And they're all blowin' exhaust into the air and workin' hard along that crack on the map. They're pullin' down the overpass. *Freeze frame.* They're grabbin' at the ground and movin' buckets of earth and dumpin' it in those trucks – and my eyes are gettin' filled up and I ride around the machines whoopin' and yellin' until two burly-lookin' guys in helmets, they chase me away.

So I turn to home, and I'm ridin' hard like the devil, but I'm praisin' the angels – and I don't know how long I'm takin' on this nine-minute ribbon of road, but I don't care, cos the machines are movin'. That one piano note in my head turns into a full song, with big timpani drums, brass horns and a frickin' violin. And you should see me. I'm ridin' even harder but I can't see nothing. My eyes are runnin' over like the Great Mekong River that feeds the delta – but I'm laughin' at the same time and talkin' to myself.

"Frico Beaumont! You're a goddamn genius! Ha! We did it! We did it!" And I can smell the last shovel of cement and the first coat of paint already. Cotton-ball clouds, they're on the move, and the summer sky is so blue and so close I can jump up and pinch myself a piece.

Meanwhile L-Island is too damn far away, and when I finally get there, I drop the bicycle on the train tracks and I don't care about the Gulf Coast train comin', cos I'm like a brand-new version of my pops, runnin' into the yard from the train tracks and screamin' out over the footbridge.

"Valerie Beaumont! Pops told ya! Ha! And *I* told you!"

And I just want to see Valerie's face when she's eatin' her words with her dinner, so I burst into Ma Campbell's house, and everybody's sittin' around, including Tony. This is it. I stand in the doorway sweatin' and almost unconscious. They look up at me like I'm crazy. I point at Moms across the room, grinnin' between the tears.

"I told you!"

"What?"

"I told you!"

"You told me? Who told *you*?"

That's when I realize she's been cryin' too.

"You know about it?" I ask her.

"Yes. Your Aunt Bevlene told me today. Who told *you*?"

"Nobody told me. I was there. Saw it with my own eyes."

"You saw it? How... Where?"

"Out at the crack..."

"Out where?"

"The crack – on the map."

And now everybody's extra ugly, cos they're confused as well as in tears, and I can't imagine what my face looks like.

"The boy flipped," says Pa Campbell.

And Moms is lookin' at me like that day in the backyard. She's feelin' sorry for me again. Her lips are tremblin' around a cigarette.

Doug wipes his eyes with his sleeve and gets a little impatient. He didn't even make it sound good.

"Sit down, Skid." The grin is still on my face when he drops the bomb:

"Belly is dead."

"What?..."

"Your cousin's dead, man."

I think this must be a joke, like that crab-crawl-mermaid thing, but that would be cruel. Cruel like Ma Campbell's insensitive ol' clock that keeps on tickin' through all these tears.

Twenty-Seven

Some of the night had been left behind to stare down the day.

I'd have been empty of any expression as we drove back from the funeral in the rain if it weren't for Mrs Halloway's class and her magic words that "adequately described complex things", includin' feelin's. I woulda been in love with her if she had a little more meat on her bones, that lady. Anyway, the day of the funeral I was numb.

NUMB

That word was like a "NO TRESPASSIN'" sign in my head. A warnin' to any kind of emotion that wanted to come around and loiter a bit. But soon all the emotions invaded and yelled and tore down the "NUMB" sign.

Tony was drivin'. And the whole way back from what was a twisted road trip, I'm going over my life in my head. I felt fragile when I thought about Belly just dying like that. Fell out of a tree, you believe that? Then, when I saw some of the trees in Decatur, Georgia, I understood. Tall as hell. Like Decatur is the city where all the tall trees come and stand together. Rows and rows of giants at the side of the road, competin' with the buildin's.

They made me feel small. And fragile. We were all growin' *fragile*. My whole crew. We were not invincible. I thought about how I used to wonder if Frico's sketchin' worked on gunshot wounds. Maybe not. That all seemed like so long ago, and I saw all the memories in black and white, like those new photos Frico was developin' in the dark room at school. New still-life photos of the most beautifully beat-up things:

261

dry driftwood from the Gulf, rusty train tracks. Abandoned conch shells. Pa's Campbell's wrinkled old face. A cracked ceramic cup and a broken bumper car out at Pontchartrain Beach amusement park. The place had been closed down by them, so that ride, it just sat there, right where the last kid left it. The paint was breakin' off in a pattern like varicose veins.

Now, Frico ain't no poet, but he wrote this in his portfolio: "Blessed is the one who seize the beauty in a broken thing". He spelt "sees" wrong – and I thought it was sappy and wanted to barf, until I really thought about it. And I missed that girl Mai again, for about a second and a half, even though she smashed me into pieces. I finally told him about puttin' on his glasses and all the things I saw through it. He laughed and watched the drops on the window chasin' each other against a sad, grey background.

"What are you seein' outside now, Skid?"

"Rain. Dark clouds. Perfectly crappy day."

"I'm seein' exactly what you're seein' right now, only twice as big."

And he laughed again. The quickest, saddest laugh I ever heard from anyone in my life. And I wanted to hug him, but that would have been weird.

Then all the way in, with that squeakin' windshield wiper cuttin' a path through Alabama and Mississippi, I saw my cousin Ainsley Belle aka Belly in front of me. We left him lyin' in a muddy field of red dirt that was crowded with other horizontal people – cold, lovely, imperfect people.

Now, no matter how good a funeral might be, you can't ever say it was "a success", or people will hit you over the head. It was a good experience, though. Everybody was there. Harry T had no hairstyle. Peter played the piano in the church in flip-flops, cos his foot was all swollen for some reason. Marlon "McCozy" came all the way from Rochester with back-up singers taller than himself, and sang a song he wrote as a tribute called 'Love Does All the Heavy Lifting' – and it wasn't half bad, y'know. Sounded like Elton John and Air Supply – no, really. He just came over to us and said "Hey, you play, right?" as if he didn't know before or was too much of a star to remember stuff. Well, he gave Peter Grant the melody, and they practised it twice in the pastor's vestry – and that was it.

> I'm so glad
> that love does all the heavy liftin'
> heavy liftin'
> love does all the siftin'
> through the hurt –
> it turns it into somethin' good
> somethin' good.

Apart from Peter puttin' too many jazz chords in it, it was a hit, if you can say that about a song you sing at a funeral. We Beaumonts all wore topknots, as a sign of respect for Belly, but I'm sure some people thought we were in a gang or somethin'. That's people for ya. Ignorant as hell. Then, when we were in the graveyard, Doug, he took a bottle out of his coat pocket. He said it was dirt from the swamp, cos before Belly died, he wished he could get to "touch the swamp dirt again".

So Doug, Frico, Harry T, Marlon, Tony, Peter and me, we all stood above the burial vault and we poured swamp dirt from our hands into the grave. We weren't in New O'lins, so there was no chance of second-lining and brass bands, but Tall Horse with his red eyes, he hit his wristwatch and hollered out "Time, time!" to his work buddies. So they lined up a whole bunch of tractor trailers inside the cemetery on both sides of a driveway. Then, when that black Cadillac was comin' through with the casket, those guys, they revved the engines and rattled the trucks and honked the horns and gave ol' Belly a twenty-one-truck salute that was so cool and touching I just bawled like a baby. Aunt Bevlene never liked that too much, though. She was way down in her soul. And

I don't think she went for that "swamp dirt poured into the grave" thing neither. Prob'ly she thought it was too Taino, and she was one hardcore Baptist. It wasn't a Taino ritual, to tell you the truth. If we were really goin' to do an ancient Taino interment, the law wouldn't allow it. Cos that would mean we'd have to curl ol' Ainsley Belle up in a cave with all his worldly possessions and prob'ly a few pineapples for his trip into Coay Bay. He was only eighteen, so he didn't have much in his name. Matter of fact, he had a lot less than he started with, considerin' I made the goddamn cargo train annihilate his bicycle.

I remember the preacher – soft-spoken ol' guy. Frico took a picture of him, partly cos he looked so broken down. But that preacher, he said somethin' that stuck with me. Almost made me say "Amen!" He said this whole earth is a "dark place still filled with all kinds of flowers", like Gethsemane... or Eden after "the Fall". Wow, that guy had a way with depressin' words. I mean, it wasn't the most encouragin' thing to say, but it put a beautiful image in my head anyhow. I know Fricozoid thought so too, cos he didn't take the preacher's picture until he said that.

Anyway, I couldn't wait to get back to the swamp, even though those big-boned Mississippi Valley girls at the funeral made me want to hang around for a coupla days. I could bathe in their muddy drawl and listen to their bracelets rattle all day, no lie. And they smelt so good. It was a little annoyin' how they kept sayin' "Who dat? Where yat?" like they thought all people from Louisiana speak that way. I wished my San Taino patois was up to par so I could confuse them. They grilled some serious sirloin, and fed us and asked about our topknots and the dirt-pourin' and what not, and wanted to stay "in touch". But look, you really shouldn't encourage the women you meet at family gatherin's. And if I have to explain why, then maybe you shouldn't be invited to family functions in the first place.

More importantly, it had been eight or nine days since I ran into L-Island like a madman. All that time the machines were out there at the crack on the map, workin'. I was anxious to see what was happenin' and, out of habit, I got the urge to call a conference about it. Then I realized that the life of conferences and callin' up the crew was a long time and one funeral ago.

The changes happened fast. We moved out of L-Island early durin' those eight or nine days. I turned sixteen the same week. It was September Nineteen Eighty-nine. Tall Horse had an apartment on – of all places – Hayne Boulevard, and he said he'd rent it to us. Oh man. You shoulda seen Moms just shakin' her head and lookin' around and smilin' real sad when she walked into that place, twenty-one years late. We left Ma and Pa Campbell in the swamp, but they had arranged for their people from Arizona to get there around the time we came back from the funeral.

When I woke up, the rain had stopped and the car was crunchin' gravel. Only Doug and Tony stayed awake the whole way. A song was stuck in my head from listenin' to Tony's music the whole way. You know when you wake up and it's only one line that keeps goin' and goin' and you can't stop it? Well, the way to stop that is, you've got to conjure up that cassette player in your head and see yourself pushing that imaginary stop button. Or just imagine yourself smashin' the damn thing. That's how I stop it. Anyways, I rubbed my eyes and realized we were not on Hayne Boulevard. Instead, we were headin' into the swamp.

"Momma left somethin' back there," Tony said, lookin' all around.

I tried to see where we were, and I couldn't tell if we had passed where that overpass used to be or not. I looked for any sign of the machines. They were gone. All they left us was empty pink sky and New O'lins in the haze behind us, but I couldn't tell the distance with no overpass to mark it with. Nothing remained: no excavator, dump truck, nothin': just a great, big, gapin' hole – a wide canal that stretched in every direction and never ended until we got into the L-Island. And in that wide-open, empty wilderness there was nothing but water grasses and marsh and new water wellin' up like blood in a fresh bruise. Oh, and birds. Waves and waves of egrets and blackbirds and waterfowls – by the hundreds – not flyin' home, but pickin' up after the machines, feedin' and settlin' into trees I hadn't noticed before. I was confused. Maybe at that very moment the machines were headin' back. You just don't leave a wide trench open for miles. I looked across at Frico: he was asleep and snorin'.

Then way ahead, we saw the smoke. L-Island was burnin'. Not blazin', really, but smoulderin' in the sunset. We could smell it. Smoke hung in the trees – and you could see the glow of fire without bein' able to tell where it was started from.

Moms woke everybody up and told Tony to be careful as we ended the ribbon of road that now had more marsh on both sides. Ma and Pa Campbell – we all thought of them at the same time. Or maybe it was because Pa's old truck was abandoned at the side of the road and his wheelchair was turned over on its side, in a ditch. Moms started chanting. The truck keys were still in the ignition, but those two old people were nowhere to be seen. A wind came through from behind us and just up ahead, the smoke rolled away and we saw it – a drillin' rig: fluorescent lights all over the tower like a multi-eyed monster. The rig was on the exact same spot where the Benet house used to be. All around it, there were more contraptions inside the chain-link fence.

Well, that whole thing just looked like an overnight growth of steel forest standin' tall and strange in the smoke and mist – or the deck of some invadin' ship that brought the fire into the swamp. One light blinked on top of the tower, as if the rig was waitin' for orders. Bushes had been cleared away, so a reflective sign glowed in the Honda headlights. At the top of the sign was that little green logo from the TV infomercial.

Tony spoke up, so soft it scared you.

"That's a natural-gas drillin' rig. But there's no one any-where."

"Don't get out."

We didn't need Valerie Beaumont to tell us that.

We turned at the train tracks into L-Island. Tony cut the engine. As soon as the car had rolled down the slope, he flicked on the high beams, and those car lights showed you a place that would make you gasp for more reasons than the smoke in your lungs. "Desolate" is the word. No sound 'cept for the tyres in the dry riverbed, one weakened cricket and the broken creek pourin' into the earth. Smoke everywhere. In the distance, the Campbells' house had no lights in it, and the crab crawl – the shack we used to live in – leant for-ward into the dead pond that was now really a big puddle. Dead alligators were on their backs in the mud. They were swollen and looked like cylinders you could roll around. I was halfway through lookin' for my father's bones out there in the pond before I realized that I had been doing that for weeks. As the water level fell, I'd climb into the tamarind tree, lookin' into the pond for bones or clothes, relieved to see nothin' but the rusty tin roof toasted by time. In the smoke now, on the surface of the dark water, orange and blue flames appeared and vanished like mischievous spirits. This was hell.

Jerusalem. Jerusalem.

"More like *methane*, Momma. That gas has been comin' up from underground this whole time. Let's go."

"Hell, no. Not until we know where those old people are. Doug, you stay with Skid and Frico. Roll those windows up. Tony, come with me."

They walked in the beams from the headlights until they disappeared at the turn of the L. So, I'm there thinkin' we needed a knife or a rifle or a sketch pad and a pencil for protection. But Doug and Frico, they're fascinated. They were sittin' there, reminiscin' about a tyre swing we used to have on the tamarind tree that swung you out over the water and back in – and you should try not to fall in with the gators.

That's when I turned to see, by those ghost lights on the rig, that our tamarind tree was uprooted, chopped up and hauled away, maybe for firewood. Only the tangled roots of it lay exposed above the dirt, half on the bank, half in the pond, the wood white and the last of the fruits cracked and scattered here and there. There were more trees flung down, or stampeded through, like somethin' large had come in and forced itself on the place. All that was not broken was beaten down or limp and still flappin' in the wind. And the piano started in my head again. It swelled up into a big ol' church organ that was holdin' a high note at the end of a stanza, but there was no chorus comin'.

Twenty-Eight

We had left one dog, the scale model Frico built and the second-place map of "New Orleans 2020" in the swamp. The scale model and the map were right where Moms had hung them in the Campbells' house. She forgot them cos she was so focused on those boxes she packed that night after that little squabble with Pa Campbell. Anyway, when Moms and Tony got to the house in the dark, the dog had disappeared and the house was fresh on fire: the source of all the smoke.

Later Tony said Moms just walked into the fire like she belonged in it. She called out for Eleanor and Lobo Campbell a couple times. Only a cracklin' fire responded. He said she grabbed the scale model and the map off the wall and walked out like it had been cool in there, and there was no soot on her white dress and head wrap. Then, when they were hurryin' back past the crab crawl, they saw a doused fire and heard voices. Inside the crab crawl, five men had their hands tied behind them. They'd been stripped down to their boxers and had cloth bags over their faces.

Moms and Tony climbed down into the house and tried to free these guys. When they pulled the cloth bag off one guy, they saw that his mouth and nose were covered with a strip of cloth. Soon as they tried to talk to him, he shook his head and looked wild in his eyes and pointed with his face tellin' them to get out, get out now. Well, Moms decided that it was all too weird, and she'd get the hell out and alert the cops as soon as we got back into the city. She was still worried about Ma and Pa, but Tony said she just grabbed his arm and said: "We're leavin' now and never settin' foot here again."

So, meanwhile, we're sittin' in the car keepin' our eyes peeled for Moms and Tony, and we're relieved when they appear in the headlights again, walkin' fast from the bend with the scale model and the map in their hands. The smoke, it gets thicker and starts driftin' across the path.

Now, I gotta tell you, that nauseous, drownin' feelin' Suzy Wilson had? Well, we all felt that way, heavy, even though we rolled up all the windows like Moms said. So, at first I thought it was the methane messin' with my head, but then suddenly Doug and Frico, they saw the same thing I saw at the same time I saw it, and in a chorus we all yelled out the first four-letter word we could find on short notice.

"Tony!"

Someone – no, some*thing* – had crossed through the headlights right in front of the car. That boy needed to get in the car and move it right quick.

"Did you *see* that?"

Doug was not keepin' his usual cool, and Frico was halfway out the car door. I didn't blame them. If you saw what we saw in the darkness and the smoke you'd wet yourself whether you had powers or not.

Op'a.

Human form – six feet tall – no face to speak of – vulture skull – big ol' glassy eyes shinin' – a beak that rounded out into a snout – hunchback – walkin' machine-like – leather skin like a bat's wing and jet-black from head to foot. Turned his whole head at the last second to look at us – dead expression – the car lights reflectin' off both of his eyes – before he slipped away into the curlin' smoke.

Tony and Moms walked up. They might as well have been runnin'. They had their hands over their noses. Anyway, Frico, he gets back in the car, and we're chattin' like crazy all at once about the spirit. We're not makin' sense.

Moms turns to us and chucks the map and the scale model into our laps.

"One at a time!"

Then she cuts us off with instructions to Tony on how to drive like hell and cussin' about five half-naked men in the crab crawl. Great, we got spirits collectin' navels and faces and Tony can't start the damn Corolla quick enough. He dips the headlights and we're reversin' out of hell when Op'a, two of them now, appear in the rearview. We look around and they're standin' side by side in the dry river bed beside the footbridge, waitin'.

"Floor it!" Doug shouts.

He doesn't floor it. In fact, he put the brakes on. Yes, Tony stops the goddamn car, addin' dust to smoke and darkness and gas. Now, Tony is gettin' out of the car – Moms is pullin' him back in – Doug is tryin' to get into the driver's seat. Hell, we're *all* tryin' to get into the driver's seat.

Suddenly voices are all around us, speakin' in bubbles or from the spirit world. Moms steps out the car and starts walkin' toward the Op'a, hands to the sky, callin' on the Lord. Tony takes his chances with the woods. We can't believe he ran away and left his mother. We grab the stuff and get out the car, collect Moms, and we all follow Tony high-tailin' it into the trees. I'm at the goddamn front, no lie. We're safely under the trees when Ma Campbell – yes, Ma Campbell – she appears out of thin air, I swear. Now, that old woman is standin' up straight, floatin' on the surface of the damn creek. This is a nightmare.

"Psst. Skid!"

Short, old, dead woman callin' your name in the swamp. Run the other way.

My whole family keeps movin' towards the spirit of Ma Campbell standin' on water. They drag me and the stuff in my hands along with them. But I'm still pointed in the other direction, believe me.

I turn around, and Ma Campbell is actually hoverin' above the hole where Herbert and Orville went to hell. That's even worse. I knew Ma was headed to hell from that hush-puppy-fryin' incident. My hair is standin' on end like a blowdryer's goin' through it by the time we get right up to this woman floatin' above a hole in the earth – the same hole Moms made us swear never to go near again.

Well, Moms, I thought she had no interest in talkin' to the dead. But she's askin' Ma Campbell's spirit all these questions – meanwhile Op'a are appearin' from behind cypresses, mumblin'. One charges towards us. I cover my navel. Frico swings around. He's got his camera hangin' round his neck. The Op'a is closin' in, and my brother, he's straight shootin' with his camera, poppin' the fluorescent flash all over the place, lightin' up those suckers rapid-fire. You should see spirits duckin' into bushes and gettin' back behind trees to escape the light. By the time my pupils get readjusted from all that flashin', I realize that only Fricozoid and me are standin' at the creek.

A hand reached out of the hole and grabbed my foot. I screamed like a girl. But it was Moms' hand. They all went down into that goddamn hole. She's pullin', Frico's pushin', and I fall into hell with them. When they finally get me down in there, it wasn't all that bad. It was a cave, man, a *cave*. That sinkhole had opened up into underground caverns. Frico's lighter came out. Tony said with all the gas around that's a bad idea. He started blabbin' about limestone caves and groundwater in Louisiana and the fallin'-away of the rock caused by frackin'.

We were sittin' on a rocky ledge, and the creek was pouring past us down into the darkness of the earth. Behind us someone groaned. My breath got stuck in my neck, but it was good ol' Pa Campbell lyin' there on a limestone ledge, shakin' and coughin' his head off. Ghosts can't cry, so I was happy when Ma Campbell burst into tears in the pitch black.

"Valerie, it was horrible. Lobo got wet. We saw all these people come and set up overnight – and they were frackin', and the earth was shakin' and – oh, Lord – suddenly there

were gunshots and voices comin' around the bend. They set
our house on fire and we ran out the back. I was pushin' Lobo
in the wheelchair when we saw them roundin' up the frackin' men. They stripped them and ordered them into the crab
crawl. We got in the truck and got as far as up the road before
Lobo's chair fell out the back of the truck and I stopped to
pick it up. Then, when they started comin' up the train tracks,
we just pretty much crawled into the mangroves and found we
could slide down in here."

"Who was doin' this, Ma?" Moms' voice in the dark.

"Couyon!" Pa Campbell's voice jumped in. "He's back" –
cough – "him and his goddamn goons attacked the men over
at that drill rig. The tower appeared overnight and he was in
heah snoopin' around with his punks by noon the next day,
for godssake!" – *Cough. Cough.* – "Now they're tryin' ta take
over somethin' they don't know jack about. Somethin' that
was illegal in the first place!"

"Calm down, Lobo."

"Go calm your son down, I told you a'ready Ellie."

The lighter comes on again. Tony is holdin' it – against his
own common sense. He just had to get a word in.

"That drillin' is illegal?"

"Yep… Yew all… better believe it."

We all jumped, cos that answer came out of the darkness
deeper in the cave. A voice echoin' from another dimension
or somethin'. Frico's lighter went on again. A vulture skull,
shinin' eyes and a snout pushed out of the darkness, right
beside us.

Pa Campbell threw a shaky punch at the thing. The creature
grabbed the old man's arm and dragged him away into the
darkness. You could still hear it talkin'.

"Yew… heard your waaf. Take it easy… Lobo. All of yew."

Familiar voice. This was Broadway's Op'a, for godssake.
We were screwed.

Everybody held back. But then Pa pushes back out of the darkness with a big leathery arm around his neck followed by Backhoe Benet's face. The ugly O'pa face was now in his hand – and a green logo was on his chest.

"Gas mask. Oil-company hazmat suit. Thought so." Tony took less than ten words to destroy the O'pa.

Backhoe Benet let Pa go and rearranged himself in the cave. The leathery suit squeaked.

"I told yew, Valerie. It was time to go. I sold this place... a little while back. Then the people... the company that... bought it... said they'd work somethin' out with the occupants."

"Well, they sure did."

"Anyways, after they acquired it... they heard that the State wanted to turn this whole stretch into conservation lands. Well, from experience... I know there warn't much gas under here to speak of, but the company, they thought the opposite... so they came in and started without any preparation and after just a few tests. Matter of fact, the deal hadn't even been sealed yet when they started."

"So...you just *happened* to turn up here today, Cap'n?" *Cough*.

"I came ta see for maself if they'd gone ahead with... frackin' the place. People been complainin'... for months on the east side of the swamp. I'm partly to blame. Now they're right here in the west. When I got here t'day, the company's men were in these gas masks and suits... cos of the methane in the air... and the frackin' chemicals they been floodin' the damn place with. Well... I got here just in time to see James Jackson ambushin' the whole operation and takin' the suits. I hid in a company truck and put one on. Was the best way to hide. Soon as I could, I went down a hole before he could count his gang members again. Crawled on my belly and found myself here."

"Well, Benet, I haven't trusted you in years – and I still don't – but you just said theah's a hole out of here?" Pa was ready to get out.

We crawled for a couple of feet underground until we could stoop, then we could stand and carry Pa Campbell. Benet had a light on the hazmat suit that showed you a few inches in front of your face. I couldn't believe this big cavern was under our feet the whole time we lived there. I could have stashed a million things down there.

Tony and Benet were up front with Pa Campbell. Tony held him under the arms. Pa would only let Benet hold down at his legs, and he watched him the whole time. I thought about the friends huggin' in the picture up in that volcano. I reckon it was like a photo torn in the middle that couldn't be put back together.

Well, by this time we're all not doin' so well, especially when we walked around a small underground pond and it bubbled with gas. We had to feel our way around it while carryin' the old man.

It wasn't easy, but right after that we could smell the smoke from above ground again. Soon we popped up into one of the dry shrimp ponds over at the Lam Lee Hahn side, about a hundred yards from where we went down the sinkhole. If you saw us, you'd high-tail it out of there, cos we were comin' out of a hole in our funeral suits and Moms was wearin' white.

Pa Campbell was babblin' about the cave when Benet gave Moms the mask to put over her face. She gave it to Pa Campbell instead. Frico stopped for a second at the hole we'd just come up through. He flicked on the lighter and dropped it. With a whoosh, a tall column of blue fire leapt out of the hole like a genie. In a split second the flame sprayed out of the hole and then curled at the top like it was a wave. The base of the flame disappeared, leaving only a ball of pure blue fire hangin' above Frico's head. You could smell his hair singeing. Moms grabbed his shoulder, and he grinned. She was worried the flame gave away our position. We could see the old Ford truck through the trees. There was no sign of James and his gang.

We scrambled up the slope into the truck. Tony was in the driver's seat. Ma and Pa were in the front with him. Moms flung in the wheelchair, and when we were all tumblin' into the back of the truck, Tony, he just floored it and took off.

We saw Couyon and his thugs coming out of the mangroves and climbin' up onto the road and runnin' behind the truck. In the night, they looked evil in those hazmat suits, worse than O'pa, cos now they had guns out.

I could tell which one was Couyon. You couldn't tell who any of the others were without seein' their faces. They looked funny, like a bunch of vultures. It wasn't a joke when they cranked those pistols, though. "Condition One" is a sick sound. Especially when you can hear it from afar – and cocked in a chorus. Everybody lay down in the back of the truck. Everybody 'cept Skid, who was still not on board.

As soon as I was climbin' into the truck, Tony took off, and I had the scale model in my hand. So I couldn't dive in, or I'd prob'ly crush the thing. So I'm runnin' beside the truck, holdin' the scale model with one hand while Couyon and his fools are behind us, and Tony is speedin' up. All of a sudden, everybody has a goddamn suggestion, but I'm hardly hearin' them above my heartbeat blowin' up in my ears.

DOUG: Get in.

FRICO: Jump in, Skid.

I put the scale model in before me.

DOUG: Let it go.

MOMS: Let it go, Terence.

MA: Hold on, Skid.

PA: Hold on, Skid.

Then Frico, he just reaches over and knocks the scale model out of my hands. I'm lookin' back at it tumblin' and rollin' behind us when Benet and Doug, they reach across and they lift me right up into the back of the truck like it was nothin'. Benet was holdin' me weird, like he did with Broadway and Squash at the sinkhole, so I sort of wrestled myself away, but slowly. And he looked off, back at the fadin' gang and that damn light winkin' at the top of the drill rig. Then everythin' was smoke. I was waitin' for gunshots. I didn't get why they didn't shoot. Prob'ly because of his mother. Maybe there was an angel there. Or we were ridin' with the Devil himself.

Moms was cryin', Benet tried to touch her. She glared at him. I could hear his Rolex. I imagined them takin' it off his hand when they laid us out like those alligators, if they'd caught us. Then Moms, from the back of the truck, she tapped on that rear cockpit window, and Ma slid it open.

"I need a cigarette."

"Last one," Ma said.

"Yeah, last one."

She covered it from the wind. It smelt like somethin' roasting. The puffs were almost invisible 'cept for when it just escaped from her burnt lips.

Salt air dragged the cigarette smoke away. It pulled my topknot, whipped my hair into a mop and dragged some tears out of the corners of my eyes. I looked off into the darkness that went on for ever. You could tell that there were animals out there in the thousands – I couldn't see them, but I imagined most of them with folded wings, huddled together on branches. Crickets called after us the whole way, and somewhere along the dirt road, Frico reached into his pocket and pulled out a handful of dirt. He put his hand over the side of the truck and let the wind take it from his open palm. He kept his hand out there for a long time, until all of the swamp dirt Doug had given him at the graveside was gone. Then I realized it took us twenty minutes to cross that crack on the map – twenty minutes. So I got suspicious, and when the strip of road finally ended and we burst into the orange lights of the city, I looked over at Frico for a long time. But he was now busy fiddlin' with the back of the wood-and-glass frame that held the sketch of New O'lins. I saw him slide an envelope out from behind the sketch: Teesha's birthday card. That was the new hidin' place. The boy knew I'd been readin' his stuff. Whatever. He put his back flat against the rear window and opened the card, holdin' it firmly in the breeze. By the looks of it, he had gotten way past "Dear Teesha" – and every time we slipped under a street light, he wrote a bit more. I made out the last few lines:

...couldn't think of what to get you for your birthday. It took me a while, but Skid helped me out. Just looked at it one last time. It's a big surprise. I can only tell you that it has birds all over it. Lots and lots of birds.

You will love the birds.

Then, when I looked over at the map for the first time since the competition – I mean really looked at it – it hit me like a brick. *One inch equals just over a mile and a half in real life.* I could measure it even without a ruler. That boy Frico Beaumont had moved the crack on the map. He hadn't taken it out like I thought he would: he'd moved it. And not even forward into the swamp, but backwards. By more than ten minutes, I reckoned. The bastard. Matter of fact, it's best to say he extended it. Now it was wider and longer and stretched into New O'lins. A whole new place in Louisiana where birds and the fish and gators could start again and maybe even the annoyin' swamp rats would have somewhere to stay. As far as Frico was concerned, the city wasn't broken in the Seventies: the swamp was. So he fixed it. As best he could. And made a wildlife refuge for his girl-friend. Neat idea. She'd love it. She was a strange bird her-self, no lie.

And me? Maan, I was pissed and proud at the same time. The guy's a genius. You can't beat a genius. So I just sat back and listened to Benet's Rolex and watched the highway rollin' away like a black carpet behind us. Out of the corner of my eye I could see him, beside me, Frico Beaumont, my brother, sketchin' the swamp back into the city.

SKID

The sequel to Roland Watson-Grant's acclaimed debut novel *Sketcher*

ISBN 978-1-84688-319-4 • £12.99

AVAILABLE JUNE 2014

Having left the Louisiana swamp behind, the Beaumonts are finding it hard to settle into the big city. As he unpacks the boxes after their move to Eastern New Orleans, the now sixteen-year-old Skid finds a diary which had belonged to his older brother Frico. Among various other family secrets that emerge from this discovery is the startling revelation that "Skid" is a hoodoo word of ominous significance. This throws Skid's mind into turmoil and prompts him to launch into a quest for the real meaning of his name and the very foundations of his own being, an adventure which will pit him against his own brother and lead him to encounter Claire, a mysterious girl who seems to hold the answers to some of his questions.

Heart-warming, funny and poignant, *Skid* – the second volume in Roland Watson-Grant's Trilogy of the Swamp after the critically acclaimed *Sketcher* – continues the exploration of a young man's coming of age in today's broken world.